THE MONKEY-PUZZLE TREE

THE MONKEY-PUZZLE TREE

Elizabeth Nickson

BLOOMSBURY

First published in Great Britain 1994

Bloomsbury Publishing Ltd, 2 Soho Square, London W1V 5DE

A CIP catalogue record for this book is available
from the British Library

ISBN 0 7475 1812 2

Typeset by Hewer Text Composition Services, Edinburgh
Printed in Great Britain by Clays Ltd, St Ives plc

TO MY FAMILY AND
ESPECIALLY TO ORSON

AUTHOR'S NOTE

In 1953, in response to the communist threat, the CIA, under Allen Dulles, instituted a series of experimental programmes in mind control. Over the next decade, the CIA channelled ten million dollars, in fifties dollars, through 144 universities, fifteen research facilities or private companies, twelve hospitals and three prisons for the purpose of research into mind control. Almost all the experiments were performed on unknowing American citizens.

The most extreme series of experiments took place at the Allan Memorial Institute, a psychiatric hospital in Canada, connected to McGill University and the Royal Victoria Hospital. Allen Dulles needed a physician who was willing to carry his experiments to their furthest stage, but recognized that if Americans realized that their tax dollars were paying for experiments upon Americans, there would be serious reprisals. Canada was close enough to the States to monitor, and happily, the Director of the Institute at the time was Dr D. Ewen Cameron, a Scots-born American citizen.

Ewen Cameron became a world-renowned psychiatrist. He founded the World Psychiatric Association, the Canadian Psychiatric Association, and was President of the American Psychiatric Association. He had been the American psychiatrist chosen to evaluate the sanity of Rudolf Hess to stand trial at Nuremberg. He wrote and published widely and was a born administrator.

In 1979, a group of psychiatric patients of Dr Ewen Cameron launched a public interest case against the CIA for experiments performed upon them, without their consent, while they were seeking psychiatric help for relatively minor complaints. This series of experiments was called MKULTRA, subproject 68.

This is the true story against which this fictional story is set.

The Monkey-Puzzle Tree is a work of fiction. Yet it would be misleading if I did not say that the bones of this story shaped the emotional climate of my childhood and its 'true-life' aspects certainly determined what I became. My mother was a patient of Ewen Cameron. She had suffered postnatal depression during the fifties, which at that time was treated by bludgeon blows to the psyche, rather than with sleep and drugs as it is now. I met Ewen Cameron and he was a subtle and constant and, I believe, malignant influence on my family life until he died.

Given a personal connection to the Montreal experiments, as they are now called, I was distressed that so few people knew about them. Much good non-fiction has been written about the CIA's mind-control programmes, especially about Dr D. Ewen Cameron and his experiments. The story has so many tempting dramatic elements: the invasion of Canadian sovereignty by the US; an 'evil' psychiatrist; LSD and other mind-expanding drugs; brainwashing; the CIA and so on. Yet people outside Canada, and indeed, many within the country, had little idea of the story. The patients of Ewen Cameron became, on the eve of winning their extraordinarily brave battle against the Agency, marginals, split off from 'normal' culture, ignored. Why?

I reasoned that people in general recoil from mental illness, particularly severe mental illness. The plaintiffs, at the time, were aged, exhausted from their fight and the battle to maintain their balance in the face of a terrifying past. But in Victoria Ramsey we have a character, young, beautiful, well equipped to take on the world. She, I hope, is a character that we all know, or want to know, or would want to be, and through her we can somehow experience the feeling of being trapped in Ewen Cameron's treacherous web.

So, I chose to tell this story as fiction, using the devices and textures of fiction in order to tell the story in the round. The mother in my story is not my mother. The members of the family are not my brothers or my father, and I make the usual disclaimer that, with the exception of named public figures and the surviving plaintiffs in the case, any resemblance to persons living or dead is purely coincidental.

Part 1

MARCH 1988

ONE

They found him in his loft. It was a few days after the full moon and False Creek had been lit up like a ghastly carnival. A logger, returning home from a hard night of drinking, had spotted the silhouette against the window. He broke into the place and hauled him down from the rafters.

I loved my baby brother. Sometimes I loved him more than myself. When we were young I'd often take a punch meant for him, or try to. So when my mother asked for help, I thought of him, not her.

She called me at my office and I very nearly didn't take the call. She had come to New York a month ago and I had had more than my fill of her then. I shouted at my assistant for putting the call through without asking. Then I picked up the line. I always felt as if the receiver was about to bite me.

'Cathy?' Catherine, call me Catherine.

'Yes, Mother?' I was abrupt.

'Oh darling . . .' A sigh relaxing into a pit of misery and then she was sobbing.

That I wasn't expecting. She could whimper and whine and complain and sigh with the best of them, she chiselled and picked at us endlessly, but she hadn't cried for years. Not in front of me anyway.

'Mum, get hold of yourself. What's happened? How's Daddy? Is he ill?'

'No, darling, it's Brian,' she said, voice catching. 'He's tried to kill himself.'

My fingers went numb around the receiver. A weird feeling. I imagine the blood rushes to your heart. I shook my free hand, then switching the receiver to it, shook the other.

'Tried means, I suppose, that he didn't succeed,' I said. Feeling was returning to my fingers but I was suddenly freezing cold. I leaned over and turned up the heat on the radiator. Shock. I was going into shock. My free hand patted papers on my desk top searching for but not finding comfort. A blanket, a bed, a hot-water bottle. Noticing my hand hunting aimlessly shook me back to reality, but I still felt as if I'd just whiffed pentathol.

He was not dead, she told me, but very nearly. Taken to the Vancouver General and put in a ward filled with borderline psychotics, he finally called my parents and she called me.

'All right, I'll catch the very next plane,' I said.

'Cathy?' She hesitated. 'It's almost four years, darling.'

'Mother, you were here last month, for God's sake!' I stopped, took a deep breath and tried again. 'I'm sorry, I didn't mean that. I'm . . . I don't know. Scared, I guess.'

'He's going to be all right, Cathy. But he needs to see you. You used to be closest.' She was cajoling me now.

'But why?' I said in a moan much like hers. 'Why did he try something like that? It's not like him, he's never been – '

'I don't know, Cathy. Depression, perhaps. He and Yvette haven't been getting along.'

'Yvette?'

'His girlfriend, or whatever you call her.'

'Oh right. I haven't met her.'

'You haven't been home for a long time.' Her voice was carefully inflectionless.

'Well,' I said. 'I'll come home now.'

When I put the phone down, I kicked the filing cabinet twice, hard enough to dent it. My assistant poked her head in and I asked her to book me on the first flight to Vancouver.

Then I sat down and leafed through my diary, backwards and forwards to see what I was going to miss, needed to re-schedule, what had already happened. See, there it was, proof. She and my father had left New York just three weeks ago.

Her uncle, Dr Arthur Westley, or West as she called him, had died at the formidable age of 103. He had left an immense amount of money, the quantity of which astonished us, to a university. My mother had been thoroughly shaken. He had been her anchor and hope; her father had died when she was fourteen and her uncle had stepped into the breach. He had paid her way through university and sheltered her later, had always told her she was his daughter. He had put himself through medical school in his thirties, then strode on, unblinking and stork-like, through the war years as head of the British General, through society doctoring in New York to a comfortable and seemingly endless retirement in the arms of a rich American widow on East 72nd, off Park. Neither of them had children. My mother was his heir; they told her every time she visited. She would laugh, look around her and think: Well, nice bits of furniture here, but surely not much else. West and Clara lived pretty well, the Waldorf for years, three permanent staff. Ha, the joke was on all of us. In 1952 he had put his entire savings of $23,000 into IBM. But by 1986, it was worth $80 million dollars. Untouched. Pure money, which is rare enough these days. Pure and clean and gone.

The rest of us were sad for her but forbearing. We had never really believed in West and his money and his love for her. He visited us rarely and we had rarely joined her on her trips to New York, although we idly listened to her tales of the Frick and the New York Philharmonic and good conversation on her return. Then, for the last ten years, he had been quite senile, reaching out to his nurse late at night, begging to be taken out dancing. None of us had visited then.

She had arrived to hear the will read in probate court – a symbolic gesture, she had said. I had watched her back, proud and straight.

Only the trembling hand gripping the bench in front of her had betrayed her. She stood up in the courtroom to protest furiously when her name was called, then sat, twitching and nervous, that night at dinner, unable to look my boyfriend Mark in the face.

I had followed my father down the street as we left the restaurant.

Mark took my mother's arm at the door and was steering her firmly down the sidewalk between the grease spills and busted-open garbage bags.

'I could help,' I offered. 'I could nose around, see what I could see, talk to people and so on.'

My father shook his head. 'I won't take this to any court, Catherine. It would bankrupt me and it would kill your mother.' He shot a look behind us at my mother and Mark. 'We don't need the money. And neither do you, if you're smart.'

I shrugged. I was used to these pronouncements. They had all the force of a royal decree. Besides, I was hurt by my parents' seeming distaste for Mark. To me, he was perfection in male dress – funny, easy and flawlessly polite to them.

To hell with them. I shut my calendar. That was three weeks ago and this is now, yet another crisis. And Mark wonders why I avoid my family so strenuously. If I get anywhere near them, I'm caught in a drama, but it is underplayed drama, plenty of subtext, mostly subtext in fact, and plenty of silence. I get lost trying to puzzle out the meanings. And when I'm thoroughly perplexed, completely lost, all of a sudden there's another huge crisis. They are Jacobean, my parents, masquerading as faded gentlefolk, leading diminished but useful lives in their mocked-up copy of a plantation house off Oak Street in Vancouver.

Surely, this attempted suicide was another hollow gesture. Brian saying look at me! Nobody's looking at me!

Mark says I'm a tough cookie. If so, I tell him, I'm a tough cookie on a permanent vacation. I tidied up my desk, and wrote notes for my assistant. My job was not very demanding; they wouldn't miss me if I left for four months. I was working for a second-string dance company in Greenwich Village, doing their books and sorting out their touring contracts, brokering arguments with the occasional star they import to beef up their audience. I also dealt with the press forays they needed to make. As a burnt-out former member of the press corps, I was uniquely suited to the job.

My assistant poked her head around the door. 'You can pick the tickets up at the airport, Catherine. There's a flight at six o'clock, direct to Vancouver. You've got plenty of time to make it to JFK. And that guy from Washington called again. A private matter, he said.'

'You're a doll,' I said. 'Thank you.'

'Family problems?'

'Yet again. I've written notes on everything pending. Get that idiot from Brussels to sign the contract, will you? It has all the points he wants in it now.'

'No problem. Don't worry about us. What should I do about this guy?'

'What guy?'

'Catherine, I just told you.'

I held out my hand. 'Give me the number, and I'll try to reach him. If I don't and he calls again, put him off. Family stuff.'

She smiled, scribbled on my desk pad and tucked the number into my briefcase. A quick kiss on the cheek and she was gone.

One thing a burn-out needs is a good assistant. The other is a loving mate. Of course, usually by the time you've reached the state of nervous exhaustion you've trashed the mate and been fired from your job. All I lost was a career.

I had become that most anomalous of journalists – a generalist. I was supposed to be able to manage an interview with the senescent owner of a private museum and his fifth wife who bore fresh bruises from an eye lift or a recent battering with the same ease as a round-robin weekend of torture victims – the revolving door decanting another set of stories of rape and upside-down crucifixion on the family lawn. When an editor asked what I knew about a celebrity or an issue, somehow, horribly, I always knew a lot.

I wished not to know. Not any more. Not anything. Not the opposing sides of any question, not the latest fad from Venice Beach, not the next big thing of anything. I wanted nothing, to watch Lifetime TV, to do yoga with PBS, to drive a red jeep Cherokee to the local Safeway and buy everything with Nutrasweet in it, as Cher advised.

But you can't jump off a high-speed train without hurting yourself. I quit and then I collapsed. I was so tired that I couldn't sleep for months, just tossed and turned and wandered around our loft, looking at things. I spent the days half out of bed. It had taken almost a year to start inching my way back to the semblance of a real life and even then I was part woman, part Victorian neurasthenic. All those little deaths meant I walked carefully through life, picking my way through minefields.

My life was filled now with calculations. I was nearly thirty-seven going on seventy-seven. I planned meals and exercise and sex and dinner parties, measuring my energy out. My nerves fried up at the slightest provocation, and I had to go to bed. Noise bothered me and I wore ear-plugs a lot, especially to sleep. If light was too bright, my eyes ached; then I got a migraine. I was capable of only a half-day of work, as long as it wasn't too strenuous, and I needed eleven hours of sleep a night.

Mark was endlessly patient with me. He didn't care that he wanted to marry a cripple – he simply loved me. He'd met me just before the crash, at a Whitney opening of a group of Canadian artists, who were seeing the event as an overdue canonization by the superculture. They quietly mocked the consulate's participation by running a soundtrack from a tape loop of poodles pissing on tin. I had seen Mark standing by one of the poodle paintings, tall and hungry-looking, hollow-cheeked. He was already losing his hair, but what there was was blond and fell over his collar.

He was laughing, something I was to learn he did a lot, and his hazel eyes searched the crowd restlessly, lighting up when they fell upon me. He walked over to where I stood and I liked him instantly. He had had some of his work published in their magazine and had become a friend of the artists. He showed me around the exhibition, his commentary a running joke. He must have decided I was a worthy project that night because he didn't leave my side for the next few months. Whenever I was free, he was there, teasing, laughing. I threw myself into the affair with all the vigour of the truly unhappy.

For the next year, he watched my comet spin out, then soothed me through the grimmest part of my detoxification from the news. Finally, I weaned myself off five newspapers and sixteen hours a day of CNN, and I stopped reaching for the phone during the bread-and-circus spectacles by which Americans entertain themselves.

In the past two years, we had become each other's best friends. We had one of those relationships that seemed both odd and enviable to outsiders. We did everything together, we were twinned. We talked three times a day, we didn't make a move without each other.

Which made my solo booking of a flight strange. But when I went home that afternoon to explain, he lifted his head from his drawing board and smiled.

'Of course you should go alone. The last person you need around is me.'

I kissed him. 'I'll be back as soon as I can.'

'Sooner than that, I hope.' He went into the dressing room to pack my bag and I fiddled in the kitchen. He knew better than me which clothes would soothe my mother's eye. I would pack to offend.

The cab arrived just as the tea was ready. He carried my bag down the stairs and kissed me long and hard. A ragged cheer rose from our resident street person. I giggled and fell on to the stiff plastic shroud of the back seat.

It wasn't until the cab turned on to the Van Wyck Expressway that the fact that I had almost lost Brian hit me. I leaned back in the cab, shut my eyes to the lights bearing down on us from the other lane. I could see him then, only thirteen when I left home for good. Two tears, unfamiliar and grudging, squeezed out from between shut lids. Why? What had happened to my little brother that would drive him to try to hang himself? What?

He had one of those smiles. A young man's smile, bashful, duck-your-head to hide your pleasure, a slight drawing in at the neck, the ends of the mouth curved up helplessly, while another side of him tugged his mouth down.

My first memory of him is a photograph. There we are, the four of us, in that classic pose. Mummy home from the hospital, exhausted by a job well done, baby in her arms. Chintz frames us, the bedspread, the curtains, a chair. My other brother Ross and I leaning on the side of the bed, gazing at this new arrival. Where had he arrived from so suddenly? How would he change things? Not much at all, they said to us, but in fact he changed everything.

The smile was to arrive later, at ten or eleven. We mostly adored each other then. I experienced life partly in order to tell him about it.

I checked in and got a boarding pass. Before I knew it, I was standing at a bank of telephones, dialling the Vancouver operator. A series of crabby negotiations with hospital staff, then I heard a voice.

'Who is this?' I demanded. 'I want to speak to Brian, please. This is his sister.'

'Catherine, this is Yvette. I can put Brian on, but it hurts him to talk.'

'Oh hi.' I paused. Of course he couldn't talk. 'It's OK, don't put him on. How is he? Tell him I'm coming out,' I said in a rush.

'He's all right, considering. Just a minute.'

'Catherine!' It was him. Ragged, but it was him. He cleared his throat. 'Sorry. Where are you?'

'At the airport, on my way there. But I wanted to know how you are.'

There was a rustle. 'Yvette wants . . . I'm not sure . . .' More rustling.

I took a deep breath. 'Why not? I don't understand. Brian, tell me, what happened? How are you?'

'Have you had any calls from Washington?' It was Yvette.

'No. Oh yeah, some guy. I don't know who he is.'

'Go see him.'

'What? Don't you want me to come there?'

'Go see him and then come here. Please?' Her voice was shaking now. 'For Brian.' Then lower. 'And me.' She sounded desperate. Her voice was hoarse, filled with tears.

'OK.' I would have agreed to anything. 'Why?'

'Hang on.' She covered the telephone with her hand and I could hear the muffled sound of sheets moving and low voices.

'Is there a fax machine in the airport?'

'I imagine there is. Why? Yvette, what's going on?'

'Hang on.'

'What's going on, Yvette? I'm really worried.'

'Brian is all right. He has bad moments, but there is a reason. He promised he won't try it again, but he needs you to help and he'll explain when you get here. It'll only take a day.'

I was silent.

'Catherine? It's important. He needs you. We both do.'

'All right,' I said slowly. 'It's not as if you've given me any choice.'

A reluctant giggle, quickly muffled. 'We want you to find a fax machine in the airport, then call us. We'll fax you the stuff. When you have it, call the man in Washington. It's not too late there, is it? Oh, only four-thirty. Well, we have time.'

'What the hell is going on?' I pronounced each word separately. 'What am I going to tell Mother? She's expecting me tonight.'

'I'll let her know. What we are sending you will explain a lot. Now, go find a fax machine.' The phone was dead in my hand.

I stood there at the phone bank, calculating. I could just do it. My suitcase had been checked, but I had enough in my briefcase to get me through a day. My ticket was refundable. I could get to Washington easily enough, just change terminals. I even had an Admiral's Club card left over from the days when I travelled constantly. There would be a fax machine for businessmen there. I turned and walked towards the departure lounges.

The fax machine was in a corner and not busy. I called Yvette back. 'Wait a couple of minutes, Catherine. I'll go to the hospital fax now. There are some twenty odd pages,' she said.

'All right.' I felt passive.

'Why don't you call Washington and tell him you're coming?'

'Not until I see what you're sending.'

I stood, waiting. The lounge was empty except for a waiter

leaning against a counter in front of a stack of white china cups. I walked over and he poured me some decaffeinated coffee. The fax machine beeped and I returned to stand guard. Shiny pages unfurled at a snail's pace and I caught every one as it fell. There were twenty-nine altogether and I took them to a banquette, spread them out and sorted them.

There were copies of newspaper stories from *The New York Times*, the *Washington Post*, the *Globe & Mail*, the *Ottawa Citizen*, and a half-dozen others. I had xeroxes of bios from *Who's Who*, career outlines of people I'd never heard of, xeroxes from the *Physician's Desk Reference* on the effects of certain drugs, and copies made from the *DSM-III*, the third edition of the *Diagnostic and Statistic Manual of Mental Disorders*.

Brian was a packrat as a child. When he studied astronomy at school, models of the solar system littered every flat surface in his room and pull-outs from *National Geographic* were taped to the walls. Later, when he developed an interest in etymology, I insisted that his door be locked, lest any of the bugs in there creep out across the hall into my room. He was an obsessive researcher, wasted in his current profession as taxi driver.

I picked up the sheaf of stories from *The New York Times*.

The first was dated 2 August 1977. The title type was larger than the usual sedate *Times* headline: 'PRIVATE INSTITUTIONS USED IN CIA EFFORT TO CONTROL BEHAVIOUR'. It was a long story, complete with charts mapping control mechanisms and a drawing of North America showing the location of each institution in which the experiments had taken place. In bold type, featured, the writer said, for the unrelenting and extreme nature of the experiments, were Ewen Cameron and his associates at the Allan Memorial Institute of Psychiatry in Montreal, Quebec, Canada.

I slid off my seat and walked over to the counter and poured another cup of coffee. I took a sip, then placed the cup back on to its saucer. The coffee was bitter anyway. I walked back to my reading.

The CIA programme was called MKULTRA. Its aim: to learn how to control human behaviour. Its methods: experimental drugs, electroshock and various other procedures that resembled nothing less than torture. This was a classic *Times über*-piece, Pulitzer material. A reporter called John Marks had gathered 2,000 previously classified CIA documents and put together a picture of the programme. I read it in growing horror, my pulse fluttering. I finished it and lay flat on the banquette and waited until I couldn't wait another moment. Then, without getting up, I pulled the rest of the clippings towards me. I flopped over on to my stomach and kicked off my shoes.

I picked up another muddy library xerox, again from the *Times*. Dated 5 December 1980, it was short, hidden away in the 'World Notes' section: 'FIVE CANADIANS ASK $5 MILLION FOR BRAINWASHING BY THE CIA. The suit filed in Federal District Court here in Washington said that, from 1957 to 1963, they were given the hallucinogenic drug LSD and extensive electroshock treatments to wipe out behaviour patterns.' All the patients suing, it went on to say, had sought treatment for psychiatric troubles.

I knelt then and pushed the rest of the pages aside. The thrust of what he wanted to tell me was contained in the two *Times* stories.

Dr Ewen Cameron had been our mother's doctor for twenty years.

I called the hospital again. Yvette answered. She sounded tired.

'OK,' I said. 'Who is this Wheeler fellow?' I had found the slip of paper with his name on it in my briefcase.

'He's a partner in a law firm in Washington. They are representing Cameron's patients. Did you see a bio of Joe Rauh in the papers?'

'No.'

'Well, find it. He's famous and good and it's his firm.'

'And you think . . . what?'

'Brian thinks she was involved. Some strange things have happened to him. He's also dealing with a lot of guilt. She went into the hospital in '57, a couple of months after he was born. He thinks it was his fault. Obviously it isn't, but . . . look . . . please. We've been arguing about it, and I say that the more we know the better he'll be.'

'What strange things?'

'Not on the phone. Just meet with them, Catherine. They've talked to Brian about your mother. You're a journalist. This is your world, not his. You know what to ask, you can navigate easily. You'll be OK. You're used to this kind of thing. You used to do it every day. Just go and talk to them.'

'Then I'll come out.'

Maybe I imagined it, but she lightened for a moment. 'Good. He's felt better since he heard you were on the way. I'll see you soon.'

'Yvette, my suitcase was checked through to Vancouver.'

'I'll ask your parents to pick it up for you. Don't worry.'

I thanked her and we hung up.

The call was easy. Tom Wheeler said he had been waiting for me and claimed delight that I was on my way. We made an appointment for the next morning. I put down the telephone, and shaken, found my way to the appropriate terminal.

In the shuttle, surrounded by bureaucrats reading newspapers, I fought for control of myself and won. I read all twenty-nine pages, tried to fix names and places and dates and failed. I set them aside, pulled out *People* magazine and stared blindly at the pages. By the time I stepped outside National Airport, I was shivering and my thinking was chaotic.

It was raining. I checked my watch. I caught a cab, told him to take me to a moderately priced hotel, near Union Station where they have passable room service.

Twenty minutes later, we had pulled up in front of the Bellevue Hotel on E Street. I checked in and went to the room.

'I'll call in tomorrow. Everything's OK,' I said to our machine at home. I didn't leave the hotel number.

I fell asleep to the strident razzmatazz of *Entertainment Tonight*.

TWO

Tom Wheeler and Joe Rauh worked in an office on Connecticut, half-way down the street from the White House. The building was dull. You didn't have to shut your eyes to miss it. The entrance on Farragut Square was taking in a long stream of men dressed in business suits that ranged in price from thousands of dollars to the cost of a K Mart special. It was still raining.

I was early and stood staring at the building directory. Joe Rauh's office was on the tenth floor. I felt uneasy. I had read Brian's copy of Rauh's bio carefully. He was famous, possibly the most famous civil rights litigator of his time, and he was spearheading this case along with Tom Wheeler. I was about to meet the man who had defended Lillian Hellman and Arthur Miller in front of the House Un-American Affairs Committee, who wrote the minority civil rights plank at the 1948 Democratic National Convention and had broken school segregation in the South.

Predictably, I was told to wait. There was a scratched Plexiglas coffee table in the waiting room. It was littered with dog-eared magazines and the morning's newspapers. A big rubber plant in the corner had brown edges on the tips of its leaves and was visibly drooping. The fabric of the couch I was sitting on had started to fray. I picked at it. Polyester. All the furniture, carpeting, tiling and drapes were in tones of bureaucratic beige. This was not a law firm that enjoyed aesthetics. It was an attitude not much in vogue in the legal business these days.

A blonde woman with a pageboy scooped back by a plaid headband came out and motioned at me to follow her. I was glad Mark had talked me into nice-girl clothes. I was even wearing pearls. We took a few sharp right turns through a maze of beige cubicle dividers and ended up in a big corner office.

Two men rose as she delivered me through the door with a contemptuous flourish, as if washing her hands of me. I already felt faintly guilty, as if I were there under false pretences, applying for a job for which I was underqualified.

I forced a smile, held my hand out. The younger man was about thirty, of medium build, and had straight, dark-blond hair that fell over a pair of heavy horn-rimmed glasses. He wore a white shirt and red tie. He leaned over the desk to shake my hand. His eyes were so keen with interest that I almost felt embarrassed. He smiled back at me. A glint of something else was there. Pity? Impossible. Suddenly, I felt very young.

'Welcome, welcome,' said the larger, older man, rubbing his hands together. He waved me to a chair. 'I'm Joe Rauh, this here squirt is Tom Wheeler. He's really the point man on this; not that this isn't one of the more interesting cases I've ever brought forward, but these darned public interest things go on for years and require the dedication of a medieval saint, hey?'

I said something polite and looked around the room.

There were black-and-white photographs and honorary degrees covering half of one wall. The furniture was the same as outside, chipped veneer, we're-not-interested-in-display furniture. I peered at the photographs. Arthur Miller and Marilyn Monroe, signed.

There was a pen in a frame that had signed the Civil Rights Act into law. It had been given to Rauh by Lyndon Johnson.

I ticked over his credits in my mind. Rauh had graduated magna cum laude from Harvard Law and come to Washington to work for the New Deal. He was taken on as a law clerk by Supreme Court justices Felix Frankfurter and Benjamin Cardozo.

Rauh got up and came over to me and leaned against the desk.

'Ignore them. You know we liberals get sentimental.' I laughed and got up, read the inscription closely. The photograph was autographed by Frankfurter, dated 3 June 1939, and read, 'For Joe Rauh who exercised for all too short a time his charming authority over the judicial process of his affectionate friend.' I smiled.

The blonde woman brought in a tray filled with cups. She set it down on his desk and left. He picked up the scratched thermos.

'Coffee?'

I nodded. 'These are wonderful.' I gestured at the wall.

'Well, there was a spirit in 1935 that has never come again. You had to be in it to believe it. The idealism was so great. We had night secretaries because we would work all night. We thought we were saving our country.' A short hoot of a laugh, loaded with cynicism.

I smiled weakly.

'We've got a hearing in a half-hour 'cross town. Tom tells me you're a good journalist.'

'I'm sure I'm flattered.' Washington always sent me into Southern belle mode. I gave myself a silent talking to and we chatted for a few moments about the magazine I used to work for and the kind of stories I did for them. They did not ask why I'd quit.

'So!' This from Rauh. It sounded like a bark. 'How much do you know?'

'One of my brothers faxed me some clippings . . .' I didn't trust my voice. It was suddenly shaky.

'The brother who called us?' Wheeler cut in.

Brian had called them. Another piece clicked into place. I nodded. 'Why did he call you?'

'He suggested that your mother had been one of the experimental subjects. The dates jibed and we did some research. We now believe she was and we also think that she might have vital information – information we can use.'

'What kind of information?'

'You do realize that the MKULTRA files were shredded in '72 under the instructions of Richard Helms, who was then Director of the CIA. Also when Dr Ewen Cameron retired in '64, the Agency stopped by his house and collected four boxes of what, we know not, but we assume most of his personal files on patients and some of the stuff he couldn't leave at the Allan.'

'My brother's ill. He's asked me to help you in his place. Frankly, I'm not sure I want to. This is all a surprise to me.'

Rauh looked at me straight on. It was an uncomfortable sensation, like being raked by lightning. There was an undercurrent in the room that made me want to run.

'We'll give you some files. Can you stay for a couple of days?' he said.

'One day, possibly.'

'We can't let the files leave the city, but we could give you relevant ones overnight. But some of them are classified. Don't ask us where we got them because we won't tell you.'

'Why give them to me then?' My instinct was to cave in to any of their requests, and I was trying to fight it.

The two men glanced at each other again. One of Rauh's bushy eyebrows was raised.

'I mean, was my mother involved? On the evidence I have and given the robust state of her health, I'm not sure she was. Even if she was, even if she could become a plaintiff, she is hardly asking to be one. In fact, I think she'd view this visit of mine as a betrayal. So why let me see classified files?' Good, that was good, I said to myself.

Wheeler shrugged. 'Good point. But what about that will?'

I felt a chill. 'Dr Westley's?'

'Don't you think there was something peculiar about that?' Tom was speaking, but Rauh was watching out of the corner of his eye, while he shuffled through papers and put them in a briefcase.

'You're speculating. Besides, how the hell do you know about that will?' My voice was sharp.

'Your brother told us,' said Wheeler.

Tom leaned over and brushed my hand with his. It was meant as a gesture of comfort, but I pulled back. 'We have investigators, Catherine. We can help you and your mother.'

'Why do *we* need *your* help? My mother has never been good at dealing with crises, and the will and now my brother's illness have been more than she can take.' I was angry. 'If all this is true, she's had enough trouble, believe me, without all you guys landing on her.'

'Why don't you read the files we have, come to the hearing, meet the team?' said Wheeler. 'Then you can make up your mind. For a couple of reasons, which we'll explain later, we need a plaintiff like your mother and if we can't reach her, we'll court her daughter. And think of the story you'd have afterwards. That direct enough for you?'

'All right,' I said politely. 'I'll read the files. It would be a privilege to attend court with you both and meet your associates.'

'We first filed in 1980. We had a couple of plaintiffs then. We have five now and are looking for more. At first we wanted only background. We sent your mother a letter, but got no response.'

I shifted impatiently in my seat. I'd hoped we'd finished with my mother for the moment.

They looked at each other.

'Where are you in the case?' I asked.

Wheeler spoke. 'Val Orlikow came to us in '79 with a tale of horror. It seems that in 1950 she had suffered a bout of depression following the birth of her daughter. Eventually, she found help at the leading psychiatric institute in Canada. You know, of course, that her husband is a long-time member of the Canadian Parliament?'

I didn't. I shook my head and sat up straighter.

'The Allan Memorial was affiliated to McGill University, Canada's Harvard, I'm told. A teaching hospital, heavily endowed, with a research arm that was started by Dr D. Ewen Cameron.'

I shrugged. Some would dispute the Harvard statement, but the university was very good.

Wheeler's high light voice tripped on, ticking off the facts. 'Under Dr Cameron, Val was subjected to a number of unorthodox procedures in lieu of generally accepted psychotherapy. She was given LSD as well as other experimental drugs and exposed to what Dr Cameron called psychic driving, a procedure used nowhere else before or since, at least legally, during which tape-recorded messages were played to a semi-conscious patient, twenty hours a day, for weeks on end. She did not get better, she got worse.'

My hands were clasped between my knees and I was concentrating.

Wheeler continued: 'In the late seventies, Val and David Orlikow learned from *The New York Times*, through the work of researcher John Marks, that Cameron's work had been subsidized by the Central Intelligence Agency as part of a secret programme to study brainwashing.'

Rauh broke in. 'More than study brainwashing. They wanted to learn how to do it and Cameron claimed he had found the technique. They wanted to learn how to implant the suggestion to kill.'

'What?' I said.

'They wanted to learn how to control behaviour in a subject, to the extent that such a person would, unknowingly, kill on command, triggered by a sentence or, say, a phone message with a coded word in it.'

'Jesus,' I breathed.

'Anyway,' Tom's voice continued, 'Val's story checked out. She and her husband had been more than honest with us.'

'In 1946 Congress enacted a limited waiver of sovereign immunity for negligent acts of government employees,' Rauh explained. 'That means that the CIA operatives can be held liable for destroying the lives of innocents. It is the legal basis for our suit, but the whole thing is iffy. The CIA are trying to dismiss on the grounds that they're not liable. Yes, it may have happened, they say, but it's not the government's fault.'

'Can't have the world suing the CIA, you know,' Wheeler interjected.

I waited.

'So we got on our chargers – '

'White.'

'Polished up the armour – '

'And here we are, almost ten years later, broke and blocked at every turn,' Wheeler finished. He leaned over, pulled a grey suit jacket on and brushed his hair off his face. His grey eyes gleamed at me and I smiled back, unwillingly.

I cleared my throat. 'So what does this mean?'

'What it means is that we are suing the CIA,' said Rauh. 'We wanted to get the bastards when we started.' His voice was flat. 'Now we just want compensation for as many of their victims that have the nerve to come forward. Reagan's Washington is pro-CIA. I tell you, young woman, I took this case on for two reasons. The first was simply to right a wrong. The second was to prove to the American public that secret agencies must be curbed by some mechanism in the law. But I'm coming close to being disheartened.'

Tom cut in. 'We are trying to prove legal grounds for our suit first and we have almost done that. We have the issue of consent – no one who was admitted to the Allan Memorial Hospital consented to be used in an experiment in mind control. The Nuremberg Code laid out the grounds for consent precisely. We are trying to gather proof that the procedures used by Ewen Cameron were invasive, cruel and way beyond what was normal in the psychiatry of the time or for the relatively minor complaints of the patients he used.'

'So you're just – '

'We are gathering research on all these points. We are fighting for the right to take depositions from the then employees of the CIA, for memos and handbooks and letters. We are looking for psychiatrists who will evaluate Cameron's techniques. We are laboriously interviewing ageing and weak people about what happened thirty-five years ago. We're trying to build an overwhelming case that no one can refute.'

'I see. Slowly.'

'Very slowly,' Wheeler said. 'We get blocked constantly with court orders, mostly citing national security. But we've got four new plaintiffs, making nine altogether. A lot of the legwork was done by Frank Church's Senate Committee and the Rockefeller Commission, both of which investigated and reported on the CIA's domestic abuses in the late seventies.'

Rauh picked up. 'It is amusing to note here that one arm of

the Rockefeller family helped fund this research and another arm is investigating the damage done by research it funded.'

'Have you had any luck?' I asked.

'Finally, we got a ruling that it is governmental negligence, not negligence at source, that has the operative impact. Which means even if they weren't actually performing the experiments themselves, since they funded them, they are culpable.'

'That's the up side,' cracked Wheeler.

'The down side is dismal. Memories have faded, victims have died or their health has failed, witnesses have scattered or are dead. Most of the MKULTRA files were destroyed, as I said. Surprise, surprise. And, the CIA is trained in misdirection and steeped in deception. Even in our own operation critical documents go missing. Without doubt, all our telephones are bugged and they always seem to be able to anticipate our next move. We've had several clerks throw up their hands and leave, no notice, no reason, no references required. They just say they've had enough,' said Rauh. His deep voice resonated around the room.

'The Agency has been trying to get this thrown out from the beginning. We had one stroke of luck in January. The CIA shrink who acted as a project monitor testified that the proposal from Ewen Cameron had been solicited by the Agency. So we've got them cold, more or less,' said Wheeler.

'Tom's our optimist,' said Rauh. 'Hell, we received a slew of documents during documentary discovery that prove the CIA were aware of what they had done and were very uncomfortable about it indeed. Unfortunately, it doesn't mean much,' he continued. 'John Gittinger, the fellow Tom mentioned, said, and I quote, "We shouldn't have done it. I'm sorry we did it. Because it turned out to be a terrible mistake."'

I was lost. I needed some time to think. It was all coming at me too fast. 'That's pretty damning,' I offered.

'There are a thousand things they can throw at us to mitigate the force of that statement,' said Rauh. 'We've got another round coming up today. Would you like to join us?'

'Really?'

'We've admitted we're trying to seduce you.'

'Why?'

'We'll take any help we can get.' Rauh smiled at me, and the sting went out of his statement.

I wanted to refuse. But how could I? I had been out-manoeuvred.

Rauh heaved himself from his old leather chair. It looked as if it had seen several campaigns like this one. As did he. He was a big, good-looking, pack leader of a man. Head wolf. Chief lion. He grabbed a cane as he moved around the desk.

'Arthritic hip,' he said. 'It's like we're fighting a war. Only the war goes on for ever and we only get to fight one battle every eight months. Stamina, my dear. It's everything if you want to be a do-gooder.'

'Being a do-gooder wasn't exactly my idea of . . .' I trailed off.

'Do you have any choice?' He threw this over his shoulder as he stumped out of the room.

We cut through the lunch crowd in the lobby, and Wheeler flagged us a taxi. We all sat crammed in the back. No limos for these guys, I guessed.

'Tom is doing most of the talking this time. I'm fielding him slowly, letting them get used to him. He's as tough as I am, though he sure don't look it,' Rauh whispered in my ear.

'We're asking to settle this,' said Tom. 'We are asking a quarter million each.'

'Why?' I said.

'Why what?'

I shook my head to clear it. 'Why not take it the whole way? If it's such a convincing case, you should be able to get much more than $250,000. Look at the size of settlements these days. And maybe you could start the process towards that mechanism of control you mentioned. There should be some arm of the government that can hold a secret agency to account. It seems to me that would be precedent setting and an extraordinary achievement.'

'You'll get a taste of what we're up against today,' said Rauh and he patted my hand.

Wheeler's leg was pressed tight against mine. His briefcase

was on his lap and he went through a file carefully. A snapshot floated on to the floor. I grabbed for it, missed and tried again.

I slipped the snapshot back into Wheeler's briefcase. It was an old black-and-white, faded. It was of my mother as a young woman. We were silent for the rest of the ride.

The courtroom was small, but filled with light reflected from dozens of planes of highly polished wood. The air was delicately scented with furniture polish; even the floor was wooden and shining dark with polish. A small chandelier hung from the ceiling. I was impressed.

'The Oak Room, we call it,' cracked Wheeler behind me. I walked beside Joe Rauh, arm out to grab him if he needed it. He didn't. Energy seemed to consume him the moment we stepped out of the cab on to the courthouse steps. People stopped, some glanced from the corner of their eyes, afraid to look at someone who, in this town, under this administration, was the embodiment of the enemy. Their curiosity was palpable.

This, Wheeler informed me when we sat down, was to be a hearing on the admissibility of CIA station chiefs' testimony that they knew of MKULTRA's funding of Ewen Cameron during the fifties and sixties. The Agency was claiming that this was a matter of national security.

There were few spectators. The counsel for the Agency came in, four of them, all dressed in dark-grey suits. Their expressions were impenetrable.

'They're up to something,' said Rauh.

He was right. No sooner had Judge Penn entered and seated himself than one of them was on his feet with a settlement offer. Rauh limped up to the podium. We watched intently as the opposing counsel flipped through some papers, talked quickly. The Judge leaned forward, asked Rauh a question.

'No! A categorical no! Never,' barked Rauh and barrelled across the floor towards us, limp forgotten.

'They're offering $15,000 per plaintiff, on a nuisance basis. My

God, these men are barely human,' he said to us. Every muscle on his face was strained.

Wheeler rose to make his first motion. He was light on his feet, paced in front of the CIA counsel, red tie flopping out, his thin fingers tapping on the table in front of them. His comments focused on one thing: the public testimony of the CIA station chiefs at the time. Both men had been contacted, both had agreed to testify.

Rauh leaned over and whispered to me, 'We know that there was a formal admission of guilt by the CIA to the Canadian government at that time. And an apology.'

'How do you know?' I whispered back.

'The Canadian External Affairs Minister told us.'

'Oh wow.' It was only partly ironic.

'Guilt.' He spat out the word. 'A temporary aberration. This is a fencing match between the two governments. Real back-room stuff, boys only, deals for deals. You probably got a free Ford factory for this one.'

The CIA counsel rose to argue his point. He was pencil-thin, with a face God forgot to punctuate. The duelling started slowly, became fast and furious. I watched Wheeler in admiration. His light voice became infinitely flexible and subtle. I felt envious of such skill.

The Judge slammed his gavel down. 'I have heard the arguments from both sides. Anything else, gentlemen?'

Rauh rose. 'May I remind the court that this case has been stuck in prelim for eight years now and that our plaintiffs are old and infirm. Old before their years and infirm beyond what we can imagine. And that we, our government, representing the American people, caused their infirmity. That we experimented on innocent citizens – not terrorists or subversives, but people who were living ordinary, law-abiding lives. We deliberately violated the Nuremberg Code, a set of principles we were instrumental in setting up. The first and most important point of this code, forged in the flames of the Nazi death camps, is that the voluntary consent of the human subject is absolutely essential. That we allow the Agency to delay due procedure on this case is another example of the arrogance of government. Let it not continue by delays in judgment.'

Judge Penn's face had slowly reddened throughout this speech. The chair scraped the wooden floor as he stood.

'You'll have my answer today, Mr Rauh.'

Rauh sat down heavily after the Judge left the court. 'And I won't like it either, I'll just bet.'

The CIA general counsel rose as one man and prepared to leave.

As they passed us, one paused, leaned over and whispered. There was an amused gleam in his eye.

'You're wasting your time, people,' he said. 'No one gives a damn about those wrecks.'

THREE

We ordered crab cakes for lunch. As soon as the food arrived, Wheeler and Rauh asked me about my mother's health.

'She's all right, more or less.'

'Which means?'

'I don't know. She's always rushing around, doing things women like her do – charities, parties, tennis. I was sent to boarding school at thirteen. When I came home, she always looked good, never complained.'

'Do you remember her last time in the Allan Memorial?'

Old memories. I was silent, trying to find the words. '1962. I was eleven,' I said finally.

'By then, Dr Cameron was desperate for a breakthrough. And the first?'

'I think she was also in the hospital in '57, after Brian was born. Cameron had started his experiments by then, hadn't he?'

'Yes,' said Wheeler. 'Funding from the CIA started then. But we think Dr Cameron had been developing his techniques for years. By '57, the Sleep Room was in full operation.'

'What was that?'

'The Sleep Room was what the hospital called the room where the patients undergoing psychic driving were kept. They were drugged into a half-sleep, so that they could not move or get up unassisted.

Football helmets were placed on their heads. Inside the football helmet was a tiny tape recorder, on which played their driving message on a tape loop. Up to twenty hours a day, sometimes for up to a month.'

I pushed the food around on my plate, shook my head.

'That's enough, Tom,' said Joe.

'Look, I don't think anything excessive was done to her,' I said. 'She's so strong. She's the healthiest of all her friends. She wins all the Senior Ladies' tennis tournaments at her club.'

Wheeler shrugged and stopped his questioning. But again I could sense disbelief.

I walked back to the office with them.

'Listen, young woman, you seem to be bright enough,' said Rauh. 'If you're interested, think about sticking around. We have a videotaped deposition coming in from Canada this afternoon. See it and then Tom will give you some reading.'

I was feeling pretty miserable. I thought about Brian. One day. 'OK.'

He shook my hand and limped back to his office. We watched him disappear.

'He needs a hip replacement,' said Wheeler. 'And the reason he won't watch this with us is that it hurts him. He is one of the grand old men of this city.'

'Not that old, surely?'

'Seventy-five is old for this fight, Catherine.'

A woman met us on the way to his office. 'It's all set up. We're waiting.'

'Catherine Ramsey, this is Mary Burney, one of our associates. Mary, Catherine is a journalist who may be able to help us.'

She looked uncertain for a moment, then spoke. 'Oh, is this your area?'

'Not really and I don't know whether I can help. But it's certainly fascinating.' I studied her. She had beautiful hair, straight, dark and glossy, which swung around a wide plain face.

'Tom, you're wanted on 2104,' the receptionist called down the hall.

'I'll leave you in Mary's competent hands.' He sped off.

'Come on, we're showing this in the conference room. It's where we meet, day in, day out,' said Mary.

I trotted obediently after her.

'How did he find you?' she said.

'My brother called him.'

'Oh, why?'

I was confused by her abrupt manner, but I decided to take a chance on her. 'They think my mother might have been involved.'

She swung around and faced me; her large liquid eyes shone for a moment. 'I'm so sorry.'

'They say they're having trouble with plaintiffs.'

'I haven't heard that. We just found another. But the more we find, the sadder and more compelling the case gets. I hope she wasn't involved. Your mother, I mean.'

'I don't think she was. Oh, she was his patient, all right, but experiments? I doubt it. She's too healthy.'

'Well, if she is, she may not have been a subject. But he was hardly discriminating. He saw everyone as a lab rat. Well, this might help you make up your mind. It's a deposition from a new plaintiff, a Jeanne Benoît. It's wrenching, so be prepared.'

There were four people waiting in a small conference room. Mary introduced me. They nodded, no smiles. Someone turned off the overhead lights. Daylight inched through faded sun strips. The video flickered and a picture formed.

The face on the screen was that of a woman in her early sixties. Her features were wooden. They didn't seem to move like flesh and her skin had a faintly yellow cast.

'Why does she look like that?' I whispered to Mary.

'We've found it's one of the effects of the drugs they were given. Any neuroleptic can do that if taken long enough, but the drugs they were given were massive in dosage and experimental for the most part.'

'What's a neuroleptic?'

'It's an antipsychotic. A drug developed for schizophrenia. Described by patients as "the chemical strait-jacket". They're much more refined now. In the fifties they were the equivalent of a blunt instrument.'

I looked back at the screen. A question was whispered to the woman by an off-camera interlocutor. The effect of this made the woman seem like a zombie. She looked straight at us as she answered, haltingly.

'I was first admitted to the Allan Memorial for depression. I had undergone a hysterectomy for uterine cancer. I was only thirty-five. When I came out of the hospital, there were terrible gaps in my memory and my depression was worse. But I would have rather died than gone back in there.

'Two years ago, Val Orlikow contacted me. I refused to help her then, but in the last two years, I have started to remember what happened. I have written it all down, as Val told me, and I will give it to you.'

Another question, whispered off-camera.

'When I left the hospital, I couldn't eat. I was so depressed I couldn't speak properly. There was a weight pressing down on my chest that nearly flattened me. I was in despair. I had no desire for my husband. I had no menstrual cycle. I had lost nearly thirty pounds.

'I went to the public clinic at the Royal Victoria Hospital and was referred to the Allan . . .'

As the voice droned on, my dread mounted. She described horrors about insulin-coma therapy, something I had never heard of. She said she had often taken up to forty pills a day. She talked about being shot in the eye with a high-powered blast of air and slumping to the floor in shock. Then she talked about being strapped into a chair, wired up and asked questions for hours on end.

The harsh voice continued, still empty of emotion.

'My first memory after treatment was of being in a deep, dark, pitch-black hole with no sense of appendages, like a worm. But I didn't know enough to know I should have arms and legs. There was no sense of solidity, like I was not on ground and I was not in water . . . there must have been something left, because there was an awareness of being. I was also aware that there had been no beginning, that this seemed to have been going on for ever . . .

'The final blow came when, two years after I left, my family doctor examined me and told me that I had arcus senilis, the white rings round the iris that indicate advanced old age. I was thirty-seven.

'I live every day fighting depression and fear. That's all. Thank you.'

The screen went grey. The room was silent for a moment, then everyone started whispering to each other. I felt a hand on my shoulder. I turned and looked up. It was Tom.

'Catherine, are you all right?'

'Yes. Why wouldn't I be?' I said, then smiled at him. But my mouth wasn't behaving properly and the smile was a travesty.

He patted my shoulder. I stood up, leaning on the chair for support. Tom walked me out of the room. 'The old man wants to see you again,' he said, once we were out of earshot.

'What for?'

'He has something to ask. Come on.'

I trailed after him down the hallway, into the big end office where Rauh sat, coffee tray all ready. I shook my head as he offered. I couldn't drink any more of the stuff.

'We'll get right to it, Catherine,' he said. 'Have you heard of the Grid Room yet?'

I shook my head.

'It was a particularly heinous form of the experiments our good doctor was carrying out. As Tom mentioned at lunch, we think that by the early sixties Cameron was desperate for a breakthrough and ready to take his experiments to the terminal stage. Most of the files on it were destroyed. We have anecdotal evidence only.'

'What does that mean, terminal stage?'

'To the point of death. He had promised his various funders that he could find the secret of brainwashing. There had been too many relapses with the psychic-driving techniques. The Grid Room was his answer to his critics, and by 1961 there were many critics.'

'Oh.'

'We think your mother was involved.'

A blow straight to the stomach. 'Why?'

'One of the doctor's assistants has come forward, off the record, as you call it, and he told us about the room.' He fumbled through his papers, found what he was looking for. 'Here.' He gave it to me. I read:

> The Grid Room was in the basement of the Allan Memorial, along with a room called the Isolation Chamber. The Grid Room had lines drawn across one wall and a hard-backed chair in front of them. At the opposite end of the room, a carefully concealed hole had been made in the wall, only big enough to take the lens of a movie camera mounted on a platform on the other side. Anyone sitting in the chair would be unaware that he or she was being secretly filmed. The room was meant to measure in a patient 'the angle of the trunk axis when sitting down', and to record on film how much 'energy output' was used by a patient when moving. Each patient was fitted with electrodes, which Rubenstein called 'potentiometers', and which would 'convert an analog signal and telemeter it to a receiving station, which was a bank of electronic equipment, including a large machine with dials and switches which he called the 'body movement transducer'. This gizmo was supposed to provide 10,000 bits of information per second from each patient. They needed to know at what hour of day a patient displayed most energy. Then they could assault the patient with drugs in order to break the patient down completely.
>
> The Isolation Chamber looked like a prison cell, with a double-thickness door and cladded walls. It was meant to isolate and disorient patients before Dr Cameron began to 'restructure' their attitudes. Patients were meant to stay in the chamber for weeks, months, and if need be years – until they were ready to listen to what Dr Cameron wanted them to hear.

I was sickened by the descriptions. I gave him back the papers.

'This man won't be subpoenaed. That was our deal. We have to use him as background. We can't get any hard evidence.' There was a pause. 'That's why we wonder whether you'd talk to your mother.'

He held up his hand to forestall me speaking. 'I know you don't want to trouble her, and that we already have enough plaintiffs for good research. But we've found no one else who was in the Allan during '62–3, at the time the Grid Room was being used constantly, who . . .'

I was surprised at his hesitation.

'Who survived,' said Tom crisply. 'Your mother survived.'

I didn't have to think about this. Not after listening to that poor woman's shame and misery.

'No way. Find yourself another pigeon.' I slid back the chair. Something, exhaustion perhaps, failure of will, my constant companion, was holding me in it.

Tom held up both hands. 'Come back to my office and get the stuff. You might want to take a day or so to read it. I'll give you my home phone number and Mary's. So if you have any questions . . .'

I stood up, so confused I didn't know what to say. I needed time to think. I followed him into his office. He sat down, pulled a fat file out of his bottom drawer and pushed it across the table to me.

'There's a lot of reading. And it's unpleasant and frightening. Do you have someone in town who you can stay with?'

I shook my head.

'Sure you want to do this?'

'I don't have a choice really. I need to know,' I said.

He studied my face for a moment, nodded once, then left the office and hurried down the hall.

I followed him, lost in a hailstorm of thoughts. My shock was turning into anger. Were these people manipulating me? How dare Wheeler try to tempt me to deliver my mother to the vagaries of the court system, to be picked over and traumatized further, with a story, with a job? Why did they want her anyway? My mother hadn't been involved in this mess. She didn't look like that woman on the monitor. She was just too strong for this to have happened to her. Now they were implying worse things had happened to her.

I stopped in my tracks. Saw-toothed memories swam up to greet me. The light in the corridor shimmered and I rubbed my eyes. What did I know? Really know? Maybe they were right.

Impossible. I shook myself.

The professional interceded. If this had anything to do with my family, anything at all, maybe I should do the story for their sakes and mine, and it would be a way to use the work that I thought I loathed. Humbug. I wasn't a crusader and I didn't buy into that cathartic shit. I was performing a favour for Yvette and my sick brother and then I was going to go back to Mark and forget all about it.

It had started to rain. I stood in the gutter, trying to hail a cab. Finally one stopped and I asked him just to drive. The meter ticked and the rain streaked the windows and I couldn't see much. But the movement was somehow comforting. Finally, I asked him to take me back to the hotel.

I love hotel rooms – the more featureless, the better, and I love them especially when no one knows where I am.

I shed my business clothes and ordered a huge early dinner from room service. Then I had a bath, and washed off the stink of the plane and the council chambers and wrapped myself in the bathrobe provided by the hotel.

The food arrived. Vegetable soup, rare steak, mashed potatoes and a big slice of chocolate cake. When I work, I go for comfort food. I turned up the thermostat in the room, turned on the TV, put the tray on my lap, and the files beside me on the bed.

I had estimated their heft carefully on the way up in the elevator. About one thousand pieces of paper – six, maybe eight hours of reading. My attention jumped between them and CNN while I ate.

Curiosity got the better of me. I opened the master-file envelope. It had my name pencilled on it. Inside there were three large files. One was called simply Dr D. Ewen Cameron. One had my mother's name on it. The third was called ARTICHOKE. It seemed the most harmless. I started on that.

My discipline had not deserted me completely. I read long into the evening, turning on lights as they were needed, piecing the story together from notes scratched on foolscap, from xeroxes of xeroxes, obtained under the '72 Freedom of Information Act, with large black lines through a lot of words, from précis of information roughly typed and initialled by Tom Wheeler.

The file did not present a coherent picture. The estimate quickly went up to twelve hours. Before long, I had put pieces of paper on every surface in the room. Finally, defeated by dates, areas of operation, intertwining government departments, I called down to room service for Post-it notes, felt pens, a pot of coffee, as a special treat, and a pack of Marlboro Lights. I started taking notes myself, and as I did, a picture began to emerge.

It was the spectre of the heroic, uncompromising freedom fighter, Cardinal Mindszenty, on a Hungarian witness stand in 1949, robotically confessing to crimes of treason he could not have committed, that escalated the fears of the old war horses of the OSS. How, they wondered, had the communists created this zombie? Mindszenty, declared a CIA memo of the time, was controlled by 'some unknown force'.

What that 'unknown force' was, and how to counteract it, became the obsession of the new cold-war warriors who were merely the old World War II warriors with a bunch of new toys and hellbent on maintaining their control. The first CIA programme in behaviour control was called, happily enough, BLUEBIRD.

It was a small step from defence to offence. By the time twenty-year-old kids from the Midwest were plopped on to New York street corners fresh from North Korean prison camps, and started busily passing out leaflets on the joys of life in a communist state, BLUEBIRD had turned into ARTICHOKE, a favourite vegetable of Allen Dulles, the man who crafted the new CIA from the skeleton of the OSS. Americans were terrified and President Eisenhower was shouting for action.

ARTICHOKE's goal was simple. It was created to discover methods to 'control an individual to the point where he will do our bidding against his will and even against such fundamental laws of nature as self-preservation'.

Bureaucratic infighting for the control of the programme was vicious. From 1949 to 1955, the programme shifted back and forth among three branches of the CIA and finally ended up at TSS or Technical Services Staff. TSS was a top-secret branch filled with Ph.D.s with lots of operational experience and not much in the way of ethics. Or rather, as Dulles said at the time, 'A recruit's ethics must be such that he would be completely co-operative in any phase of our programme, regardless of how revolutionary it may be.'

There was some attempt at co-operation with the Canadian and British governments and overtures were made to Hoover's FBI. There was no information in the file on how or whether co-operation had been forthcoming.

Recruitment of qualified scientists was difficult. A candidate's ethics, often enough, were not such that he 'might care to co-operate in certain more "revolutionary" phases of our project'. Nor was managing ARTICHOKE all that easy.

Then there was the problem of human guinea-pigs. The most convenient subjects were Eurospy trash, the junk that washed up in the agency outposts of the world: unimportant defectors, double agents, plants, etc. 'Unique research material', they were called, for they were trained, and in theory, therefore, harder to break. Nobody cared about them and they might even have useful information.

Prisoners of war were also considered ideal subjects. Dulles, after talking to Swiss drug manufacturers, became convinced that the Russians had used drugs and hypnosis to create the 'Show Trials', in which shot-down POWs in Russian courtrooms recited the miseries of life in capitalist America and the glories of communism.

Thus, the experiments started, in various separate projects. Combinations of drugs, hypnosis, and interrogation were used on Japanese, Korean and Vietnamese prisoners of war and, of course, the middle-European denizens of the shadow world. As far as could be determined, no project director knew about what was being done in projects not his own. There were no controls.

Benzedrine, Seconal, marijuana, LSD, PCP, electrosleep machines and shock were the most common tools used. After the subject had been turned into a drooling mess, unable to remember his wife's name or the year he was living in, under hypnosis it was suggested to him that what had occurred would be forgotten. Total amnesia of the experiments on the subject's part was the most critical part of ARTICHOKE's plan.

In some cases, experiments were taken to the terminal stage. The first four 'subjects' were Japanese, thought to be double agents. Rumour had it that Dulles had presided over that one himself and had them fed to the sharks way out at sea at midnight, the evening after he had scrambled their brains with alternating injections of massive doses of Seconal and Benzedrine.

Nothing provided the answers the CIA sought. No combination of 'tools' produced subjects who had been brainwashed in the same way that the American boys captured during the Korean War had been brainwashed.

By 1953, Allen Dulles was feeling hopeless. The President was demanding a weapon in the war on brainwashing. The Great American Public was in panic mode, building fallout shelters behind homes in the spanking new suburbs and stocking them with canned food. People saw communists under every schoolroom desk. The equations were simple: the threat of communism was real and dangerous. They had a tool, we didn't. They could change the way people thought. We couldn't.

Dulles realized that in order to crack the code he needed an arena in which to duplicate everything the communists could have done. Prior trials had been haphazard: on transients, hookers, drug addicts, prisoners, even on their own people in safe houses or apartments rented for the purpose. They needed clinical controls. In order to conduct such clinical trials, they needed a laboratory, ideally their own hospital, their own patients, their own Dr Frankenstein.

The dangers were obvious and enormous. If the American people discovered that extensive and terminal trials had been funded by their taxes, and carried out on their own citizens, it would mean the end of his career. It would mean the end of his brother and sister's career – John Foster Dulles was Secretary of State and his sister ran the Berlin desk; it would be the end of the historic Dulles sway over American foreign policy. It would seriously curtail the Agency's power for decades to come.

Finally all his doubts came down to one question. 'Did it have to be Americans who would be used as guinea-pigs?'

Enter Dr D. Ewen Cameron, one of the world's most prominent psychiatrists and head of his very own psychiatric hospital in Canada. Even better than this, he was a Scot who had become a loyal American, trained at Johns Hopkins University. Cameron signed on, demanding only that he would have complete control and unlimited freedom to solicit additional funds. His goal was a teaching hospital and research centre. He was a friend of Allen Dulles. He was a godsend.

When this final piece of information clicked into the puzzle, I ran to the bathroom and vomited. My stomach heaved again and again, until I was throwing up stinging yellow bile. Finally, hollow and with a foul taste in my mouth, but filled with energy I hadn't felt in a very long time, I sat back on my heels and stared into the middle distance. My eyes focused on the bathroom telephone.

I ordered a jug of hot chocolate, a bottle of chilled vodka and another pack of Marlboro Lights. I lurched back into my bed. While I waited for room service, I sat wrapped in the plastic bedspread, staring into the lights of the Washington night.

FOUR

It crept up slowly, a faint backbeat of alarm, then, sharp and hard, my heart started pounding. I was in the middle of a panic attack. I leaned back against the quilted headboard of the bed, rocking back and forth, and worked on catching an even breath. My heart raced so fast it frightened me, and then it went off track, faint and uneven. I didn't take tranquillizers any more – not since it took eighteen months to get off them. This time I would have made an exception. I prayed for room service to come.

My heart stopped hammering about a half-hour after the vodka and hot chocolate arrived. The milk settled my stomach enough to take the vodka. The sugar helped the shock. I'm an expert at food chemistry. When I started reporting, one of the required extra-curricular activities was to perfect the art of drinking to the point where you maintained reason and stayed sensate. The point was to deaden emotion, throw off all the little tendrils of panic and sorrow and hopelessness that you encounter in an average day's work. In my case tonight, it was a survival tactic.

I began to feel better. My breathing stopped stuttering and grew even. Night gathered and thickened. Lights flickered from the buildings across the street. I roused myself enough to put on a table lamp, draw the curtains.

I stared at the other two files sitting on top of the TV. I had paged through them quickly, looking but not looking. Compared to the ARTICHOKE file, these were filled with personal information, stuff about my parents' lives, my life, our history. My mother's case file looked thick and poisonous.

I drank, and slowly, slowly, I reached that treasured state of detachment.

Come on, I said to myself, as the quiet Washington night wore on, our childhood hadn't been too bad. Like everyone's, it was a pattern of light and shadow – lightly sketched, mostly forgotten images. I remembered the tree-lined streets of the village where I grew up. I remembered our dog, an enormous epileptic Airedale who only tolerated us and tried to kill visitors.

Some emotions I couldn't forget. They had stayed with me despite my efforts to blot them out. I remembered dinners filled with hilarity and rapid-fire conversation and bad weeks of hoping that Mother would be normal and that my father would be cheerful when he walked through the door.

The bad days were many. She would be in bed and he would be angry. We could tell, within ninety seconds of his return, whether he was in a rage or not. If he was, my brothers and I would retreat as far as was possible to our private areas of the house and not move or speak. On those nights, even watching television was risky.

I remembered my mother forcing the three of us to learn to ski, young and uncoordinated, trying to measure up to her extraordinary standards of sportsmanship. She believed that, if you could hit a golf ball straight, win three straight sets of tennis or ski for eight hours a day, everything would be fine. So, me at nine, Ross, seven and Brian four, and our mountain goat of a mother trekking through four feet of unpacked snow to the golf course, climbing the hills and screaming and sliding our way down, tears turning to ice on Brian's chubby cheeks. We'd hate her, but for days afterwards were red and flushed with oxygen, completely exhilarated.

I remembered the days just before the summer people arrived and the weeks after, when the months stretched out ahead of us, one party after another, parties for adults, for children, for teenagers, for all of us, all together.

Other memories rose unbidden. I remembered the odd blisters on Brian's hands. My mother said they were from his touching the ends of the fire tongs just after they were removed from the fire. He banged his head constantly against his headboard, some nights all night. I remembered his blond hair and big brown eyes, his fire. He would argue anything to the death, no matter how wrong he might be.

I pulled the bedspread over my head then and sat looking at darkness, smelling the scent of dry-cleaning fluid and other people. I couldn't face it. Yvette had said that Brian had nearly died from his guilt and terror. I preferred to suppress it, to hide, to allow these brave men on their white chargers to fight and slay the CIA dragon by themselves, without me. I wanted to go home.

I reached for the phone, pulled it towards me on the bed. I would call Mark and he would come and get me and then I could hide. Or first, I would ring Yvette and say that Wheeler and Rauh were the best in the business and were well on the way to winning this case. And then I could go home. A lump formed in my throat and I wanted to cry. My eyes stung and filled with water, clouding my vision; the tears refused to fall. I brushed them away angrily. This was too hard for me. Eleven when they took away my mother, just eleven. And for what? We didn't know. There was no reason that we could see. Ross, only nine, at boarding school, banished. Brian just six.

I moved my legs off the bed, walked across the bedroom floor to the television and picked up the file.

It was a thick, legal-sized buff envelope that was bulging at the seams. I took a deep breath, opened it, and spilled the contents on to the bed. Photographs, letters, cablegrams, more xeroxed papers with lines blacked out, her naval record, more photographs, my christening certificate, my school records from boarding school, my brothers' school records, the membership rotas at the various clubs we belonged to, transcripts of phone conversations, photographs of my parents' wedding reception, and finally, in one large glassine envelope, a medical file. My God, how did they get all this?

I picked up the medical file. Hers. I opened it, pulled out all the subfiles and laid them on the bed. One file was filled with notes written in a small crabbed hand, slanting forward. They were Cameron's notes. I shoved it aside. Another had 'Writings' marked on it. Inside were piles of old-fashioned foolscap, grey and spongy paper that felt fragile to the touch.

Another file listed each plaintiff on the inside front cover. It was marked 'Effects and Side-effects'. Transcripts of taped interviews mostly – thick, endless. One sheet, typed single spaced, neatly on a standard typewriter, fell out. 'Effects of early versions of Chlorpromazine' was the title.

Just notes really. I was about to put it aside, then one item on the list caught my eye. 'The drug drastically lowers blood pressure. Mode of action unknown, as of 1949.' Fine. What else? Allergic reactions, jaundice and liver damage, nausea and gastric distress, irregular heart rhythms, dry mouth and nose, a general susceptibility to colds. EPS, they called them – extrapyramidal symptoms. Abnormal muscle reactions. Uncontrollable and painful cramps, muscle seizures in the lower back, life-threatening spasms in the mouth and throat that interfere drastically with breathing. Uncontrollable writhing, squirming, twisting, grimacing, pacing, foot-tapping, finger rolling, rigidity and trembling, on through the whole dreadful list.

Neuroleptics had improved the quality of life for schizophrenics. No longer did they have to be restrained or lobotomized. Chlorpromazine was called the chemical strait-jacket. A memory jarred me.

I was fourteen, home from school for a long weekend, and I walked into the blue bedroom after breakfast to find her on the floor, rigid, jaw clenched and head pulled down to her shoulder. The expression on her face had terrified me and I ran to her, touched her. I remembered seeing these cramps before, three years earlier. Massage had helped. Her muscles were hard as wood. I rubbed them slightly, then harder, and as I watched her, helpless tears slid from her eyes. After about ten minutes the spasm passed and I helped her on to the bed where she slowly slid into a trance of relaxation. We never spoke of it.

I read on. As Mary had said, these drugs were sledgehammers compared to today's psychometric drugs. I reviewed what I had ferreted, over the years, from various adults. First collapse before I was born. She had been released only for a few months when she got pregnant with me. My father had been curt. I'd had to drag information from him. 'She's all right,' he had insisted.

But these side-effects, mild though they were, I had them too. I felt all this. I had arhythmia and bizarre minor liver-damage. Every doctor had remarked upon it during my recent bouts with illness. One of them had accused me of excessive hard-drug use, which I had denied angrily. I had terrible allergies, I caught every cold going, my blood pressure was so low that some doctors joked I was barely alive. Nothing serious, but it seemed that the symptoms that I had carried with me all my life were precisely the same as the minor side-effects of the early neuroleptics.

The abyss yawned wide then. Anger was the rope across the abyss and the world wasn't large enough to contain my anger. If I had a gun I would have shot my mother's initials into the ceiling of the hotel room and calmly waited for the police to arrive. I needed a fight. But girls with two university degrees do not carry guns. Instead of shooting at things, they read.

I returned to her file and spread out the subfiles, turned them over on the bed. I glanced over the diagnosis: 'Schizophrenic. Patient exhibits profound personality displacement. Prognosis: poor.' More notes, treatments tried. Multiple shocks, sleep therapy. Drugs. No names, just numbers. 1957. The year after Brian was born. More shock. LSD-25, PCP, more shocks. Depatterning. Twenty days of negative driving to complete depatterning.

I picked up another file dated 1957. Dr Cameron had standardized his treatments by then. First the patient was interviewed at length, usually while drugged. Then, still drugged, the patient was placed in a room, alone, for hours at a time, and told to write. From her writing, he constructed negative and positive driving messages to tape, for her to listen to, during the second phase of treatment, which he had called psychic driving. After three weeks of listening to a negative message, drugged into a half-sleep, he replaced the negative message with a positive message, meant to rebuild the patient's confidence. Then, he put her to sleep for two weeks, ensuring that she would forget, largely, anything that had happened to her.

In my mother's file I found her driving message, presumably played to her through speakers in a football helmet. Some of it was in her own voice, the rest in Dr Cameron's: 'You are childish and manipulative. You are a disgrace to your family and to the people who love you. You have been a failure at everything. Your children do not love you. Your husband never did. Your father is dead. You must not defile his memory by thinking of him sexually.'

I threw the thing off the bed. She had listened to this twenty hours a day, for three weeks, a tape recorder strapped inside a football helmet, and drugged immobile.

Sheaves of foolscap fell to the floor. The writing on them was in my mother's hand, crabbed, stunted, then sometimes expanded and wild. I had seen that hand, tamed, for decades, on weekly letters that found me everywhere in the world.

'I don't trust my husband any more. He wants me to be in here. I don't want them to see these writings. My father would understand. He would take me out of here and bring me back to where I was once. I was once strong and healthy. I was strong and healthy because he believed in me. Everyone else wants to use me. They don't care about me at all.

'The doctors don't care either. They want to examine my brain. I know doctors. I understand them. They ask me senseless questions and I try to give them sense. But they do not think it is important from the psychological point of view. They are the ones who are mad. I am not mad, I put myself in here but I am not mad. I know what I am doing. I am not frightened of losing my mind. I am not frightened of losing my husband. I am frightened of losing my children.'

'*I hate you*!' she had scrawled across a whole sheet of paper.

'Why don't you come for me, and save me from this? Why do you keep putting these drugs in my veins and stringing me out like a stretched piano wire, so stretched, the sound becomes dull and has no force? Why do you do this to me?

'I can't understand why you don't let my children come and see me. Don't you see how I miss them? I must leave, I must get out and see them. I must take them away. This city only understands money and power. We must leave, fly away to the sun and the prairie and live a simple life with the ducks and the geese and the fish-filled rivers. I am terrified of being locked up and losing my children. I want to leave now.

'I am afraid of people because I believe they will hurt me. I love my husband, but he believes in the doctors and I do not any longer believe in the doctors.'

The last page. Calmer, seemingly drug-free and clear-headed, in tiny writing, precise and definite, the nib of the pen tearing the paper:

'The smallest sound, like my hand dragging across the sheet in the morning, echoes like the roar of the Atlantic. My hand aches from endless writing. In the late afternoons I sit, stupefied by tranquillizers I had to kneel and beg for outside in the hall at the nurses' station, watching the sun dip into the trees behind the hospital. Sunlight fills my eyes and tiny drops of it dance behind them. Noises from the corridor behind me thunder in my brain. *God*, it hurts! *Stop* it hurting. I miss my children. I give up. I've lost everything, just let me go home.'

Her file became suddenly disorganized. There was a gap in her writing of a week. Notes made and signed by Cameron, and by the resident assigned solely to her case. Case number 50-0010-3683. Scraps of paper on which she had written. Directions from the doctors to write about specific events. I reconstructed the next few days:

By the end of the second month of treatment in 1957, someone had to dress her in the mornings. She no longer wore her own clothes, but a hospital-issue nightdress and dressing gown, and she shuffled through the hallways on prescribed walks beside a guard. 'Movements restricted and inhibited', said the record. 'Low self-confidence', said the record. Her head was lowered so as not to see anything.

She hallucinated and reported what she saw to the nurses. A skull glittered behind the face of a kind orderly, demons snatched at her ankles as she walked. The press of the starched fabric against her skin was agonizing. It felt like sandpaper.

The world was flat, featureless. Nothing seemed more important than anything else. The fact that she wanted to shake her new baby, Brian, she said to one nurse, who reported it immediately to Cameron, was equally as important as the fact that she had just re-papered her bedroom walls and stripped and sanded the banisters in her hall stairwell.

Then fuzzy images glimmered, then sharpened. She started writing again, painstakingly detailing the sounds, sights, and feeling she experienced as a six year old thrilled to drive around town with her dad, and then, the next week, she was an eighteen year old obsessed by figure skating and politics, longing to leave this boring town.

Once in a while voices rose from her past and shouted at her. Hollering imprecations and accusations – hating her, making her feel filthy and tired and worn out with guilt. She wrote down what the voices said.

Her reason, her ability to build a logical argument about anything, disappeared. Logic was no longer interesting. There were so many other things that had meaning.

'If only it did not hurt so much,' she wrote. 'I hear everything that goes on in the hospital. Layers of sound rise from the basement to the tower. I hear screams and cries and whimpering and the murmuring of nurses. I can distinguish the sharper voices of the doctors, giving orders. I hear the hesitant whisper of the occasional outsider, a visitor. The traffic, a half-mile away on Peel Street, is deafening. I ask for ear-plugs. Then I hear the throb of my blood moving through my body; the rush of the fluids in my sinuses, the fall and lift of my lungs, the thunder of my heartbeat. I am exhausted from all this sensation.'

Suddenly the writing changed and her script slanted forward, the pressure on the pen harder, as if she had woken up.

'I must tell my side of the story. It will help me. Please understand what happened. My days are filled with fear and endless horrible sound, and my nightmares are one long line of terrible images. I only rest in the afternoons – don't you see? My mind is only blank then and I wait for it, I plan for it, I know I can survive, if I have those empty afternoons. I have the drugs in the morning, always different, I never know what I am going to see or feel. Then I write, if I can, until you tell me to stop. Then, you take me back to the room and lunch is brought in. And then I have another needle, a delicious warm soft drug that makes me smile. I am happy.

'You see, that afternoon a nurse came in with a manicure set. She is the one who gives me my shots. She sat down beside me as I watched the slow setting of the sun. "What do you want?" I said. "Can't you see I'm resting?"

'"My dear, I've just come to file your nails," said the nurse.

'I heard only the sticky sweetness in the voice and I loathed it. "I don't want them cut. This is my time for me. Go away."

'"Now, Mrs Ramsey – look at your nails. They are getting so long!" The nurse took my hand and pressed the fingers flat. She slowly trimmed a sliver off my ring finger.

'I felt as if she had scraped the inside of my brain with her scissor blade. The sound was so hard, the sensation so awful that I lunged for the hand holding my arm and I bit it.

'The nurse screamed and jumped back. The chair tipped over and her instruments scattered all over the floor.

'Now those were satisfactory sounds, I thought. They felt good.

'Scuttling back to a safe distance, the nurse bent and swiftly gathered up her scissors and files. She says that I laughed then. Perhaps I did. Red in the face, she rushed out of the room in a curious backwards scrabble.

'I laughed. I'm sure I did. And I turned my face back to the window. The colours of the setting sun bathed me in light. So soft they were, so different from the garish shades I see when I don't have the tranquillizers. I wondered what there would be for dinner.'

All this and more was in her file.

She had tried to escape the next morning. Spat out her pills and yanked the IV out of her arm and waited till she was sober. Then, in her hospital nightdress, down the corridor, up the stairs to the side door, the fire door, then out on to the icy steps, sliding down, falling, the ice scraping her bare legs.

Dr Cameron prescribed curare and she lay paralysed in a basement room for two weeks.

Dawn was streaking the night sky before I finally passed out. My hands were still clenched around the papers.

FIVE

When I woke, it was nearly noon. My body felt as if someone had stretched it on a rack, taking time to rip the muscles and separate tendon from joint. I lay on the thick impersonal mattress of the hotel, anaesthetized by sleep and a hangover and a day that had refused to end until I had collapsed with exhaustion. I made an effort to think. I was slow and I couldn't feel much of anything, but anxiety thrummed and my mind was running away with me.

Who was she? I hated her. I loved her. She had formed me and I had left her the moment the door opened and I could form the sentence saying I was leaving.

She had grown up on the prairie, the empty middle of the country, a place I had never seen. A prairie chicken, a prairie hen, a prairie dog, these were the epithets she hurled at herself on days when things weren't working right. She was born with dark hair and blue eyes as pretty and chill as the Atlantic on a hot summer day.

We had heard about the virtues of her father, who had seen the future and bravely – for it was the depths of the Depression at the time – called it good. She had loved him with no small passion, and had sat listening, during his Saturday coffee mornings with the other powers in their forgettable city, to the man who loved Roosevelt and Shaw and Bertrand Russell. I never knew him, but I wished I had.

I heard about his brother, her uncle, another angular Scot, the famous Dr Westley. He was her hero and a kind of protector. She taught us success was something to be fought for, worked for, something to be desired. But we were spoiled by our father's world, a place he belonged to by virtue of birth and his achievement in the paper business, where success meant lots of money and a name that spoke of eighteenth-century land grants, where hard work was laughed at and the popular were those who managed to sit in a swing all day, waited on hand and foot.

I knew my grandmother, my father's mother, whom we were all taught to call Muffie, had hated and resented Mother. The war between them was relentless and I had often been caught in the middle.

Mother had come to Montreal at the end of the war, had graduated from university with a first-class degree, a supergirl of some proportion, decorated during her Naval service, beautiful and sharp, ready for action. She had let slip that it hadn't been easy for her then. Those days were fast forwarded. There was no inspirational message for children in that time, and all her stories of her past were designed to teach and warn. No opportunities for young women, or women of any age. The men were returning from the war. She was told to dream of refrigerators.

She had met my father and, after a giddy courtship, married him. I had dizzying mental pictures of hotel ballrooms, the men in black tie, bright women in full bloom, all young, all celebrating for the first time since 1929. Twenty years of gloom to make up for. Then the wedding and a difficult adjustment to married life in the upper reaches of society, where the women played dumb, and the year unfolded in a stately procession of formal events.

I knew some dreams had died. What they were exactly, I did not know.

Here I had to stop. That was all I knew. That was all I knew about my mother. I swept the bedclothes back and stepped out on to the plush peach acrylic carpet. I drew back the curtains and stared down at the street. It was nearly lunchtime in Washington.

What a strange city. Southern and lush by implication, but, in point of fact, so cool, so colourless. Black, white, grey, beige. The women weren't wearing any jewellery, or it was so discreet as to be unnoticeable - gold shell earrings, a tiny bracelet, a pearl lapel pin. They walked, decorous and composed, but purposeful. I called room service and a cheerful voice took my breakfast order and admonished me to have a pleasant day. While I waited, I took a quick shower.

Why didn't I know more? I had never met her father. I had met my maternal grandmother a few times, but all I remembered was a small stiff, wiry hairdo of a woman with a pinched mouth and a very straight back. She was born on the farms in Ontario. Those eastern fields, lush and fertile and green, had not softened her. I had met a couple of never-married great-aunts from the farm. But that was it. My mother's history and her family had been excised as neatly as if they had been cut out of a book with a switchblade.

When had my abject love turned to dislike, aversion, and finally crushing rejection? I knew that she had been a brisk and efficient mother much of the time, loving and warm-hearted, especially when she thought we needed her. That sometimes she seemed wrapped in a delicious private world that we longed to enter with her. That she had seemed successful, a model of success even, in Foster, Quebec, where standards of hostessing and housekeeping and the sporting life were high indeed. She appeared to be content and adjusted, at least in the forefront of my memory. These reports looming out there in the room seemed bad science fiction. Sure, she had black times, when we used to tiptoe around. My memories of those were so dim as to be non-existent. But then there was my flight, first at thirteen to boarding school, then finally, the absolute break at eighteen. What was I running from? I had told myself it was my father's world, that claustrophobic, luxurious world that hobbled active women and turned them into docile brood mares. What if there had been another threat?

The door opened noiselessly, and a tray was deposited on the table. I heard a whooshing sound as the room was reordered slightly and soiled dishes removed. When I emerged from the bathroom, I felt almost human.

Except that my memories were pouring back and I was suddenly eleven years old, all over again.

I knew why it was returning now. The Midnight Ride, as we called it, had divided us. Though we struggled on, that night and its aftermath had finished the life of our family.

It had been a cold autumn that year. But we often had freezing months in the Eastern Townships and the memory of the long summer of '62, golden and hot, warmed us. Besides, the houses were built for cold and were cosy and welcoming. When Brian and I could forget the early banishment of Ross to boarding school, we loved coming home from the village school, knocking the snow off our clothes and sitting beside the fire. She would play the piano for us and I remember dancing to Chopin and, my favourite at eleven years old, Debussy. Brian would tease me, but then sometimes join in and the dog would groan in his stupor, head as close to the pedals as possible.

Where was my father? Gone, in a fury. Away, he was coming back, she told us. Maybe. He travelled. He had responsibilities and maybe this time he couldn't come back because his responsibilities had finally worn him out, we told each other at night upstairs. I couldn't say I felt sad. I liked being her best friend and Brian liked being her protector. I dreamed of captaining the boat in the club's races that summer and argued about it with Ross on the phone on Sunday nights. We joked that the real captain would never return, just send money.

And then he came back. Suddenly maniacally cheerful, he vowed to make a go of it. We promised to be better. And began again our tiptoeing around. There were still rages and slamming doors, but she smiled. The blue bedroom seemed fraught and angry, tempest-tossed. I peeped in mornings before school and saw the twisted sheets, the upholstered pillows from the chairs all over the floor.

That night they had a fight to end all fights and we listened, upstairs, our rooms separated by the long corridor that overhung the stairs. She was screaming at him and we shuddered at her defiance. More doors banging, voices raised, then finally, silence. And we slipped into an uneasy sleep.

Then, shsh, she was bent over me, finger to lips. It was still dark outside.

'Mummy?'

'It's all right, darling. We're going out.'

'Who?'

'You and me and Brian.'

'Where?'

'Aunt Creetie's.'

I complained a little for I never liked getting up and certainly not before dawn. She laïd out my clothes, packed a few in a bag she carried, and left me to dress. I did and sat on the bed to wait for her, resisting the temptation to slide back under the covers. There was something in her voice. We tiptoed down the stairs, through the basement where the dog, ears so alert they were criss-crossed, joined us. Brian kept one hand clamped around the dog's mouth so he couldn't bark or whine. The freezing garage. She pulled open the door and we looked out. The night was absolutely still and black. One streetlight pooled yellow on the snow at the driveway corner and fat snowflakes fell and melted on our faces. A new moon hovered over the trees, but was shrouded in snow cloud, leaving only a white soft glow.

She hurried us into the car. We fell, bumping and padded, into the back seat, and immediately struggled up to a sitting position, unwilling to take our attention off her for a moment. She struggled with the ignition and gave up. The car wouldn't start.

She put both hands on the wheel and lowered her forehead on to the freezing plastic. She was whispering and I inched towards her, trying to listen. I couldn't hear much.

'God damn them for ever. God damn . . .'

I slid back in the seat, looked at the window with all the little castles and winter scenes drawn by Jack Frost.

'Mummy?'

'Sorry, yes, Brian?'

'What are we doing? Ruff is shivering.'

She dragged herself up and turned.

'Sorry, my darling. I'll get this started.'

She pumped the gas three times, and held her breath as she turned the key.

Nothing. Battery dead. That click was familiar to a northern child.

'Mummy?' Brian spoke.

'OK, kids, the adventure is getting even better.'

'Why? I'm cold.'

'You'll warm up when we start walking.'

'Mum, no, please. I want to go back to bed.'

'Shut up, Brian, or I'll put you back in bed. Then you'll end up with your grandmother. Would you like that?'

Brian shuddered, buried his head in Ruff's fur. Muffie always treated him with disgust. It was me, the only daughter in two generations, that she loved. I had been told that endlessly and, before I stopped pretending I was a good little girl, I had suffered through many afternoons of shopping at Holt Renfrew, then tea in too delicate porcelain cups and horrible cake with candied fruit in it, in her hothouse apartment, then returning home to a mother whose face stiffened when she saw mine.

'All right, let's go. Up and at 'em.'

'Mum!'

'I mean it.'

She flipped the door handle and got out. She wore a fur coat and a fur hat and sheepskin-lined boots and her eyes were shiny and bright. The moon was full. The clouds that had obstructed it had drifted away across the frozen sky.

We left the garage by the side door and trudged along the salted driveway out on to the road. Green light blinked off everything, the sheet of snow covering the neighbours' lawn.

'Brian, hold your sister's hand.'

'OK, Mum.'

I felt a docile hand tuck mine inside his jacket pocket. It felt good to be out here, away from the thick, chaotic air of the house. I wrenched my hand away and we ran ahead together, sliding on the ice. The dog bounced after us, like a deer in the underbrush – sproing! I laughed.

'What time is it?' My laughter made me feel braver.

'Only three, darling.'

'Three in the morning?' I was staggered by this thought.

She giggled. 'At what other time would you stage an escape?'

I smiled back, only a little worried.

She marched down the road, setting a brisk pace that challenged us. But we were sinewy and strong. We trotted along and elation rose in the back of my throat. The dog skittered ahead, sliding on the icy patches, galloping back, as delighted as I was.

Brian caught up with me, as I huffed and puffed behind her. Already steam flew from the innards of the snowsuit.

'She's nuts,' he whispered loudly.

'Is not. We're running away.'

'From what? To what?' he hissed back. 'Look at her.'

I did. Her square back looked stiff and uncompromising and somehow very lonely. She strode along, the Diana of the eighteenth fairway. People used to crane their necks from the bar terrace to watch her progress up to the green.

'We're running away because she wants to have another life, and not be stuck out here doing nothing. It makes her cry. I understand. You don't.'

'No, I don't. It's not so bad. People laugh at us when he's gone.'

'That's stupid.' But I knew that my nightmares had begun right after he'd left the house, at the end of the summer.

She had nightmares too and had taken to sleeping with a long candle burning by her bed. Some nights I would meet her in the living room, in the middle of the night, and we'd sleepwalk our way to the kitchen and silently make hot chocolate.

'You're horrible,' I said to Brian.

'Yeah, but what are we going to do? She doesn't have any money.'

'So?'

'We'll have to go to some public school.'

I was silent at this. I liked the idea of public school. I didn't want to go to boarding school, not then anyway.

'I wish Ross was here,' I said.

'Me too. We'll have to live in an apartment.'

I gasped. 'No way!'

'Yes.' He was adamant.

Apartments were beyond the pale. Even I knew that. Nobody talked to children who lived in apartments.

'And forget riding.'

I punched him in the arm and skidded up to Mother. 'I wish Ross were here,' I repeated to her.

'Do you miss him, sweetie? I do too. But you know, he'd be worrying us all to death right now.'

'Are we leaving here for ever? I'll miss it. It's . . . it's . . .' I didn't know what it was. It was all I knew. I saw the icing-sugar snow on top of the spars on the sailboats moored in the harbour and the soft mounds of white that used to be canoes beached for the winter on the sand. The place was ghostly. I stopped to look, mouth open. She took my hand, pulled me up the long hill to the golf course.

'Shall we sing?'

Brian shook his head.

'Remember when I used to take you kids skiing up here?'

'Yes,' we chorused.

'Fun, wasn't it?'

A mumble or two.

She strode on.

'See, she is nuts. I was only three. I nearly drowned in snow. And that weird food? Everybody thinks she's weird.'

'You're just scared.'

'Faster now,' she called to us.

'Mum, I'm tired. Can we go back?' said Brian.

'Traitor,' I said. 'I'm fine,' I called.

She looked at our faces, then away.

'But look at the golf course. It's fairyland tonight. See how the moon is sitting down by the 7th green? Isn't it fantastical and magical? Can't you just see Russian ladies in their sleighs, with their tinkly laughs and handsome cossacks racing over the snow with their white horses galloping?'

'What kind of horses, Mummy?'

'Oh dear. Arabs?'

I nodded. 'Yes, they would have had Arabs.'

'Mum, what's a cossack?'

'It's a dashing soldier, Brian, with a glittery uniform with silver buttons, and gold epaulettes and a huge curving sword like a Mongol's.'

We stood staring down over the golf course, our eyes lit by visions.

'Come on, only a few more minutes till Creetie's. Don't you remember her house isn't far from the golf course?'

'Is hers the little castle with the moat?'

'That's right, Brian.'

'Oh boy, I always wanted to go there, but there were no kids my age there. Great!' He threw his wool hat up into the air and caught it. 'How long are we staying?'

'A couple of days. Till we sort things out.'

'Then what?'

'The city, I think.'

'You mean I don't have to go to boarding school like Ross?' I said.

'That's right. No more boarding schools. We'll send you to a good private school in town, with your friends.'

Brian raced ahead with Ruff, skittering and playing tag with the bewildered dog. 'I'm happy,' he shouted back. 'I'm happy. I don't ever want to go away from you.'

She waved to him. 'Me neither,' she shouted back.

I tucked my mitten into her glove. 'Me neither, Mummy.'

She smiled down at me. 'Of course not. We'll get a nice little apartment on the mountain in the city and you can ride on the mountain.'

'And you won't be upset any more?'

'Nope.'

I squeezed her glove, then ran ahead to join Brian.

She walked on, a slight figure under the tall yellow streetlights. The houses on either side were set far back from the road. Nevertheless no light glinted behind the trees. Even the floods were turned off. The city people were gone. Only the stalwarts, the true town fathers, came out on bleak fall weekends like this one.

Their drive loomed ahead. A stone turret, with rectangular slits for rifles so the family could hold off intruders for weeks, until reinforcements arrived. Tonight, for the first time, I wondered who the attackers would be. The French? Or maybe Indians. No, they wouldn't fear the Indians.

They did fear the French. Witness the mockery and taunts, the casual insults, the constant running down of anything French Canadian. The kindest thing that any of them had said was that, of course, the French Canadians had a folk culture, but that theirs, imported straight from the good old British Isles, was high culture. Elevated culture, godlike, ascendant. I hated them.

She squared her shoulders. 'Kids!' she called. 'Come here now. Leash the dog and bring him along. Good behaviour now, all right?'

We slid up to her on the dark icy driveway. She gave us each a hand, marched up to the dark-shadowed doorway. More carefully rough-hewn fieldstone, more rifle slits, big iron grating. She picked up the giant black iron knocker. It was shaped like a lion. She lifted it high, let it fall. Did it again.

Brian pulled at her hand. 'There's a bell.'

'Ring it then.'

He did.

We waited. Nothing happened.

'Knock again, Mum,' said Brian.

'Louder.'

She did and Brian leaned on the bell. Presently, a light went on inside. Click. Another light went on over their head. Peering though the glass, we saw a figure stumble and slip on the shiny wood floor and then head towards us, face concerned and irritated at the same time. Dr Donald McDougall, Creetie's husband.

He turned, after seeing us; his mouth opened and shut again. Then he fumbled with the locks on the door. Creetie appeared from the corridor, doing up the sash on her dressing gown, brow furrowed, then lifted, and smiled when she saw Mother through the glass window.

'Finally,' said Donald, as he managed to pull back the heavy door. 'Thought I'd never get it open. Well!'

'My dear!' said Creetie as she slid towards us in furry pink slippers. 'My dears! What's happened?'

Mother's shoulders slumped. 'You've got to help. They're going to take the children away from me.'

Silence from the two adults in the door, and suddenly I was more afraid than I had ever been before.

Then, without warning, she lost the strength in her legs and pitched forward into Creetie's arms.

We were ushered into the kitchen, undressed and given hot chocolate and then put to bed by an awkward Donald. I stayed by the doorway of the bedroom and listened while he called my father. A terse, whispered conversation, none of which I could decipher, then silence. Eventually we both fell asleep in their funny little guest room with its demure twin beds and dotted Swiss curtains.

The next morning, she was not to be found. 'In bed, dears, she's exhausted,' said Creetie kindly. 'Your daddy is coming to fetch you. And Muffie too! Isn't that nice?' It was not the first time I'd seen pity in an adult's eyes and it was not to be the last. I shrugged and was silent and ate the excellent pancakes and bacon. Brian was red-faced with embarrassment. It was not long after that my father came to get us, set-jawed, grim and silent.

And it was five whole long months until she came home again. Shaky and not remembering whether I'd had my birthday. I had.

And after that, she became cold, dutiful, perfunctory, locked deep within herself. Unreachable. Faced with the choice of living with Muffie in town and going to private school or boarding school, I asked for boarding school and holidays with friends, returning home for awkward reunions, where she, shamefaced, would try to be my mother and I would try to be her daughter. And we would pretend that abandonment had never taken place, that morning when she had not appeared for breakfast and had disappeared for ever after, gone in her essence.

I had never asked what had happened. I had accepted the explanation offered by Muffie that she was sick, and set my face towards the world, counting the years and months until I could leave.

Perhaps it was time I asked her. Perhaps it was time I knew the facts of her family, and of ours, of the will that broke her heart and the final mysteries, the hospital stays and her marriage. Perhaps it was time I went home, for the first time.

With this stern resolution in mind, I called Tom Wheeler. The receptionist took a few moments to find him and while I waited, I rehearsed what I would say.

'Catherine!' He sounded delighted to hear my voice. 'Are you all right? Have you read everything?'

'I read as much of it as I could stand.'

There was silence. 'Yes? And? What have you decided?' he said, after a long pause.

'I'll try,' I said grudgingly, and wondered at myself. 'I mean, I'll go home and ask her if she'll consider giving you a videotaped deposition. But that's all.'

'That's a start.' He was still bright. 'And Catherine, something to think about. Joe had a brainwave yesterday evening and made a few calls. The executor of your uncle's estate is a lawyer in New York.'

'Yes.'

'He's a known associate of Bill Casey.'

'So?'

'Bill Casey is head of the CIA, Catherine. When he took office, he warned everyone at Langley, down to the guards at the gate, that the spirit of Allen Dulles once more walked the complex. The nice, soft, confessional Agency of the seventies is dead. Casey is fighting the secret Third World War.'

I sat down on the bed.

'Catherine? Are you still there?'

'I think so.'

'We know that, in January 1982, Casey received a report on the mental state and financial status of all our plaintiffs, as well as any of Dr Cameron's former patients who could well become plaintiffs.'

'And this means?' I was drawing him out intentionally. The panic was too close and I didn't want to start hyperventilating again.

'Casey was a tax lawyer for extremely wealthy private clients in New York City for twenty years. He wrote or edited twenty-four books on tax and investment matters. He knows about every rich private estate in New York City. Do you think he would miss your uncle and his connection to your mother and to MKULTRA? Can you put it together now?'

'You're saying that he had Dr Westley's will changed? Wasn't he afraid the connection would be too obvious?'

'You didn't catch it, did you?'

'No. No, I didn't. Wouldn't have even thought.'

'I suggest you do some thinking now. We'll do what we can to help.'

I was silent.

'Catherine, in 1972, Richard Helms was DCI, Director of Central Intelligence. You know from your reading of the files that Helms was a major player in the Agency's mind-control programmes. On 20 September 1972, the station chief in Ottawa reported that one of Cameron's former patients, Dr Mary Morrow, was actively pursuing her legal action against the Allan Memorial Institute and Dr Cameron's estate. Helms immediately ordered a full check on the status of every patient used in Cameron's research. Was there any way, *any way at all*, that what had been done to them could be traced back to the Director? Incidentally, three months later, all the successors to the programme that involved your mother were shut down and all the files that they could find were shredded. And five months after that, Helms was replaced.'

I mumbled something about calling him in a few days, and hung up the phone. My tongue felt thick and heavy in my mouth, and I had pin pricks in my hands and feet.

Bill Casey, CIA Chief, appointed by Reagan, scourge of Central American communists, had in his spare time hunted down and immobilized dangerous Canadians like my mother and my ancient, senile great-uncle. I couldn't believe that the paranoia of the old CIA hands could have penetrated that far.

I lay back on the crumpled sheets.

SIX

A coven of black umbrellas hung furled on the railing on the steps down to the plane, but the sun was arched high in the pale-blue sky, and the passengers of San Juan Airlines didn't need them.

The plane was very small, a Dash 7, designed for short, propeller-driven hauls alongside the whitecaps of the Olympics to small-industry towns, logging camps, and haunts of environmental activists.

There were eight of us, all uninteresting-looking, me paler than usual, skin stretched so tight against the bone that my face hurt. I'd been waiting in the Seattle airport for two hours for this shuttle to Vancouver. I kept yawning. I had done more travelling in the past forty-eight hours than I had in two years and my body was in full rebellion.

Dutifully, we each identified our luggage as we climbed aboard and the attendant pitched the bag into the hold. When he tried to take my briefcase, I wrested it away from him. I had copied some of the more relevant papers from Tom Wheeler's file on the hotel Xerox machine and I wanted them with me. The engines hummed, propellers whirled and we were on the runway, waiting our turn. Little planes leapt into the air around us, seemingly from standing starts. As soon as we were aloft, the sea glinted below us, the terrain so enormous and impressive. I lost myself in it for a moment. White cliffs and blue sea and dozens of tiny flat islands lay sleeping in the sun. All those good people, unexceptional, privileged beyond their knowledge, lucky lucky lucky.

We flew along the snow-covered range, mountains punctuated only by navy-blue sea. Welcome home. My big empty mute country, the one with the staggering visual effects.

'Excuse me?' said my seat mate.

'Sorry. Was I talking out loud?' We lapsed into silence, he no doubt convinced he was about to die with a lunatic.

I hated coming here. I felt exposed. In New York, I could hide – I was one of that thick crowd of provincial runaways, anonymous. Here, I belonged and I hated the feeling.

The gleaming city, melodramatic in its setting, beckoned over the last, heart-sinking range – glass towers, more white-capped peaks, the coastal range this time.

It was to this city that we fled when my father retired. A new city, where nobody knew us. A city where we could start afresh.

Vancouver Airport was an undistinguished two-storeyed semicircle, painted grey and pink, those reject deco colours of the late seventies. It looked out on to a delta where the Fraser River dumped melted ice cap into the Pacific. Beyond it, uninterrupted by the arrogance of man, rose the inevitable, inescapable mountains.

I was wandering around the grubby arrivals hall, wondering at the Hong Kong Chinese with their fleets of Vuiton luggage, when she tapped me on the shoulder.

They had both come to the airport to meet me. My mother's face was almost yellow and my father was drawn and thinner than ever. He took my bag from me, though, and carried it out the door. I thought of those muscles under the flesh of his arms, how gnarled and hard they once were, so strong that they still served him, even in his mid-seventies. I put my arm around my mother. She was shrinking on me. Her mind was wandering.

'It'll be all right, I'm sure. I'm sure he didn't mean to.' She did not ask where I had been for the past twenty-four hours.

The shock she had sustained was visible. Her pupils were dilated. I wondered whether her doctor had given her anything. Then I dismissed the thought. She wouldn't even take aspirin. She probably hadn't been sleeping.

'I suppose I can't see him tonight.'

She shook her head. 'He's getting stronger now. He apologized to us both this afternoon and says he's glad you are coming back for a while.'

'Only a week.'

'At least you could come. Ross is too far away. I haven't told him yet.'

'Better not until Brian's improved and can write himself.'

Father honked his horn as he pulled up to the airport door. We got into the car. She insisted I sit in the front, even though I couldn't see anything.

'How are you, Daddy?' I asked, as we pulled away.

'As well as can be expected, Catherine,' he grunted. 'Glad to see you, though.'

I flushed with pleasure. Such words from him were rare.

'Did he tell you why he did it, Mum?' I turned to see her face.

She shook her head. 'Yvette had left him. That might have had something to do with it. Though she's around every day at the hospital.'

'Poor Mother. All your children have such unsuitable mates.'

She managed a small laugh. 'I don't see why either. You are all so normal. You with a graphic designer, Ross marrying a Thai and Brian with a Metis, for God's sake!'

'Do you still say that half-breed babies are idiots, Dad?'

'Not after Ross married Kumi and had two children.' The ghost of a smile.

'Well, thank God for small mercies. Do you like Yvette, Dad?'

'Seems all right,' he said. 'Nice enough.'

'I don't know why she left him,' Mother said. 'Yvette and Brian had been together for four years. You know he picked her up off the street from Medicine Hat. He talked her into going back to college and she was doing really well. I thought they were happy together. She's eight years younger than him, you know,' she said, leaning towards me, voice fierce suddenly. 'I liked her. I thought she had both feet on the ground, and that the mix of French and native would be exotic enough for him. He still likes to be seen as a rebel.'

'Yes, I thought she was good for him too,' Father weighed in. For him, such a statement was an accolade.

I didn't know where to go with the conversation. I didn't know how much they knew, if anything. I didn't even know if Brian had spoken to Mother about his concerns and his research.

'I still have hope for them,' she said.

'I'll try to find out what happened tomorrow morning.'

'Take my car. The keys are on the table in the hall. Your father's off early to one of his charities.'

We lapsed into silence. It was dark outside and the drive was a long curl down streets I didn't remember. By the time we reached the house, I was exhausted and went to bed.

The next morning I woke up with a start, and sat straight up in bed, shocked by where I was. The bedclothes were damp. I checked my watch but it was still on eastern time. My bed was high and narrow and I remembered then almost sliding out of it during the night.

I had slept in this bed from the age of six. It was a pretty pine spool bed, surrounded by old polished pine furniture just like it, and all covered by a slick of beeswax. Pink-and-white shepherdesses frolicked in meadows in the print that hung on the windows, covered the cushions of the little couch. The pink rug I landed on was soft and padded, and I remembered how much and how often in the past twenty years I had reluctantly missed the gentle surroundings she always created around us.

I showered and dressed quickly. My suitcase had been retrieved from the airport the day before. As I left my room, my mother called me. She was in her bed, a tray on the table beside her. Her room was brightened with yellow-and-blue Regency striped curtains and yellow-and-blue chintz covered every available soft surface. Her room was a garden.

'I haven't been able to sleep since he called,' she said. 'I can't remember being so upset. It's nice that you're here. I feel better. I slept last night, finally. You look sweet.'

I looked down at myself. Mark had pinned every outfit together, so I could dress by numbers almost. Clothes buying and house decorating were his domain. I saw I was wearing a soft red-and-blue kilt with a red V neck sweater and pearls. The jewellery had been in the pocket of the blouse.

I kissed her on the cheek. It was cool to the touch and very soft. 'Where's Dad?'

'Gone already. He'll be back for lunch. You go down there yourself, darling. You can get breakfast on your own, can't you?'

I nodded. 'Shall I take the tray?'

Downstairs the rooms were silent and filled with sunshine. I had never lived in this house and I walked through it, wondering, touching old things I remembered from childhood. The floors were blond oak, inlaid with darker strips of walnut, and gleaming. Over them, she had laid a green carpet. The immense monkey-puzzle trees outside filtered the light and every room was lightly scented with the eucalyptus that grew like a weed in the garden.

I sat at the table in the breakfast room and waited for the coffee to drip through the filter. The wallpaper in this room was green-trellis tracery and the furniture white-painted wrought iron. Everything spoke of peace and stability, a kind of contentment. I pulled the morning paper towards me and wondered how soon I could leave.

Her keys were where she said they would be. I picked them out from the ticket stubs, old address books and leaflets from local decorators.

'I'm off!' I called up the stairs.

'All right, darling. Drive safely.'

I vaguely knew where I was going and I drove slowly down the hill, feeling my way. The hospital was on Cambie Street, an old limestone building built a hundred years ago. It was joined by a soaring modern wing, filled with light. Brian was in the modern wing, in a private room, insisted upon by my parents.

'Gee whiz,' I said, as I entered. 'You're pretty well set up here.'

I got the smile, and a lump rose in my throat.

'Catherine, thank you for coming.'

I kissed him lightly on the cheek and sank into the one armchair in the room. It was too low, the cushion too soft, and I felt trapped in it. I looked at him. His skin was so pale it was translucent and he was obviously very tired.

'So!' I said. 'How are you? How's your throat? You were sounding pretty hoarse on the phone.'

'Better by the hour. I keep drinking. I eat honey by the spoonful. It helps. Talking helps too.'

There was a pause, he looked out the window.

'I watch the Hobie Cats run down here, in front of the wind usually. They tie up on False Creek. Wish I was on one. Like catamarans, they're so fast, it's like flying.' The sound that came out of his throat was harsh, ragged.

'Brian.'

'Remember sailing on Brome Lake? Wasn't it fun?'

'Brian.' My Lord, he was talking about twenty years ago.

'Don't you wish we could go back there?'

'No.' My voice was sharp.

He looked at me then. His hazel eyes were dark and there were immense circles under them. I averted my gaze from the purplish bruise that circled his neck.

'So now you know,' he said.

'Yes.'

'Quite a tale.'

'Is that why this happened?'

'There were several reasons. I was alone, Catherine. There was no one to talk to. Yvette had left. She said I was obsessed and that she was drowning in my crisis.' He paused, looked out the window. 'Fair enough. I was a madman, seeing ghosts in every corner.'

'What reasons?'

'We don't ever really talk in this family, do we? There's so much to hide, so much we don't understand.'

'That's like a lot of families, or so I suspect.' I hauled myself out of the chair and sat down on the bed beside him. 'I'm trying to talk. What reasons?'

A long pause. He didn't meet my eyes. 'It was my fault, Catherine. She went in after I was born and he was doing the experiments then.'

He looked at me. His eyes had teared and he was twisting the sheet around in his hands. He fought for control. I held his hand. 'I felt so terrible and so confused and alone, then I thought: This is what it's like, you start to lose it, you slip your moorings. And I thought I was going to spend my life bouncing in and out of a mental hospital, and I couldn't stand it. I'm not crazy, am I?'

The world slipped. 'No! You're not. It was just shock and sorrow.' I leaned over and hugged him. 'No, Brian. No.'

'Why not?' he whispered. 'Why isn't it my fault?'

I let him go, and faced him. 'It's not your fault because you were a few months old. How could you be responsible for anything that happened when you were just born?' My voice was hard. I tried to sound certain and strong, like Father.

There was a long pause. He twisted his head away from me, lips thinned. I got up, went to stand at the window. Clouds had covered most of the sky and there were fewer sailboats.

I turned. 'How did you first find out about what happened to her?'

'There were some stories in the *Sun* that started me off. I went through the library, put together everything written about it in Canada, then I called a library in the States and they mailed me most of what I sent to you. Then I called Tom Wheeler. He checked it out and told me she's on the list of those used in the CIA experiments.'

'And then you spoke to her?'

'Yes. We went out for lunch.'

'And?'

'She treated me as if I was ten years old. What was I talking about? Nothing happened to her. Why didn't I get a proper job?'

'So she knows a bit?'

He nodded. 'What did they say in Washington?' He leaned over and picked up a bottle of apple juice.

'They want me to ask her to give a deposition. They think she knows about the Grid Room.'

'What's that?'

'A particularly extreme form of torture he dreamed up. It happened in the early sixties.'

'What do you think?'

'I'd like to know what she thinks. And I'd like to know what happened. Was she a patient? Was this stuff done to her? Was she really ill, or was she a subject?'

'Be careful. She's still shaky. The will really upset her.'

'You never believed in that, did you?'

'No. Well, yeah, sure I did. I guess I never really thought about it. West wasn't a part of our lives, but he was important to her. And I believed, equally, that she was important to him. The inheritance was to be her justification for all the trouble she'd brought to the family. So it was important, very.'

I looked at my brother. His face was grim; there were harsh planes etched on it that I didn't remember. No wrinkles, no signs of ageing yet. He was only thirty-one, but where I once had read indecision and weakness, I now saw resolution.

'You're starting to look like Dad.'

'Maybe he looks the way he does because he stood up to all this stuff alone for all these years.'

We sat quietly for a few moments.

'Cath?'

I shook my head, wordless.

'I've scared you.' He sounded surprised.

'No, it's funny, but I'm not scared.' But I was lying.

'Let's be honest, at least. You're scared because you worry that I'm crazy like her. And you think that somewhere in you sits that insanity and that it might come out if the surface is scratched. That's why you don't come home. That's why you can't face this. Relax. Believe me, she's no more crazy than I am or you are.' He lay back on the pillows, reached for the juice.

I handed it to him and caught a glimpse of my face in the mirror over his bed. It was white and pinched.

'She was never mad,' he said, with effort. 'Don't you see that? Exhausted, confused, in need of support and help and a few good honest friends, but not mad. Come on, Catherine. You've seen the newspaper stories. Many of the patients he experimented on had minor problems – alcoholism, menopausal anxieties, postnatal depression.'

'Her hospital records don't say that, Brian. They say she was nuts.' I got up and walked over to my briefcase, pulled out a sheaf of papers.

'Where'd you get those?' he asked, eyeing them.

'I copied them from the files the legal team gave me.'

'I thought hospital records were private.'

'They're about our mother. Who has a better right to them than we?'

He shrugged. 'Who has ever consulted us?'

'OK, what about this?' I read from her diagnostic sheet. '"The patient stated that she failed to develop any understanding of her difficulties and felt quite disillusioned by the course of treatments. This seemed to us probably to represent her underlying hostility which was present not only in respect to all her therapists, but also with respect to authority figures even during her childhood and her girlhood years and may well, we thought, constitute a serious problem in the satisfactory carrying-out of therapy and adjusting to the life of a married woman with children."'

Brian's voice was tight. 'So what? Seems sane to me. Didn't like treatments. Cameron retaliated by worsening her diagnosis.'

'Brian, I'm trying for objectivity here. Listen to this: "The patient is now beginning to slip again. She has become anxious, unclear in her thinking, and while her orientation is now rapidly returning, it is clear that the schizophrenic thinking is also coming back."'

'So what treatment did they propose?'

'Gamma 50 LSD-25 and 10 milligrams of Desoxyn.'

'A moderate-sized hit of acid combined with a little speed. I'm glad he's not working in this hospital. For how long?'

'For several weeks.'

'Then?'

'She wrote stuff down. I have samples of what she wrote. But they took it, spliced it and put it on a tape loop. Cameron's voice. Then they put her to sleep for three weeks, or at least almost to sleep, and played the tapes over and over.'

'His standard treatment. What was on the tape?'

I closed the file, leaned over to put it back in my suitcase. 'Stuff about how she was a failure at everything, then positive messages about success and loving her family. She must have been a mess.'

'Can't you see how terrible that must have been?'

'Of course, it scares the shit out of me. But there must have been something very wrong with her. There had to have been.'

'She may have had problems, but she certainly wasn't schizophrenic. He did that to everyone. Christ, he thought menopausal women were schizophrenics. He thought alcoholic men were psychotics. He believed everyone, even well people, could be "improved" by his techniques. It wasn't her fault.'

I stared out the window. I could see tiny whitecaps on the waves.

'Catherine? What are you going to do?'

I sat beside him on the bed. I resisted an impulse to grab his hand and hold it. I tried to smile.

'I don't know. Try to talk to her.'

He nodded his head. 'All right. I'm tired now. Go home and ask her. Then come back tomorrow afternoon and help me get to my apartment. We can talk more then.'

I got up from the bed. He was nearly asleep or seemed to be. His chest rose and fell slowly. His eyes were closed.

I waved at his sleeping form from the door, and shut it behind me.

'He's asleep,' I said to the nurse at the counter down the hall. She nodded at me blindly. 'Room 305,' I said, in case she didn't know. This time, her face was comprehending.

'He is exhausted. The doctor said he needs a lot of sleep,' she said.

'Oh.'

'He's a nice kid,' she said and she smiled.

No one was in when I got home.

The house hummed around me. I could hear the tick-tock of the grandfather clock over the rinse cycle of the dishwasher. The branches of the monkey-puzzle tree rubbed against the arched windows of the dining room. It was a lovely room and I went into it. Three perfectly arched windows, floor to ceiling. The walls were painted a sunny butter yellow and red-and-green chintz curtains that hung from the curved wrought-iron rods made it a colourful room, not overwhelmed by the heavy mahogany dining-room furniture. The window ledges were white and wide enough to sit on. I crouched there, looking out at the mad, dark-green tree.

No one ever discussed my mother's condition with us. It was taboo. No one ever sat us down and explained why suddenly one day she was in the hospital, and why one day, a few months later, she would reappear, pale and strange.

A car drew up in front of the house and my mother got out and came down the walk towards me. I went out to meet her. Her arms were full of packages.

'Oh dear,' she said, as she came through the door and handed me the packages. 'Thank you.' She shrugged off her coat on to the chair in the hall, then took the packages from me, and carried them into the kitchen. I trailed after her, feeling sixteen again.

'I bought good old-fashioned scones for tea. I'll bet you don't get them in New York.'

I shook my head.

She bustled around the kitchen putting things away, filling the kettle with water.

'Linden or fennel?'

'Real,' I said.

'Ugh, caffeine. Not for me. But I've got some Earl Grey back here somewhere.'

I helped her set up the tea tray and after the water boiled I filled the teapots.

'I saw Brian this morning,' I said.

'How did he seem to you? I think he's much better. It was only a momentary fit of depression and loneliness – don't you agree?'

A passing thing to hang yourself. It seemed to me that it took some forethought. You needed a rope for one thing. A damned good reason for another.

I carried the tray to the sun room. The flower boxes were filled with begonias. Not my favourite flower, but they looked nice, mauve and pink and deep pansy purple. She followed carrying a brown pot.

'I've found some jam I made last year. Apricot – your father loves it.'

'Thanks, Mum.'

We sat in silence for a while, looking out at the garden. The upper part of the garage peaked like a witch's hat and was completely covered in ivy that grew over the trellis like a weed.

'Great garden, as usual, Mum.'

'Oh Cathy, I'd so love to have you all out here. I wish that West's will wasn't so strange. If I had more money, maybe Ross could come here with his family and find a job teaching. Maybe you and Mark would come for summers. Summers in New York must be so draining. And I could help Brian out more. The poor kid. I go over and over the will in my mind. It keeps me awake at night. What happened to that poor man? I called his housekeeper, Florence, you know.'

'You did?'

'Yes, and she was most illuminating. Said that she didn't trust his lawyer and financial adviser. That he was completely senile near the end. Used to lift his arms up to her and ask that she take him dancing. And there were strange men around all the time. Men she'd never seen before.'

'Maybe Clara's people?'

'No, Clara took care of her family. She had a lot of money of her own, you know. No, Florence said that these men just showed up out of the blue about five years ago and would come over, shut themselves in the study with him for hours at a time.'

'Interesting.'

Tears started to seep from under her closed lids. 'Oh Cathy, what have I done?'

'Mum! You haven't done anything!'

'I've ruined your lives.'

'You have not. Come on, don't be sad.' I knelt at her side, and held her hand. 'It's just the juxtaposition of events. Brian and West together. Why not go and lie down for a while? Come on.'

She stood up unsteadily. 'I wish we could be friends again, Catherine.'

I led her up the stairs and into her room. 'We are, Mummy. You know we are.'

Her eyes turned to me. Cornflower blue, navy-blue centres, filled with tears. 'Thank you, darling. I'll rest now.' Her voice was childlike. I drew the drapes and shut the door behind me.

How was I going to stand the rest of the week? I tried to call Mark, but he wasn't in. I left a message on the answering machine.

That night, my father and I ate alone, in the den, from trays, while we watched *MacNeil/Lehrer*.

When the sign-off came, I took my tray into the kitchen and started putting things away, running water into the sink. He had followed me and was helping.

'Why do you think Brian tried to hang himself, Dad?' I asked.

His hands stopped moving for a moment, then started again.

'Probably an inherited weakness. These things get passed on.' His voice was as impersonal and hard as a police officer's.

'You're kidding.'

He shook his head.

'Her problems really took a toll on your life, didn't they?'

He looked at me and his eyes were filled with shock and something else, an immense gratitude that someone had finally understood how much he had lost. My eyes teared up and I tried to hug him. It was like trying to hug a tree. I turned and pulled on a pair of rubber gloves.

'I don't think Brian is mentally ill,' I said.

'What the hell would you call it?' We were back on familiar territory.

'I think he was upset over the newspaper stories about Dr Cameron and his connection to the CIA.'

'That is all a bunch of nonsense. Brian should have more sense, if that is the real reason, which I doubt. Those stories are overblown and overwrought, if not completely fabricated. Just what I'd expect from the press. That man helped your mother, for the most part.'

'What if he didn't? What if the stories are real, Dad?'

'I won't discuss it with you, Catherine.'

'But – '

'And I don't want you discussing it with your mother. She is my concern, she always has been.'

I was silent. I diverted the conversation to the evening news and we had a brief tussle over the stock market. I was stupid enough to say that I thought the '87 crash signalled the end of a decade focused too much on materialism. That statement earned me a ten-minute lecture on free markets and capitalism. I went to bed with a headache.

The next morning I was at the hospital before visiting hours started. I prowled around on the ground floor, had some wretched coffee in the cafeteria and bought him some magazines.

On the stroke of ten, I was outside his door. His face lit up when he saw me. I shut the door behind me and put the magazines down on his bed.

'Did you try?' he asked.

'I couldn't. She was too upset.'

'Have you had time to think it through? Doesn't it make sense to you? She wasn't crazy, they drove her crazy.' His voice had real urgency.

'I don't know, Brian. I've seen what one of the subjects of Dr Cameron's experiments looks like thirty-five years later. Mother doesn't look like that.'

I walked towards the window, my back to him.

'Just ask. How long are you going to wait?'

'Don't push.'

'You could spend all spring here waiting for an opportunity. The performance remains flawless and impenetrable. Nothing happened. Nothing ever happened. Nothing will ever happen. We are perfect. We are eccentric and perfect. It's in our genes. Daddy's family were perfect English eccentrics who built a country while being kooky. Come on, Catherine, jump in the deep end. Learn to swim.'

'Fuck the hell off.'

'Now that's more like it.' He turned away. I grabbed his sleeve and he turned to face me, worry in his eyes.

'Bastard. Creep.' I stared out towards the Pacific. I wanted to be out there, out in the middle of nowhere.

'You haven't much choice,' he concluded, not without a little triumph.

'Haven't I?' I hissed and stalked towards the door. I slammed it behind me, but forgot that hospital doors are on hydraulics and only whoosh.

'See you this afternoon.' I could hear his laughter following me down the hall.

I barely concentrated on my driving and I got there in double time. She was on her knees in the garden and I watched her working. The phone rang and I dashed to pick it up on the first ring. No use disturbing her before I had to.

I said hello.

Silence greeted me. I repeated myself.

'Catherine?' A male voice came on the line.

'Yes?' I replied.

More silence.

'Hello?' I said, impatient.

There was no response.

I replaced the receiver and stepped outside.

She looked up. 'How is Brian?'

'Better, I'd say. He wants me to pick him up this afternoon and take him home.'

'Good, he's on the mend. Did the phone ring? Who was it?'

'No one.'

'Oh, him again.' She laughed. I sat on the steps and waited. The air was pleasant, lightly scented with forsythia and cedar. The neighbourhood was very quiet. The phone rang again in the house, harshly, once, and then stopped. Mother didn't even lift her head.

I hadn't been able to force myself to plan what I was going to say, even how I was going to approach the subject. And, I still didn't know what to think. I was restless. I stood up, went back inside, wandered around the lower floor of the house, looking at things, opening drawers. How was I going to put this?

At eleven sharp, she came in, changed, and started to make

herb tea for herself. I helped, or rather, tried not to get in the way.

'You know, I didn't even know how to wash dishes when I left home,' I said.

'So what? That's hard to do or something?'

'No, but you never let me in the kitchen.'

'Didn't I? I can't remember.'

I carried the tray into the sun room and we sat in adjacent chairs staring out at the monkey-puzzle tree, which didn't have much to offer in the way of entertainment.

'Mum?' I said, as I accepted a cup of rosehip tea. I loathe rosehip tea. Her muffins were sugarless and made with wholewheat. A monk's tea break.

'Mmm?' she said, dreaming. 'It's so nice to have my only daughter around. I envy my friends whose children live near them. But you and Ross are doing interesting things. I do wish Brian would find himself a real job.'

'Yes,' I said. 'But there's something I have to tell you.'

'You're getting married!'

'No.' I laughed in spite of myself. 'I'm thinking of going back to journalism.'

'Oh,' she said, disappointed. 'I do like Mark, you know, even if your father doesn't appear to be jumping with joy. He's an original.'

'Yes, well. The story is in Washington.'

'Really?' She turned her eyes towards me, attempting interest.

'Yes, and you might be involved.'

There was a very long pause. I sipped at the bitter tea.

'What makes you think that, Catherine?'

'I don't think it, Mother. The legal firm does. They think that Dr Westley's will was subverted, that Dr Cameron performed experiments on you and that the CIA are behind the whole thing.'

There's nothing like spitting out the whole melodramatic scenario in one long damned sentence. I didn't know how else to do it. Splat, right in your face, Mum. All the ugliness and horror in your life in one sentence. Subject, verb, nouns, proper names.

Her cup and saucer clattered as she put them down on the glass table. She sat there, immobile, staring straight ahead.

I waited. The few crumbs I had swallowed were stuck in my throat.

Finally, 'Mum?' I said.

'Just a minute, Catherine.'

'OK.' I felt ten, no, I felt younger, six years old maybe, naughty and waiting to be punished, and at the same time confused and hurt beyond reckoning. I squirmed a little in my chair.

Time passed. I sneaked looks at her. She was thinking all right, her mouth was working, almost convulsively, as she tried to absorb the shock without acting it out. Then, suddenly, she got up, and went out the door, down the steps, across the terrace and into the far reach of the garden. Gone.

I was terrified. What if I'd pushed her over the edge? What if this was the first chess move, the first toppling domino? And this time I'd be to blame. A fit of trembling seized me and I too got up, wrenched open the door and in a few long strides joined her. I touched her on the shoulder. The muscles under her skin were bunched with tension. I could feel her age and approaching frailty and my heart contracted slightly. I had hurt her. How could I have done that to her?

'I'm so sorry. But everyone thinks it would be better out in the open.'

She turned a furious face to me. 'Everyone? Who is everyone? Tell me, does your father know about this?'

I shook my head. 'Just Brian. And the folks in Washington, of course. Mother – '

She turned away violently. 'Thank God for that anyway.'

'Mother, please. Talk to me. Tell me what happened, please. Let me tell you what the lawyers think. They're some of the best in the world. Please?'

She turned to me. Her face was older, drawn and grey with exhaustion.

'Go inside, Catherine. Let me stay out here alone for a few moments. Then I'll come in and we can discuss it.' Even her voice had aged.

A few minutes later I saw her walking up the steps of the patio towards me, hands sunk in her pockets, her head bowed, walk purposeful.

'So,' she said, sinking into the chair beside me. 'What are we going to do?'

'Whatever you like, Mum,' I said. 'Whatever makes you comfortable.'

'Then I choose nothing,' she said.

'What do you mean, nothing?'

'I mean, we do nothing. We do not get involved. We let it pass us by. You had no right to go to Washington without my permission.'

Angered, I stood up. 'May I ask why? If these people are right, our family was bludgeoned by Dr Cameron and the American government.'

'Sit down, Cathy, and stop the histrionics.'

I obeyed, unwillingly. 'Don't you care? Aren't you angry?'

'Yes, I suppose so. Maybe I am. I don't really know any more. It was a very long time ago and I don't remember much.'

'Me neither,' I said. 'But it's not all that long a time ago. These men say they think that your uncle's will got tangled up in this.'

Her face hardened. 'I can't believe that. I'm sure it was just the university working on a sick old man.'

'Believe it, Mum.' I told her about Casey and Helms.

'You think that they stole West's money because they were afraid of what I might do if I inherited it?'

I nodded. 'Exactly. If you had that money, you could finance one hell of a public-interest suit.'

'I see. What do you want me to do, Catherine?'

'Consent to be interviewed. They'll come up and do it. Tell them what happened to you. The stuff he did to you. Did you sign anything? A consent form? Did Dad? The case is being built on the issue of consent. You guys didn't offer to be guinea-pigs. Then, try to remember what you lost from it. Memory, skills, knowledge, health, whatever.'

'Impossible.' Her answer was immediate, her voice pleasant. 'It's out of the question, of course.' She rose, impassive, not a hair out of place, dressed in a lamb's-wool sweater and tweed and pearls, the very image of slavish conformity to her class.

I heard a humming intensify around us. It rose, deafening me for a moment, then finally, blessedly, it began to abate.

'I'm sorry, Cathy. You'll just have to put it behind you. I couldn't do that to this family, not after everything I've suffered and that your father has suffered. You can have no idea what we've been through with this. Now we have a few years of relative peace. We can afford the way we live now. We have our friends. What would they think if we plunged into an ugly battle with the US government? I know that means almost nothing to you, but it means almost everything to us. We'd lose everything we have, everything that means anything to your father. He has suffered so much for me, you have no idea.'

'An impressive speech, Mum. Sounds like you practised it.'

She smiled. 'I'm not stupid. I read the papers. I had an idea it might be needed some day.'

'Too bad you couldn't drum up some courage while you were practising.'

Those blue eyes were glacial. 'Perhaps when you collect Brian, you might take a few of your things and spend a few days with him. You can talk it over. Try to see it my way, for once – just try.' She walked over to the door. 'Now I'm going to the tennis club. Shall we say Saturday for dinner, Catherine?'

And she swept out of the room, impressive and stubborn as iron. I sat, watching the place where she had disappeared. Then, finally, I got up, went upstairs, packed a few things and left.

Brian was sitting in the visitor's chair, suitcase in front of him, waiting. He looked spent.

'I'm all checked out, ready to go,' he said.

'Good. I told her.'

'And what did she say?'

We walked down the hall to the elevator.

'Nothing doing. She balked. Froze me out. Told me the past was past, it would ruin her life and so on.'

'And you said?'

'I pushed her, but she refused to budge. She told me to leave. I don't know, it's her life, Brian. Maybe we should leave her to it.'

He waved at the women behind the nurses' station but, when he turned his face to me, the look on it was almost fierce.

'How delightfully old-fashioned you are, Catherine. Don't you see how this affects every moment of every day of your life? Why don't you live here? Why have you never lived here? Why did you leave home at thirteen? Why did I? Where is Ross, your other "adored" brother? Why don't you live down the street happy as a bug with someone just like yourself, doing useful things for the community and breeding happy children – happy children just like we were?'

The doors to the elevator opened. There was no one in the elevator to hear us. I shook my head again. 'She told me to stay with you till Saturday. I brought some things. They're in the car.'

'Good, there's some stuff at home I want you to see.'

'Like what?'

'It will help you reclaim your past.'

'Why would I want to do that?'

'I've pinched all her old scrapbooks, even the ones from college. You can spend the next few days meeting your mother, probably for the first time.'

'You are completely mad.'

'Now there's an original joke.'

'Sorry, Brian.'

The doors opened on the ground floor and we stepped out together.

SEVEN

Traffic was minimal; it was still before lunch. I drove slowly down the hill. I wasn't familiar with this part of Vancouver. His building was on a seedy hidden road that bordered a landfill, between two of the bridges. Entire neighbourhoods had been built since the last time I'd been here. False Creek with all its perfect little condos and town houses was only a few blocks away. The accretion of restoration had the area firmly in its grip. But Brian's building, an old warehouse, was pristine. Home for decades to box companies and woodworking firms, it sagged, unreclaimed, like an old drunk.

The building had been painted deep red once, but the paint was peeling in wide curls off the crumbling brick. I stood at a metal door while Brian rooted around for a key, under the rubber mat, under a broken clay pot that stood near the door, and then, methodically, he felt along the top of the one small window, boarded up near the door. He brandished a key.

The place was enormous and immaculate. One threadbare kilim covered the floor, but it was vacuumed and the unvarnished wooden floor was swept. I glanced upwards, then quickly averted my eyes from the rafters. The kitchen was clean, and everything was in perfect order. I walked around like a cat checking out new territory. Brian disappeared down the hallway and I followed him slowly, looking at the posters he had put up on the wall. He went into the bedroom. I heard the springs creak and the television switch on. I went to the door of the room and looked at him. He lay on the bed, remote control by his side. He was staring at the ceiling.

'What am I going to do?' I said.

'I don't know. Make some tea or something. I'll bring the stuff in from the car in a moment.' He returned his gaze to the ceiling.

'I'm sick of tea.'

'There's some vodka in the freezer.'

I made an impatient noise and walked over to the window. How many days till I could leave? Should I just get on a plane and go back to New York? Should I call her and apologize?

That stopped me. Apologize for what, exactly? For asking her to tell us the truth? For asking her to stand up for herself?

I twisted myself away from the window and went back to the bedroom. 'I'm going to go out and get some lunch. Where can I go around here?'

'Go to Fourth Avenue. It's one trendy eatery after another. Bring me a sandwich, will you? And come back and eat it here. There's some stuff I want to show you.'

My heart sank but I nodded and grabbed my bag. I couldn't get out of there fast enough. A familiar feeling was coming on. Fog, smoke and mirrors. It was like driving very fast in the pitch black without headlights. I wanted to go very slowly. Stop, in fact, pull over to the side of the road, and fall asleep. I was down the stairs, and striding along the trash-strewn street towards the car, before I recognized that I'd felt like this before, when I was young. The feeling that came from parental proximity. A kind of stasis, of paralysis, bound by invisible soft cords.

I shook myself, got in and drove towards Fourth and found myself in the middle of a tie-dyed heaven. Crude hand-painted store fronts competed with old-fashioned hardware stores and awnings with cute modern names. I walked into the Lazy Gourmet and ordered two smoked-chicken-salad sandwiches on semolina.

'Pasta salad?' asked the cheerful salesgirl. I nodded and asked for two double espressos to go.

When I arrived back at Brian's loft, he was waiting downstairs, sitting on what was left of the clay pot. He rose and gestured towards the trunk and I opened it for him.

'Can you carry this?' I took a box from him, tucked it under my arm. He hoisted another and my suitcase. 'You can have the bedroom, unless you want to stay in a hotel.'

I shook my head. 'Can't afford it anyway, especially after this lunch. Besides – ' I didn't want to admit to him, not right now, that I wanted to know what he had to show me.

He was happy with the sandwich. As we ate off the kitchen counter, he darted around, bending over as he arranged the scrapbooks in the order he wanted me to read them. He went into the closet he used as an office and came out with a book, which he opened. He turned down the page I was meant to read and placed it carefully beside a yellowing newspaper announcement and a couple of slips of paper he patted carefully flat.

He pointed to an old cardboard book with a faded pink ribbon closing it. 'This one has all Mother's letters home in it. These next are the courtship and early married days, their military service. Surprising number of clippings. Nice ones of Dad when he won the DSO and so on. She was real cute.'

I paged through the letters, while I ate. I was starving and wished I'd asked for a Nanaimo bar at the Lazy Gourmet.

'Chirpy style she affected, eh?' I said.

He laughed lightly. 'You'll get into it. Great coffee. I'll drive like a demon all afternoon.'

'You're not going back to work? You can't. You just got out of the hospital.'

His face looked drawn. 'I want to. Besides,' he continued lightly, 'I have to make a living. I'll be back around seven and take you out for dinner. You can get me through dispatch at the cab company.' He laid a card on the kitchen counter and was out the door, carrying his coffee cup and a pager.

I looked at the papers and books spread out on the rug like a feast. I sat on the sofa, eating the pasta salad from a plastic container.

I put her letters home from college beside me on the sofa. She was diligent, a worker, and there were many accounts of academic and social triumphs. Some snapshots were included in the letters. A laughing dark girl, face round and vulnerable, and filled with eagerness and fun. The letters were hopeful in the face of every tiny or imagined defeat. She studied history and political science and had deciphered these mock sciences with ease, translating them into the inexorable advance of reason and goodness.

She lived and breathed hope and the will to help, to spend her life working in government or politics. In spite of my waning anger, I found them unbearably poignant and put them aside, saddened by all that bright promise worn down to a nub of endurance.

I hurried on to the next scrapbook, career and marriage. In this one, Dad figured largely. Big shot of him in full military rig, including ribbons and hat. A photograph of her as a Wren, shining upturned face, fun-looking, the kind of girl you'd want to stand next to in line because you knew she'd crack jokes. A dry yellow newspaper cutting about the colonel's military exploits, accompanied by a snap of him marching down Sherbrooke Street in Montreal, 'at the head of his troops'. The expression on his face was serious and I recognized it.

I sat back. All these photographs, meticulously dated, placed in order, captioned, glued in leatherbound volumes, represented hundreds of hours of work. The thought struck me: what if they were an exercise in memory retrieval, of pasting over the blank spots with imagined life?

The darker mother appeared in my mind then, hair streaked with grey, thin face haunted by unnamed ghosts, lying in her rumpled bed, muttering to herself. The grim recital of I am, I am, I am, in order to survive. Her arena shrunk, believing her mind destroyed, her strength gone, taken from her. I couldn't really remember this mother; perhaps I was imagining her.

I slid off the sofa to the floor, shut my eyes and blindly put my hands out. What would I find?

A microfiche birth announcement, not in one of the scrapbooks, but placed there by Brian for me to see. There was a cash-register receipt attached to it with 'pd, thnx' scribbled on it in ink.

I wondered. I read it, it was dated 14 October 1949, before I was born. 'Born to Victoria and Ian Ramsey, a son, John, 8 lb, 14 oz at the Royal Victoria Hospital, Monday. Felicitations to the happy family.'

I dropped the paper. A son? I stood up, walked around the place. She had a son and we didn't know about it? What happened to him? Where was he?

I went into the kitchen, filled the kettle and put it on to boil. Then I walked back and picked up the next piece of paper. Same origin, microfiche copy, receipt attached. A death announcement, fourteen days later.

I lost my balance. I carefully inched back and sat on the sofa. So? So? I said to myself. So what? Lots of people have abortions, miscarriages, cot deaths. I paged through the scrapbook. There were no snaps for that year and then, two years later, a shot of her with her mother at home, faded, tired, her dark hair hanging below her shoulders, lank. She was wearing a shapeless house dress and I was in her arms.

The kettle boiled and the whistle shrieked at me. I got up, lifted it off the burner, rummaged through Brian's cupboards and found some ancient camomile tea. I put a tea bag in a mug and poured boiling water over it. A dead child, indeed. Brian had marked the trail clearly. I returned to the sofa, picked up the book he had left for me, examined it. The book was E. Fuller Torrey, MD's revised edition of *Surviving Schizophrenia, A Family Disease*. Torrey, I was informed by the back cover, was a clinical and research psychiatrist in Washington, DC, an adviser to the National Institute of Mental Health, and it listed a couple of dozen other credits, including nine books. I was duly impressed and turned to the chapter titled 'What Schizophrenia Is Not'. Brian had turned down the page subheaded 'Psychosis Following Childbirth'.

It seemed that in every thousand births schizophrenia-like symptoms can develop in a mother. She may hear voices that tell her the baby is defective, kidnapped, or dead. I stopped reading for a moment, and sat, telling myself to breathe. The cause, I continued reading, was still unknown, although in recent years, said Torrey, most attention has been focused on possible biochemical factors, especially the massive hormonal changes that take place following childbirth. Treatment, these days, wrote Torrey, is mostly with drugs and sleep and a normal mummy appears after about three weeks.

What the psychiatrist did not say, but what I guessed, was that a mother hearing voices in 1949 was usually put in the loony bin, diagnosed as a dangerous paranoid schizophrenic. And that postnatal schizophrenia could be further aggravated by the fact that the child had died.

A tear slid down my face on to the page. Those triumphant military faces, that tumultuous wedding lavishly recorded in the society column, all that late-night studying, the ambition, those cheerful, hopeful good letters . . . to end up with this death and then madness, then imprisonment. The thought that all this ruin and confusion was caused by a misdiagnosis of schizophrenia rather than postnatal depression was awful, and for the first time in as long as I could remember, I let myself cry. I swept all the paper and books off the sofa, buried my face in a pillow, and cried myself to sleep.

When I woke up a few hours later, the sun was listing towards the horizon, and it was around four o'clock. My tea sat cold on the table in front of me and paper was strewn all over the floor.

I paged through books that showed my life before I had memory. My birth announcement. A daughter! Congratulatory telegrams, a shot of me asleep in her arms in her bed at home. My fists were up, covering my mouth. Then there was Ross as a happy chubby baby, surrounded by lots of strange adults beaming at him. Holidays I couldn't remember. But we seemed to have enjoyed ourselves. Dad washing the car with an old-fashioned hose and a chamois, Ross playing with a black-and-white spaniel. Then I started picking up things I recognized. A cousin's face, an upholstery fabric that had survived, a dress that my mother wore.

Fast forward. I picked up a leatherbound book, thick and heavy, green morocco, tooled front cover and a beautiful thing. I opened it. Foster.

I start and it is then that the memories flood back: sense

impressions, smells, colours, the colour green mostly. An almost terrifying sensation, one image after another, like large colour photographs unfolding inexorably in front of my inner eye. I shut my eyes, force darkness. I open them and the images assault me again. I give in, let them come. The pictures begin to move. Heightened activities, lots of people, and fun. But a shadow overhangs this move out here, a shadow that I felt then and could feel, even today.

Jump cut forward, five years to 1963. I see myself, my grandmother's child already, prim and well behaved, delighting in the failure of manners in others, always trying for that social one-upmanship that formed my father's mother's entire existence. I am there, in the living room in Foster, bay window, piano, chintz and silver, to see my mother, just home from five months (five months!) in the hospital. I am reluctant, Muffie insists, not so secretly proud of my reluctance.

My mother is sitting there in the window, thinner, face with planes making expressions I am not used to. She looks smarter somehow, wily. She turns towards me and her face registers a millisecond of dismay as she marks my pink-flowered blouse, my cute little skirt, my adorable shoes, my desertion. Then irony takes over and I feel my spirit fly to her side. I smile at her and she holds out her arms. I run to her and kiss her oh so soft, slightly yellow skin. Muffie hurrumphs and lights a cigarette and starts to fence.

'I can't thank you enough for all your help,' my mother says, formal in intonation.

'I did it for Ian.'

'Of course, you love doing everything for Ian, don't you?' Her face was pleasant.

'Hurrumph.'

'And Cathy looks so pretty.'

'Someone had to clean the child up,' says Muffie.

I watched this, interested, but hardly riveted. I was glad Mother could keep her end up.

'We must plan your birthday,' she said to me. 'What would you like?'

We had celebrated my birthday over a month ago. She had called from the hospital, shaky, but her voice had been warm and teasing and she had listed what we were going to do when she came home.

'Catherine has had her birthday,' said Muffie, upper hand gained once more.

'Of course,' Mother said.

'Don't you remember, Mummy? You called and said that we were going to get some new grown-up furniture for my room from Mr Carpentier's barn and that you'd teach me to refinish.'

She rocked back and forth in her chair a little, her face twisted with effort. I was terrified, and sat waiting for the next move.

'Vicky?' said Muffie, warning in her voice.

'Yes, of course, I remember now. Just be patient with me, sweetie. They say that everything will come back, leaking its way into my brain.'

'OK.' I sat on the arm of the chair as close to her as I dared. 'Can I stay here tonight with you?'

Her face lit up. 'I don't see why not. Is Ian staying here or with you, Muffie?'

Muffie grunted and left the room, her face a mask of fury.

Then another memory, shards of memories, later on, that year and the next few. I went to boarding school and felt outcast, able to come home for one weekend every four weeks and the usual holidays. Sometimes, she did not even come to get me for that one weekend. I sat and waited, surrounded by the terrible pity and contempt of teenage girls, but no message came.

Or when I did come home, I was confronted by lethargy so deep that she would not get out of bed, or mania that had us whirling around the village from one event to another till she collapsed and was unable to get us home. I had no patience for her recovery. I hated it and I started to hate her. She was unpredictable and scary and I promised myself that as soon as I could I would get away and spend time only with normal people. I began my pathetic hunt for replacement adults, sane ones, who would nurture, protect and advise me. As I grew older, my rejection of her became a rejection of all she had experienced. This, I swore to myself, this would *never* happen to me. To ensure that it wouldn't, I made myself into everything that she wasn't. If she did it, I did not. If she could not do something, I whipped myself until I mastered it.

I shook myself. Bad. Dark alleyway. Think of something else.

Brian had more research for me. I picked up a copy of Dr Cameron's entry in *Who's Who*. Impressive, two and a half columns long. But it didn't explain much that I wanted to know. Who was Cameron that he could steal the life of my mother without any guilt or self-doubt? I had read the Washington research. This had been a dominant question for the legal team. The son of a Scots preacher, intensely competitive, ambitious beyond belief. 'There, but for God, went God,' said patient after patient. It was testimony to his personal magnetism. His secretary had said that so pervasive was his presence that you could always tell on entering the building whether he was in it. He permitted no sloppiness. If your slip showed or if your stocking had a run in it, you'd hear about it.

Val Orlikow, the woman who had brought the suit, called him terrifying, awe-inspiring. He spoke courteously, but towered over people. He used this. She came to worship him, but when she resisted LSD, he was cold and abrupt. He had no time for weakness or indecision. 'Make up your mind. Do you want to get better, or not?' And she would hold out her arm for another injection, ready to spend another ten hours in melting terror.

What weakness had this man seen in my mother? What breaking point had he recognized?

God, I had met him! I'd forgotten it till now. He was there now, in front of me. Tall, unbelievably tall, and dressed in a grey suit. Grey eyes, staring down at me, no warmth whatsoever, analytical, judging. I was afraid. I wanted to hide behind Mother. I shook his hand – dry, fine skin, and I curtseyed. But I couldn't speak. I was too afraid. I had the impression of danger, of very thin ice.

How could someone greet the frightened child of a patient and have no warmth in him? He had not even bothered to fake warmth.

Another critical question posed by the team had been why had no one in his profession blown the whistle? There had been a lot of doubt and many questions. The answer they had come up with was the Emperor's New Clothes syndrome. Cameron was so competitive that he became too important and impressive to question. If you doubted him you were taking on the Canadian Psychiatric Association, the American Psychiatric Association and the World Psychiatric Association, organizations he had headed up and two of which he had founded. Or you were questioning the value of all the first-class graduates he was turning out. Lastly, and most importantly, doctors who blow the whistle on their brothers are, for all intents and purposes, signing their professional death warrants. The profession was reluctant to criticize Cameron because he made them, found them funding, appointments, status. The Canadian Department of Health and Welfare funded him, the National Research Council funded him, the Rockefellers funded him and the Society for Human Ecology funded him.

Which was another example of the Emperor's New Clothes. The Society for Human Ecology was a CIA front, busily funding mind control. It had strong connections to Cornell University and had attracted the continent's most impressive psychologists to head its board of directors: Carl Rogers, B.F. Skinner. Doubt one, doubt them all.

In the files I had received from Wheeler, the legal team mocked at Cameron's science. His lack of research skills was one of the bricks the team was using to build the case. Cameron believed that he could break the personality up into little bits, like a watch, and repair it – a very crude assumption. Basically silly, said a shrink they deposed. 'How can you expect someone to change behaviour if they can't remember it?'

By the time Brian banged into the apartment three hours later, I was watching Oprah. He flicked the set off.

'Hey!' I protested.

'I want to know what you found out.'

I shook my head.

He disappeared down the hallway. I followed him.

'Want anything? It's 7 p.m. Legal drinking time.' He took a bottle of vodka out of the refrigerator and poured some into a glass.

I accepted the drink. 'Thanks, I need this. Could I have some grapefruit juice or something in it?'

'Coming right up.'

I'd piled the books and photos up in the corner of the sofa. He brought in a pitcher of juice and filled my drink up. I took a sip. He waited for my approval. I nodded again. He sat in the butterfly chair opposite.

'Well?'

I shook my head. 'I feel a bit dizzy. I remember that summer that you guys went wild with the air guns and I beat up on that dwarf child Meredith Tucker. I remember that Mother had really tried to stick up for us, for me especially. God, I missed her,' I said. 'I mean, I missed her the way she was then, all vibrant and funny and glorious, the best mother in the world, I used to think. Then that awful walk through the snow, the Midnight Ride. Why? And the fighting that they used to do? What was that all about? There is still so much I don't know.' I took a long gulp of the drink and waited till I felt the familiar warmth sneaking up from my toes.

'Uh-huh. And?'

'After she left us, and no one told us why except Muffie who said she was sick and might never get better, I decided to leave her and never come back, just like she left me.' I looked at Brian, and to my horror saw tears in his eyes.

'Don't you remember anything else?' he asked.

'Lots of things. Nothing important.'

'Don't you remember her pushing you? Be independent. Work hard. Find a profession. Be successful. Don't you remember all that?'

'Don't end up like me,' I said softly. 'Have an affair with a man before you marry him. Get to know him really well before you decide to spend the rest of your life with him, and keep your profession, always, it will be with you even when he isn't. Subversive statements then, said once, on the way to somewhere in the car, as if they were keys to a new world.'

'They were. The world she had lost.'

'Oh Brian, I feel so sorry for her.'

'Catherine, you always have felt sorry for her. You've just buried it.'

'Stop psychoanalysing me, for Christ's sake.'

'There's something else.'

'Something else I don't know about? I can't bear it.'

'This is a dip into melodrama. Let's just say they're at it again.'

'Who is at it? At what?'

'They're harassing us.'

'Who is?'

'I'm not sure. I think it's to do with stopping her from fighting Dr Westley's strange will. Or participating in the lawsuit in Washington. If I stretch it, perhaps to stop my research, as small-time as it is. What they are doing is baby stuff, by their lights, I'd guess. Phone calls, some guy mutters at us, hang-ups, mail delivered late, opened, roughly taped closed, as if to say, "We're watching you." Then, about three weeks ago, someone blew a pipe of air into Mother's face at a supermarket and she fainted. Dad had to go and get her, and she was ill with some mysterious virus for three weeks. Bedridden, ill, and you know that never happens any more.'

'What do you mean a mysterious virus?'

'Some bug that was very hard to get rid of. It's standard practice. If you read spy novels, you'd know about it. You can infect just one person that way. Airborne transmission of viruses. The covert agencies have been developing these techniques for years. Think of every paranoid's fantasies about the CIA, the CSIS, Mossad, MI6, and so on. They can give people the flu or even typhus, if they feel like it. It's part of their biological warfare research. Get a whole city sick and throwing up for a few days, or just that one critical group of people. They break up marriages, lose people their jobs, destabilize lives. It's called "stress creation" in the literature. Meant as just a warning kind of thing. Cease and desist, shut up, burrow into your life and maybe we'll let you keep it. Her car's been bumped in traffic and so has mine. Repeatedly.

The cab company is furious with me. Their insurance rates went up. Phones are bugged too.'

'How do you know?'

'Had a friend of mine, you know, an electronics genius with lots of equipment, check them out. He was real impressed. Kept testing again and again, first time he'd done a private home. Mostly he covers industrial snooping.'

'It's funny. While I was at home, there was a strange call. Someone said my name, then nothing. I thought – I didn't know what to think, so I forgot about it.'

'That's exactly what they want. Then, slowly, all these little things start to build into one big thing and you're scared to death.'

'Did it set you off? Did you talk to Mother about it? I just can't believe it.' I drained my glass, set it on the table, wished for a cigarette. 'I can't take it.'

'Why not? We're taking it out here on the edge of nowhere. We can take it. Why not you? Ex-supergirl, all bravery and spit?'

'Excuse me, but it seems to me you're not taking it very well,' I said. 'What makes you think I'll do any better?'

His shoulders slumped. He took a sip of his drink. 'Because, Catherine, I don't think I should have to fight this alone.'

'What do you want me to do?'

'Go work for the guys in Washington. You know the ropes down there. They won't treat you like a dumb, provincial Canuck. Do something about it. Don't just live with it. Fight it. She needs a champion. And who else but you? You can do it. You can find out what really happened to her.'

'But why did she cut herself off from me, Brian? Why is she so odd, so distant? Why is she always pushing me away?'

'Don't you see? She doesn't want to pollute us. She thinks that too much contact with her will ruin us. So she won't let us near her.'

The doorbell rang and I got up to answer it. A tiny dark girl with an upturned nose stood there. 'Hi, I'm Yvette,' she said.

I hugged her. 'I'm so glad to meet you.' My voice was muffled in her cloud of black hair.

Brian bobbed behind me, smiling. I waved and left the room for a few moments. When I came out, he had left.

'Where'd he go?'

'To get some food for dinner. I'm going to stay.'

'That's great. I'm sorry about you two.'

'Well, it may improve. Right now, he's obsessed, Catherine. I can't get his mind off it, ever.' A couple of tears trickled down her face and I hugged her. She pushed me away gently, still holding on to my arms. She looked me straight in the eye. 'Help him, Catherine. I'm sure you can. He can't carry this all by himself. It will kill him if you don't help.'

'I'll go to Washington as soon as I can,' I promised.

'I'll tell him,' she said. 'That will help.'

'Keep an eye on him?' We needed this girl.

Her soft face crumpled. 'I'll do my best. Catherine, has your family ever been happy? I can't live with his pain.'

Tears sprang to my eyes and I brushed them away furiously. I didn't know how to answer her, so I shrugged. 'I'll leave tomorrow.'

The next morning, I went to see my mother again. She was guarded, and when I put my request again, she turned me down. Despite my growing sympathy I was furious.

'Damn you. Do you know that I decided never to have children because I thought that, if I escaped your madness, perhaps my child wouldn't and I couldn't go through it again? What if you weren't ill? You probably weren't ill, Mother. And Brian – don't you realize it's this that drove him almost to the point of death?'

Wordless, she shook her head.

I ran upstairs, finished packing and left for the airport without a reservation.

PART II

SUMMER 1962

EIGHT

I sat at the airport, feeling ashamed. I had behaved like a child, throwing my weight around, withholding affection and storming off like a four year old. Why? I was lost in a fugue of bewilderment and unhappiness, unable to dig out of myself long enough to see how anyone else felt, and resentful because figuring out what everyone else felt was the clear path.

Further, I was uncomfortable. Because of my tantrum, I had to fly to Toronto and then to New York. I'd be travelling all today and way into the night. I moved awkwardly to the phone bank, fumbled for my card and called Mark. He was happy that I was coming back sooner than expected, but there were questions in his voice. I explained that Brian was all right and that I simply couldn't sleep another night under my parents' roof. He sounded reserved, the way he used to when I'd phone, high on another story, with yet another trip planned.

I neglected to tell him that I had promised to visit Washington. Not only visit, but to dig in, find out the truth of our involvement. It was my first sin of omission with Mark and it did not feel good.

I returned to my seat. I had another hour to wait. My mind was going a million miles an hour. I couldn't read. I couldn't concentrate on a newspaper or a book. I watched people for a while, but in my mind one visual imprint after another unfurled itself. I saw myself as a child, standing in the bathroom, swinging the mirrored cabinet door back and forth, watching infinite images of myself gesture. I abandoned myself to them.

My embattled family. Yes, Yvette, I remember when we were happy, or at least, together. And I remember the summer it unravelled for the last time.

In the late fifties, 'Get her to the country' was a prescription still used by the physicians of the élite. It was in Foster, a tiny village south of Montreal, twenty miles from the American border and surrounded by hayfields and stone walls and careful woods of oak and elm and maple, that our family life took shape. It was there that my brothers and I grew to a wary, ironic consciousness.

At first, our mother, as limp and grey as a well-used dishrag, staggered through the days. She was helped by a succession of French Canadian maids, who, alternately disdainful or subservient, stole small keepsakes forgotten in the back closets. It was after silhouettes of her pioneer family disappeared that some of her stuffing came back. She fired the maid on the spot and announced that, in future, she would take care of us herself. There followed months of hilarity and confusion, speckled by days of dark brooding and unreasoning fear. We caught her moods like the flu, rarely able to shake them at the garden gate. At least, until we embarked on our death-defying games.

The Village elders, that council of three wealthy families who had founded the town two hundred years ago as a watering hole for their families, would not sell us land until they had spent a year or two observing our behaviour. This was explained in an off-hand manner – forgive us for this silliness, part of the unwritten by-laws of the town. Of course, chuckle chuckle, we would be approved. But in the meantime, whispers flowed around us. Who were we? Who was our family? What had they done? How much money did we have? Did we fit in? How did we fit in?

For two years she struggled on in her little salt box of a cottage on Church Street, her battle mostly invisible to us. My father got up every morning and left in his Oldsmobile 98 for his mill not far from us, or for his office in the city. I started at the village school, Ross at the nursery school. Brian was a baby, by turns entrancing and the most irritating being in the world. When he started walking, he became one of us automatically. We three were a team.

Mornings she handled us on her own. Or tried to. We learned to dress ourselves before most children do and we learned to wait for breakfast and eat lumpy salty porridge without complaint. Ross and I were chronically late for school and our teachers learned not to complain. We learned to dissemble and we learned the inestimable relief of a shared joke, the roar of laughter at just about anything. Too many days, she was not functioning. We helped, especially with Brian; we pretended we were not helping. We missed her, wanted her, needed her. We felt resentful and guilty. We grew up soon and we grew up wild.

Two years after our arrival we were approved. One of the town fathers took it upon himself to find us some land. There were no 'For Sale' signs in Foster. We started building a house, snug in the middle of the old families' fief.

My mother enjoyed being able to tell the architect and contractor exactly what she wanted and she worked on the landscaping all one winter with one of the architect's assistants. She said at the time it was like getting a huge basket of presents after years of everyone forgetting your birthday.

Even once the house was built, we remained outsiders. We were triple outsiders. City people in a country village. Summer people who stayed on in the winter. Villagers who were accepted behind the walls that bordered and hid their giant, feathery green, soft-as-cotton-wool gardens. Privileged children capable of going off like a time bomb. Foster, an hour's easy drive from the city, was a tiny English-speaking enclave of labourers and English expats hiding in the skirts of the very rich, who protected us from the sea of French around us. We were careless of such niceties. The French were held in contempt by our elders, and occasionally mentioned as a possible future threat.

Nature sheltered us, caressed us. Even now I go back to that part of the world with trepidation. It is so gentle, so seductive. It will always be my true home. It is a children's fantasy of the country, with its gentle hills, rolling valley, deer grazing undisturbed in the fields. There was a strange cliff behind which, it was rumoured, a group of in-bred families lived. On the other side of the lake, townies raced their cars up and down the twisty lake road and dance halls fought with drive-in movies for their patronage. On our side, in the forests of the rich, pruned and planted, forgotten tea houses rotted and broken arched pillars stood mute testimony to some man's dream of a dynasty. This was a fantastic land.

In the winter the town was ours. There were few rules that needed following. School, homework, clean hands for dinner, don't upset your father. She was better the year after the house was built. She studied the piano, learned to throw good parties, read widely. Her vitality trickled into her like a glucose drip, imperceptible, but even the colour in her cheeks returned.

We became known as the wild Ramseys, the uncontrollable ones, the ones with The Mother. We were tolerated, laughed at, watched with the knowing eye and treated with careful hands by villagers who knew everything. They knew we carried a congenital disease. These were our salad days – they might not come again. Because of that, perhaps, we were forgiven more than we would have been ordinarily. Winters we were village folk, gentry, perhaps, but still villagers, theirs. It was almost the only true gentleness we ever knew outside our mother's despairing love.

It couldn't last. By 1962, we were up and running as a family, and Muffie arrived at Easter for her ceremonial visit. She divided major holidays between her four sons, alternating them with the years and expecting strict adherence to Old Montreal custom which was as needful of endless preparation and as ludicrous as a trip to the North Pole in winter.

At Easter, aside from the processions to church in full Anglican rig: gloves, hats, dark suits, navy dresses for the women, hats, spit-polished brogues and black patent shoes, she wanted an Easter-egg hunt with the best-bred children in the vicinity. That year, none came.

She enquired why not.

When informed that neither Ross nor I had spoken to any of those children for almost a year, all hell broke loose. The study door slammed behind the three adults, and when they came out, my mother's mouth was twisted in a faintly rebellious sneer but she said nothing. No one did.

From that Sunday on, our weekends changed. We were on display, up, as it were, for sale. A roster of children was drawn up. Every weekend a car appeared to drive us off to play with children 'of our own kind'. We were absolutely forbidden to spend time with the village children during the week. Politeness and no further was the instruction. We broke the rule continuously.

On weekends we had no choice. What could we do? We went, awkward and shy, afraid of the big houses, English nannies, sugary smiles of strange parents.

What did we talk about with these children? Well, for one thing, we didn't have to talk. Their days were arranged for them by the clock and there was so much activity that there was no time for anything like making friends. Associates, that's what we were, in training for the larger associations of big business in the city in the time to come.

We played tennis on cracked courts and swam in pools heated to no more than 68°F. We sailed small boats and we went for crocodile walks and took painful training teas with strange elderly women. It was amazing the programme that my grandmother was able to effect from a distance and with so many parents so much younger than she. To us, it was an example of the awful power of the grown-up.

We were divided up. Boys to one family, me to another, was the usual arrangement. Ross and Brian fitted in fast, finding a family of boys that conformed to Muffie's stringent qualifications, up on the Conference, an agglomeration of big cottages up on a hill, so closely (for Foster) jammed together that they were nicknamed a conference back in the nineteen-hundreds. So Conference Hill became their haunt. They were lucky.

I began to go regularly to the Tuckers', a family who at that time owned almost every major newspaper across Canada. The Tuckers were very stuffy.

One Saturday, I stood dressed in a plaid tunic and white eyelet-stitched blouse, tugging at the uncomfortable clothes, and refusing to put on white stockings until Mother sank back on her heels with tears escaping from under her lids.

We weren't supposed to tire her. Ross shoved me and I put the stockings on.

'I don't see why I have to go. I hate Meredith and Frumpy. This is the weekend! Why can't I go riding?'

'You can ride tomorrow. Catherine, you know why we do this. Your manners were getting rough from copying all those village kids.'

'It's just Muffie. You don't believe that.'

She brushed a dark strand out of her eye. 'Actually I do. You all could do with more polish out here in the sticks.'

'Oh Mummy!' I was despairing. I hated this with an absolute passion. 'I'm never going to spend time with people I don't like when I'm a grown-up.'

'Me neither,' said Ross.

'I hope you two are right. I hope you're in that position.' She smiled wearily. 'Now, the cars are in the driveway.'

I trailed behind, grabbing at her hand. 'How does Muffie afford these cars, Mum? I thought she was broke.'

'Catherine, you are too old for your own good. Some sort of favour is being paid back, I imagine. Who knows what goes on in your grandmother's world? I don't know and I don't want to.'

'I love you, Mum.'

She bent and hugged me. 'Me too, Cathy, my darling. Now be good.'

'I'll try. Do I really have to go?'

She sighed, but it was a sigh of sympathy. 'Let's try one more weekend. If you really hate it I'll take it up with your father. Just make a little effort, darling. Try to fit in.'

I wanted to try, really I did.

I arrived at the Tuckers' and, faced with another rainy, early spring Saturday morning with Frumpy's dough-boy face and droopy eyes and Meredith's stupid snobbery, something else took over.

The trip to the Tuckers' was long. They lived on a huge estate twenty miles south of the village, right on the US border. The house was almost two hundred years old, at least the core of it was, and built as a country residence for a gentleman. Now I would recognize it as mock Palladian. Then we thought of it as the temple, glorious in its grace and confidence. The house made the Tuckers appear elevated, intellectual, more evolved than we were, we village peasants, neither fish nor fowl.

Of course they were no such thing. Some long-distant relative had built this house after a triumphant tour of the home country. Came back and built a little England smack in the centre of the French Canadians, no doubt thinking they were charming peasants who would serve him well, just as soon as he could intimidate them into service.

The house was reached by a long cobblestoned drive that ended in a slow curve. Forsythia hedges bloomed everywhere and weeping willow in a long stream guided visitors down to a slow-moving wide river on which the Tuckers carefully bred black swans. Beyond the house stood a miniature version of it, the stables. Then beyond that staff quarters, three houses descending in size, the largest almost as big as ours. And, as I was made to acknowledge each time, the Tucker house in Montreal was equally as impressive and the Tucker house in Barbados extraordinary. I would come home and recite the laundry list of Tucker possessions cynically, until someone told me to shut up, for God's sake. I was merely trying to debrief. It was all I heard during my Saturdays there; Meredith and Frumpy were as impressed by their parents as their sycophantic nanny. Once they made me memorize the list before I got lunch.

It was cold enough to merit indoor activities, but the Tucker nanny wouldn't hear of it. Exercise was mandatory for children every single day. We had a choice of riding in soaking rain or swimming in the barely heated pool in soaking rain. We chose swimming.

We changed quickly into uncomfortable elastic bathing suits and made a fast scamper down to the pool. The nanny was a Mrs Larratt. I couldn't believe that she'd ever been married, she had such a moustache and was so mean. She told us she would call us in a half-hour and she wanted us to keep moving until then.

We had no choice. It was so cold. It was warmer when we were completely submerged and moving our limbs back and forth. There was a ball, but throwing it back and forth meant lifting your arms into the cold air so we crouched in the shallow end, wrapping our arms around ourselves to keep warm.

After fifteen minutes of freezing in the rain, Meredith's black heart manufactured something that would really hurt. Who knows? Maybe she merely wanted an excuse to get back inside.

I knew from experience that Meredith didn't censor her remarks. In the way of children repressed at home, violence and cruelty leached out in company of her contemporaries. I was always ducking her cracks about our poverty, our pathetic family, the village school, the scum we spent time with during the week, and finally, our mother.

I tried to drown her.

I know that I did because that was what I was told I had done. The incident is still fuzzy, more than twenty years later.

From what I was told, I threw myself on top of her from the diving board. Then I used all my force to hold her under. I was big for my age. Frumpy was struck silent with shock, then dashed out of the pool for help. I held Meredith under until she went limp. Then, I left her floating on her back, and walked up the pool steps and into the house, wet footprints on the silk carpets, and announced to the grown-ups having morning coffee in the peach and pale-green drawing room, 'Meredith's had an accident.'

Disassociation from reality was what it was called. For months, I didn't open my mouth at home except to eat enough to keep me alive. My silence was called truculence by my embattled and bewildered father, but it wasn't. I simply couldn't remember and that fact scared and embarrassed me.

The nanny was fired. I was never invited to the Tuckers' again. I drifted back into my village crowd and only at the gates to the house would my silence return.

NINE

It was only then that we became friends. That spring, the spring of Meredith and Frumpy, after I lost my ability to speak, I started sitting at the counter in the kitchen, while she prepared dinner, and I'd listen. She began to fascinate me, locked as I was in my unwilling silence. I heard the minutiae of her day, her little loves and tiny dislikes, her jokes and her fancies. I studied them and fell slowly in love with her.

I can still hear her speaking to me, for she was often lonely, she said, and she liked to talk, to hear the sound of her own voice, strong and certain, as she tried to bring an eleven year old out of her shell. She said it meant I was sensitive, and, contrary to the rest of our crowd, to her, sensitivity was a gift. I encouraged her, sitting, head in hand, staring at her. I knew I was hearing things that my friends didn't hear. I was receiving the secret knowledge of the adult.

She was a monologist; she had been condemned to spend her life commenting upon it, describing the fibrillations of her feelings, reaching for understanding. What she wasn't telling me, she was writing in her diary, scribble scribble, the mouse that refused to give up. She wrote stories about us, for us, then read them to us, and we were flattered beyond words that we had been immortalized. And despite the limitations she lived within, she was happy then, I knew it.

I had been badly frightened by Muffie and her insistence on conformity. I worried about what else our future threatened. I saw Mother as a potential ally, if only (and this is a curious thought, the convoluted reasoning of a panicked pre-adolescent) I could protect her enough. I began by watching her, and that spring I spied on her, listened at doors, scrabbled through her diary, if she had not remembered to lock it in her strong-box.

Then, sure as summer drought, the fear began. The certainty that I was going to lose her grew. I started to shadow her, insisting silently that she take me everywhere, appearing mute every morning after a party, waiting for the stories. When the phone rang, I crept near the door and listened to her side of the phone calls that came from her friends, all tall, athletic women like her, dressed in pink madras and blue chambray shirts, wearing peaked caps to keep the sun off their faces, though tiny lines streaked from their eyes, white tear tracks through dark tans.

You see her, now, don't you? A tall, dark woman in her late thirties, well proportioned, with strong arms and dark eyebrows and a dazzling smile. My brothers and I worshipped her that year, squirmed around her feet like adoring puppies, for she was in her prime, in command of her rather considerable self, and magnetic for it.

And when it all fell apart, Ross, Brian and I sat piecing it all together, sharing information, conversations overheard, diaries and letters read in secret until we had puzzled out what had happened. I give you the story of that summer of '62, the unedited terror of my youth.

We stood at the bowed window at the back of the house, looking down the slope at the bower under the grove of fir trees. It was a perfect day for working in the garden, she said. I nodded. I stood far enough away to seem detached, but close enough to be her audience. She was in a mood today. She shook her head and laughed.

'Housewife, mother, occasional socialite . . . I catch a glimpse of myself in the mirror these days, Catherine, and laugh. I've merged, or maybe even mutated. I've become one of them, flushed from days spent outside, freckles sprinkled across my nose, hair in a practical bob. Look at me!'

I looked. She was dressed in the uniform: deck shoes, khaki shorts, sleeveless madras shirt. She looked like everyone else. I shrugged.

'I know!' she said. She had taken to reading my mind, no doubt to keep the conversation going. 'The disguise is so perfect that only once in a while does real life loom in front of me. Only once in a while I say something so wrong that I silence a room.'

I pretended I hadn't heard, stood looking at my feet.

She turned. 'I'll have to change before we start. Why don't you begin on the grey garden?' I nodded and wandered down, grabbed a spade and weeding bucket from the shed.

This garden was my favourite – hers too, I thought. I'd been working alongside her all spring. The others – the rock garden, over by the boys' favourite place to hide, the formal gardens at the front of the house – were all more or less finished. This one was filled with wild flowers and herbs. I had learned the names: oregano and Queen Anne's lace, tansy and hyssop, artemisia and bee balm and scabiosa – none of them the kind of plant that proclaimed the gardener a talent – this was the hidden garden that needed coaxing.

She set down a tray of tiny plants and slipped into her place beside me. In the kitchen, the phone rang.

'Ignore it,' she said to me. 'Let someone else answer it.'

I said nothing.

'Oh you're right. No one's in. My, how popular the boys are this summer already, and the season is just starting.'

I looked away. I was not popular. The boarding schools had let loose their charges five days ago and families had started to arrive. Filled with energy and plans and party schedules, mothers drove around the village in a tizzy, bent on booking blocks of lessons. No one called for me.

I had driven around with her weeks before, booking the best lessons. That, she said to me, with a grin, was one of the benefits of being stuck in the country. It made up for some of the condescension in the voices of the summer mothers. She also could practise on the golf course the second it was ready, which inevitably put her miles ahead of the women whose game had grown creaky over the winter months, despite trips to Bermuda and North Carolina.

'I have a new hair idea for the Spencers' tonight. I hope it won't look too provincial against all the city extravaganzas I'll be up against.'

The phone stopped ringing. I wondered where the boys were. They usually landed on it, with shouts and shoves and cries of 'It's for me, you ligger'. Ligger. I wondered where they'd got that expression and what it meant. I could barely keep up with them these days. They were growing so strong. Strong and funny. Ross was growing taller by the minute, but his delicacy made him seem girlish, almost pretty.

'I had such an argument with Ross yesterday,' said my mother suddenly. 'He's different from Brian; he's willing to argue any subject into the ground. He has my colouring – dark hair, dark-blue eyes, a determined chin.' She rubbed her eyes suddenly, streaking dirt across her face. 'Is mine still determined? Or has it submerged itself in docility and social grace, becoming a little pointed and petulant? Silly.'

I dug into the ground ferociously.

She shook herself. 'Bad subject, dark areas, stop.'

I drew away from her then and sat on a rock just a little behind her.

'Don't worry, Cathy. In the past five years, I've learned how to pull myself away from the brink. Self-analysis of any kind opens doors into rooms filled with things I just don't want to see. Shadows. Now, I deal with them as efficiently as I can. It's just like planting this garden or raising you kids to be strong and resilient. Or becoming ladies' captain at the golf club.' She paused and seemed to think for a moment. I held my breath. 'I've learned. I write my doubts down. I take them to Ewen in the city and then he takes care of them. Somehow if you write them down they become much less important. The one thing that still bothers me, the shadow impossible to ignore, is you, Cathy.' She was still facing away from me.

I stiffened.

'You haven't really spoken for three weeks. That's a long time, darling. It's been three weeks since you had that run-in with Meredith. Can't you tell me what happened?'

She looked at me then.

I turned my face away, picked at the moss.

'Well, it doesn't matter. But you know, you barely acknowledge your father and you're spending all your time with village children. Your grandmother is furious.'

I couldn't help myself. I snorted. She smiled at me.

I knew tales of my assault had made the rounds of Montreal. It wasn't going to be an easy summer for the Ramseys, my grandmother warned, in a relentless stream of phone calls. 'Bugger off, Muffie,' Mother had said more than once. A big huff and an insistence that she speak to Father would follow. Then he, puffing on a cigarette, eyes rolling, would pretend to listen for five minutes, would offer her some money and put the phone down.

It had become one of their favourite rituals. A martini, a cigarette, then the maid would call us for dinner, which more often than not would end up in hilarity, mostly at my grandmother's expense.

Through which I sat silently, trying not to smile. My grandmother was somehow making my parents happy with each other. And I guessed that somehow my father was proud of me for standing up for myself. In fact, he had said so one night. Time enough, he said, for me to learn the manners I would have to practise for the rest of my life. Give her a year or two as a hellion, at odds with this manicured playground. Only fair. Boys would civilize me and time enough for that.

I immediately decided no such thing would ever happen.

My mother loved him those nights, I could tell. She hummed doing the dishes the next morning, even said once she was glad she had married him. Despite his icy detachment, his military precision, his rages when he was flouted or mocked, underneath he was kind and understanding – didn't I see that? I did. The boys were enjoying him, pestering him for drives around town, sailing trips. Ross had won the chance to crew for him in the boat-club races and even I was jealous. He could be a lot of fun, especially when he was kept away from my grandmother.

My mother sat, hands around her knees, back to the garden, looking up at the house.

'You know, Cathy, this house really made us happy, your father and me. It cemented us.' Her mouth twisted into an ironic pout and I almost smiled at her. 'Once, of course, we had been approved by the village committee, those three towering demigods. Actually, they were really nice to us. Once we were approved they went to great lengths to find us the right property. When Ian told them that we wanted to build our own house, there were careful enquiries about what kind of house. How big, what would it look like? Then they retreated for two weeks.

'I know you hate them all, sweetheart, but look what they found us, this big hunk of field, on the main road, on the same street as all the big houses. Acres of forest stand behind us. Beyond the forest, the lake. Even your favourite place, the pony club, is close, only two fields away.'

She waited for a response. I kept my mouth firmly shut.

The pony club was on the property of an ageing playboy bringing up his daughter on his own in a big old colonial house with a battalion of housekeepers and, of course, the pony-club mistresses across his driveway. I knew my parents loved it here. Despite my desperate class war, I admitted to myself I would hate to leave.

She turned away from the house and started digging again.

'It's hard, Cathy, when you don't talk. I worry about you and I hate it when I can't stop thinking, remembering, sorting worries, reviewing them endlessly. It's almost as if my mind has a will of its own, that it decides the only way for me to be is constantly to recycle old thoughts. Certainly, I made a decision about you a few weeks ago. Why disturb you with it now? Patience.'

I sat up at that. It sounded like a threat.

A bird swooped down, landed on the grass beside her, chirped once and escaped, twittering with loud pride at his daredevil nature. She laughed and I smiled.

'Isn't this such a contrast to those days in that little clapboard house up on Church Street? I hate even driving by it these days, though from time to time, I wonder if there's a new couple in there now undergoing hazing. I wonder if that practice will ever die. Surely it will, surely these few English families can't hold all the cards in this province for ever.

'Those two years were the worst of my life. The first I can barely remember in detail. Just that I had spent months in a fog, exhausted and dragging my way around, falling into a sleep after lunch.

'Then, slumped at the kitchen table, trying to gather enough energy to make dinner. Ian coming home, solicitous mostly, but sometimes distant and caustic, escaping into martinis and the newspaper. Then sleep at night, sleep from which waking was impossible, even if I was haunted by nightmares that never seemed to stop. Sometimes when I woke in the mornings my nightdress and the sheets on my side of the bed were wet from night sweats and my pillow damp with tears.'

I was fascinated, afraid to make a move, afraid if I did, she'd notice me and stop.

She sprinkled fertilizer around the new plants. 'God, the routine, horrible and endless. For a while I had help. But they made me suspicious the way they skulked around the house, sneaking looks at me, poking in my drawers. I found myself counting the silver when they left for the day, listing ornaments in my head, looking to see whether the linen closet had been disturbed. But for months, over a year even, I can't remember how long exactly, I depended on them for everything: shopping, cooking, house cleaning, childcare, even, on particularly weak days, support back up to bed. There were too many of those days.

'There were weekends when Ian had insisted that I attend some party or other. The families wanted to meet me. The mother was very important, they had said. Hen pecks of anxiety would torture me for days. You see, you and I are not that different. I'd go over my clothes obsessively, then turn up overdressed. I'd learn, and dress down next time to discover that this weekend was traditionally formal. Really, I agree with you, they're ridiculous people.'

She was starting to make sense to me. Before today, all I heard was how nice they were, really, under all that junk.

'Their behaviour *is* comic, Catherine, the tiny measurements of country hierarchy, based on an arcane formula made up of breeding, family accomplishment, schools attended, size of trust fund, children's schools, position and size of country house, city house, number of cousins, how many in the vicinity, how many sailboats, horses, and dogs. What kind of dogs, what kind of horses, various connections to England and Boston, the only American city they acknowledged as having any value whatsoever . . .' She paused, took a breath.

I laughed out loud.

She looked at me, shocked, as if the fact of my presence suddenly became real. Her eyes narrowed. 'But I learned the ropes. I drank martinis, made friends with a few of them. They are human after all, and I accepted that I would probably never work again. My energy trickled back. I found interests that were acceptable and that I enjoyed.' She stared directly at me. 'I fitted in.'

I stared back, uncomfortable, frightened and, somehow, betrayed.

TEN

The Spencers' house was new too. They were one of the original families and lived in a compound that had stretched out to cover Loon Point over the last hundred and fifty years. Jack Spencer had laid claim to a spit that reached out into the lake like a chubby prawn and had built an enormous modern house, filled with modern teak furniture from Scandinavia.

The Spencers were considered very fast, but untouchable behind the shield of an old fortune and a century of public service. If the young Spencer lad wanted to play Frank Sinatra records and build an outlandish summer cottage, as long as he turned up at the family securities firm on Dorchester Street every Monday morning at eight-thirty, well, how amusing and inventive are the young.

Mother stood on the stairs in our house, where the longest mirror hung. It was not exactly full length. But if you walked down slowly from one step to the next, you could see everything, shoes to hat. I was beginning to spend big chunks of time looking in this mirror, examining every portion of my body to see where it would change, hope to God, flipping myself up and down the steps to check out the whole image. She did the same now, stepping up, then down, then up again. I sat on the top step, dressed in a white piqué dress, my dark hair rebellious under its butterfly clasp. My scalp hurt, and I was embarrassed by the way I looked. My white shoes were way too pointy.

But she looked wonderful, just the way I knew I would never look. Her dark hair was curled under in a shiny pageboy and her dress – yellow, sleeveless, with a low square neckline – had a full skirt made out of piqué, like mine, which made it stand out. Terrific for dancing, she said. She felt like Jackie Kennedy, she said. She toyed with a white handbag, wondered whether she needed to bring it.

'You look terrific, Mum,' I said.

'Why, Cathy, thank you!' She pressed her lips as if to stop herself from saying anything else. This was my first sentence since I had said I wanted to go to this party five days ago. The Spencers were related to the Tuckers and they were offering an olive branch. At the first Spencer party of the season, children the same age as Judy and Susan were invited to help pass food, carry empty glasses to the kitchen and spy, almost unnoticed, on their parents.

'I like this dress. It's very gay, don't you think?'

'You look like you're going to have a lot of fun.'

She turned to look at me and smiled. 'You look nice too, sweetie. Did you have fun today?'

'OK. Mrs Northrop showed me how to pluck a chicken.'

Added to my compliment, this was more than I had said at the same time for a month.

'Oh, did you like that?'

'No.' I laughed. 'I couldn't eat it afterwards.'

She laughed. 'I know what you mean.'

'Susan Spencer has a new horse.'

'Oh?'

'I wonder if she's going to enter it in the show.'

'That's not till the end of the summer, darling.'

'I have to know. If Cedar and I are going to do all that work, I have to know if she's going to bring that horse in.'

'Well, you'll have a chance to find out tonight.'

'I know.' That was why I was going.

The drive to the Spencers' was mostly silent. My father had

his first martini before we left home and he was concentrating on navigating difficult curves on the lake road. I sat in the back seat, watching.

'How many people do you think they'll have?' she asked finally.

'No idea. I suspect it'll be around one hundred and fifty. That's usual for the first party of the summer.'

'Enough so that everyone left out gets to hear of it,' she cracked.

'Victoria.' His voice was instantly on guard. He was her personal word cop, always staunching her wit. I wished he'd relax, join in, because he was funny too.

'Don't worry, I'm just joking. But it's true, isn't it?' she said.

'Probably.' He let out a light chuckle. 'Guess I never thought of it that way. Nice that you could join us, Catherine,' he added, and his voice held only the faintest hint of irony.

We arrived in a high good humour. He complimented her on her dress and she twirled for him as they walked up the slate steps to the entrance. She stopped at the door, her attention suddenly fixed on the house.

'Gosh!' she whispered.

It was pretty amazing for Foster, all heavy horizontal beams and wide fat space, carved out of blond wood and fieldstone. As completely different as was possible, without building an igloo, from the colonials and salt boxes and English manor house knockoffs that had been fashionable here for the last two hundred years. The heavy wood door swung open and the sounds of Sinatra teased at us. I pulled my hand free. I was terrified by all this, it was too grown-up, and seemed very dangerous. I peeked down into the main room. There were hundreds of people there, all dressed up and glossy, with stiff hair and masses of jewellery. I took a quick step back and darted for the car. She caught me and dragged me in with her.

'It's going to be fine,' she hissed into my ear.

I didn't believe her for a minute and tugged away.

'Just stay close if you feel at sea.'

I let her pull me into the house then.

The entrance gave way immediately into a wide foyer with stone steps down into a gigantic sunken living room. Floor-to-ceiling windows looked over the lake.

Everyone was standing in the living room, all long-time friends, talking, smoking and drinking. In the corner, Cassie Dundonald showed Jack Spencer a new dance step and they were repeating it over and over. My mother's mouth dropped open for a split second. She bent down and whispered that she suddenly felt as if she had been locked in a cloister.

Our hostess approached, hands held out, smile glistening, polished, seamless. I lost my nerve and edged around behind Mother.

'Now I really feel as if I've been buried in the country.' She kissed Patsy Spencer on the cheek. 'What has been happening in the world while I've been raising terrifying children and planting acres of flowers?' she said as their hostess greeted them.

'Join the party, Victoria. You've been away too long. This hidden treasure must be Catherine.' She reached behind Mother and hauled me out. 'Judy can't wait for you to arrive. She has her own bowl of onion dip and about three huge bags of potato chips hidden in her room. She thinks I don't know, but I do.' A tinkle of laughter. 'Why don't you run and get yourself a Coke? Her room's the third door on the left down the right corridor.' Obedient, I walked down the stairs, then stopped, and stood looking up at them.

Patsy Spencer kissed Dad and took Mother's hand and accompanied her down the hall steps. Her eyes were hard as she watched Mother walk into the crowd.

Mother found her best friends. They were, as usual, standing in the centre of the room, the better to see and be seen. Her favourite, a huge bony blonde named Phyllis Walters, was a divorcee. Phyllis was from the Maritimes and despite her reputation, she was always at the best parties. Mother said she guessed the size of her house and the loudly voiced conservative opinions were the reasons. That and the fact that her laugh, raucous and slightly cruel, had the effect of lightning on a dull party.

Creetie McDougall was the other. A small dark woman with

a twist to her very red lips, she was married to a surgeon who made rare appearances on winter weekends, and spent most of the summer on the golf course. Creetie had learned to play a vicious game to keep up with him. 'If I didn't,' she explained, 'I'd never see him.'

This statement invariably won a snort from Phyllis. I got myself a Coke from an already sweating barman, and ignoring the directions to Judy's room, crept closer to them.

'So isn't this marvellous?' shouted Phyllis above the noise in the room. 'We're about to have almost three uninterrupted months together. What will we get up to? All bad, I hope. Let's swear on it!'

'You've already had too much screech,' said my mother, as she hugged Creetie and complimented her on her strapless dress.

'Just because I'm from Down East, you all think I'm an alcoholic.'

'Aren't you?'

'Oh, Victoria's on form tonight. We're gonna have fun.'

'Not too much fun, Phyl. Ian's on the lookout. It's the beginning of the season – watch out.'

'Your oh-so-cautious husband makes me laugh.'

'What do you mean?'

'Never mind, what do you think of this house? Something, isn't it?'

'I think it is terrific. I haven't seen anything like it outside the pages of a magazine. It's dramatic, but I wouldn't mind living in it.'

'I agree,' said Creetie quickly.

'Oh come on, you two. You sound like a newspaper article. It's as pretentious as the Spencers', and has all the showy qualities of Jack. Look at all my money, it says. I think it's disgusting. Why couldn't he build a big old thing with shaded verandas and a cupola and a garden house?'

Creetie's husband pulled her on to the dance floor. Phyllis nodded towards them. 'Poor thing. He's having an affair with his nurse. She hasn't a clue.'

My mother looked around for me and pushed me away with

her hands waving in the air. 'Go see Judy, honey. This is for grown-ups.'

'Mum! You said!' I took a small step away.

She ignored me. I skittered back within earshot.

Phyllis continued, careless. 'It's true, you know. I'd say most of the men in this room are having one, or contemplating it. I'd watch out for Jack Spencer if I were you. He thinks you're weak. Stuck out here all winter and so on . . .'

'You are damned silly sometimes, Phyllis. Call me when you want to play golf, not cause trouble.'

She stalked over to a bunch of armchairs and sank into a wide and very comfortable square leather armchair. I immediately sat on the arm. She reached up and smoothed hair back from my face.

'What's wrong?'

I shook my head, wordless.

'I still haven't had a drink,' she said. 'Pretty good, eh? When we first moved here I had no idea how to handle alcohol. I used to get falling-down-stupid drunk nearly every time we went out. Everyone did. The next morning, people called or toured house to house detailing last night's hilarity and mistakes. The police who tidied up were always so polite.'

I smiled at her. She pushed me gently. 'Go on, honey. Go see Susan and Judy. What about that horse? You won't find out about that standing around me all night.'

I left her then and skated across the smooth dance floor. I almost slid into Phyllis, but I caught myself on the corner of the bar. The barman smiled at me and someone changed the record.

'May I have another Coke?' I said to him and he pulled a bottle out of the ice and popped the cap.

'Straws?' he said.

I nodded and took the bottle. A couple of waiters approached then and I ducked out of their way. As I swung around, I nearly backed into a group of people standing on the edge of the dance floor. They were all looking at someone and I followed their eyes.

My mother was dancing with Jack Spencer in the centre of the room. Her yellow dress swung around her and she followed him in a very complicated series of dance steps. The other couples on the floor had cleared a space for them and were watching them as they danced. I searched for my father and found him, cigarette dangling from his hand, smiling at her. She looked wonderful.

'Shame about that girl,' said a woman in the group. 'She seems so vibrant. I suppose, though, that would be part of it . . .' Her voice trailed off.

'What do you mean, Janet?' It was Phyllis's voice.

'You know, Phyllie.'

'No, I don't.' Each word enunciated clearly.

'Of course, she's your friend.'

'What do you mean, Janet?' the man asked.

'Well, she's mad as a hatter. I feel sorry for Ian. He has his hands full there.'

'You stupid cow.'

The woman turned to Phyllis, eyes bright in her puffy, flushed face, and shrugged.

'I'm not saying anything that everyone else doesn't think. And aren't you the one who drones on about our hypocrisy, day in and day out? How do you like honesty now?'

I backed away, and darted around behind the huge stone fireplace, my eyes stinging. I stood there, leaning on it for a while, pressing into it, scraping my arms and bare shoulders back and forth on the stone edges. Then I walked quickly down the long hallway, looking for the kitchen. I ran through it, found the pantry and corridor to the back door and tripped down the stone steps on to the gravel. The sky hung very close that night, I could almost touch the scrim of stars. The immense sky and cool night quieted me for a few seconds. Then, I threw the Coke bottle as hard as I could against the stone wall bordering the driveway. It shattered into a thousand satisfying pieces.

I found the car and crawled into the back seat, put my cheek down against the cool suction of the plastic, and curled myself into a very tiny ball. Eventually I must have fallen asleep for I woke up only when someone lifted my head gently and tucked my father's folded-up jacket underneath my cheek.

She was talking about an old man with spots on his trousers. He was silent.

'What's wrong, Ian?'

'Nothing.'

'What do you mean, nothing? It was a lovely evening. Didn't you have a good time?'

'I did before you put on that hour-long demonstration with Jack Spencer. For God's sake, everyone was laughing at us. He is notorious, Victoria. Don't you know that? You looked like a fool.'

'It wasn't an hour. I was just trying to have a good time, make friends.' Her voice was tired, pleading. 'Your mother is always going on at me about making more friends. I was trying.'

The flick of a lighter. 'By the way, she's coming down next weekend. Insists upon it.'

'Oh no!' she wailed.

'Says we're mismanaging Catherine.'

'She means I am.'

'The child didn't even say hello to her friends tonight. Hid in the car the entire evening. She looks like an orphan most of the time, hasn't spoken for weeks, is still running around with those little ragamuffins in the village – '

'And that's my fault?'

'It's your job, for Christ's sake!'

'But, Ian, she – '

'Leave it!' he shouted and his voice held the warning of a rifle being primed.

She was feeling too good and ignored him. 'Why should I leave it, Ian? Why? Catherine is starting to talk to me, in whole sentences now. She's coming out of her shell. This place is confusing for the kids, all artifice one moment, simple and down home the next. They need to be ordinary to survive in the village school. You know Ross is always coming home, bruised from a fight with some bully who wanted to beat up the rich kid.'

'Jesus, you just don't listen.' He braked the car, threw the gear into park and got out. She sat, eyes straight ahead, in the passenger seat for a moment, then rolled the window down.

'Ian, get in.' He stood white-lipped, staring down at her, about to explode. I recoiled. She wasn't watching the warning signs. Why wasn't she watching?

'Drive yourself home.'

She waited a moment longer, but he had walked out of the pool of light from the headlamps.

'Mummy? Let's go.'

She slid over into the driver's seat, adjusted it and the rear-view mirror. There was a thump as he kicked the rear of the car.

'Mummy?'

She put it in gear and we drove away.

I was awake now, half sitting, still crouched into a tight ball, heart filled with dread. I stared out the window, and watched the night slash by in front of my eyes. I knew it would be days before they spoke again.

ELEVEN

The morning after that party, she entered my room early. She sat down carefully on the edge of the bed, smoothed the pink blankets. I peeped through my almost closed eyelids.

'Darling?' Her voice was low, almost a whisper.

'Mmpf?' I turned on to my back, opened my eyes. 'Mummy? What are you doing here? What time is it?'

'It's nine o'clock, darling.'

'Oh!' Escape beckoned. I sat straight up. 'I have to meet Rodney and Shelagh down at the Mill Pond. We're going fishing.'

'Can it wait an hour, sweetheart? We have to talk.'

'Why?'

Her voice soothed. 'Well, we have a tiny emergency. Your grandmother is coming down.'

'Muffie?' I pretended surprise. My knees came up under my chin and my brow furrowed.

'Stop it, Cathy, you were awake last night. I could feel you thinking away back there. Yes, Muffie. And coming especially to see you.'

The worst was happening. I wanted to hide. My head went down on to her knees and my hair swung forward to cover my face. Maybe, I thought, I could beg to stay at Heather's for one night, then get sick and have to stay there, not be moved.

'Cathy?'

'Yes?' The word was muffled.

'Can't you tell me what's going on? Why are you so angry with us?'

'Not.'

'Lift your head, darling, and talk to me.'

I struggled with myself. I wanted to help her, but I was caught in my own misery. I raised my head.

'We're not the same as everyone here, are we, Mummy?'

'What do you mean? You know we are, really.'

'Well, we don't live in the city all the time like the city people, but the village people never see the city people on the weekends and in the summer like we do. And some of my friends are French and the city people are so mean to them.'

'That's just prejudice and you have to learn to ignore it. We are the same as the city people because we used to live in the city. Eventually you will spend all your time with city people. You'll probably even live in the city and just come out here on weekends.'

I shook my head vigorously. 'Not me. They're awful to us.'

'Oh darling.' She hugged me. 'It's easier for the boys, I know. Girls can be so mean. Why don't you take the day off from your friends and come with me, so we can talk about it. I'm going junking.'

I felt brighter then and she must have seen that because she squeezed my hands. I had been so lonely, and I was miserable about what I'd seen last night. Her world seemed even scarier than I had imagined and I started to cry, and she pulled me to her and held on, while I snuffled into her shoulder.

As we drove through the hills and tiny hamlets of the Eastern Townships, looking for likely prospects, she talked to me, and as the morning wore on, I became more lighthearted and forgot the conversations of the night. I loved poking around in farmers' barns looking for things that had been abandoned fifty years ago, layers of paint obscuring their beauty. She could find a 200-year-old washstand buried under twenty layers of turquoise paint and argue the price down from $50 to $15 in five minutes in broken French. I'd stand and pantomime silently behind the farmer's back.

We had lunch at Jeanne's *chien chaud* stand and then I finally told her the Meredith story.

'She said you were nuts, Mummy, and that Muffie was going to take us away from you.'

She carefully put the large container of Coke down on the splintered picnic table. I noticed that some spilled on to the table.

'That won't happen, Catherine.'

'That's what I told her. But why does Muffie have anything to say about what we do or say? She's just a granny.'

'She's your father's mummy and he loves her very much, even if sometimes he isn't even aware how much he does. She has a hold on him I can't explain since she was barely around when he was your age.'

I stared fixedly at her, waiting for the next words as if they were the keys to unlock a whole host of doors.

'Look, honey, I don't know whether you can understand this, but try. It might seem like silly grown-up stuff, but it affects you a lot, so it might help.'

I nodded at her.

'You know that Daddy doesn't have much family money like all the other city people. Muffie helps. She's a social powerhouse, which is good for Daddy's business. Do you understand that, Catherine? She can get us club memberships. She arranged the property sale. She can get you all into the right schools. That's why she's so interested in your manners and your friends.'

'I hate her.' I spat a mouthful of chewed hot dog on the ground. 'That's what I think of her.'

She gasped, unsure of whether to laugh or shout.

'Catherine, they *will* take you away from me if you *ever* do that again.' She took my chin in her hand and pinched it carefully. We smiled at each other.

'We have to teach you some things so you can fool her. We only have a week, so I want your full attention.'

'What's a "social powerhouse"?'

'Someone who knows what's right and what's wrong and who is listened to.'

'Does she know what's right and wrong?'

She heaved a sigh of frustration. 'As far as manners go, she sure does, Cathy. Will you help me?'

I thought for a second, then grinned and nodded vigorously. I adored conspiracies, and especially the ones that Brian, Ross, and I plotted. This sounded like a more intricate grown-up conspiracy. Besides, anything to beat Muffie was more fun than anything I could think of.

It wasn't easy, but with a few new clothes torturously purchased and climbed into each morning in fury, and afternoons spent learning table manners, elements of conversation and positions proper to my age, I learned how to behave. Even though I loathed the clothes and made fun of the manners, I took to the duplicity with ease. Just in time, for Muffie arrived a day early.

We were sitting in the living room practising having tea. I was wearing a Liberty print tunic and a white eyelet-lace blouse. We heard a clatter on the gravel outside the door and the dog began to howl in the basement.

'Let him out?' I grinned evilly.

'No.' Mother smiled. 'Wonder who it is?'

'Halloooo!' from the hall. We got up, shooting each other looks of dismay.

'Sweethearts!' came the gravelly, smoke-filled voice. 'I got a ride with the Pecks. Such a comfortable car, a Mercedes, so I took it, just to be with my sweeties a day early. Aren't we all so happy to be together again? I do wish I hadn't promised that old Morgan woman I'd spend the summer in Murray Bay.'

She threw her arms wide, pocketbook dangling from one arm and a mohair stole arranged on the other. We each gingerly hugged a shoulder.

'Well,' said Muffie, examining Mother with a sharp eye. 'My suitcase is out by the garage.'

'Ross can bring it in when he arrives. We were just having some tea. Please join us.'

'Yes, do.' I joined in and Muffie stared at me, openmouthed, taking in every detail of my outfit. She fumbled in her bag for a cigarette.

Mother led the way into the living room, I followed close on her heels, grinning from ear to ear.

Later that night, my father had closeted himself in his den. The walls were panelled in the new vinyl stuff that looked like pine. Built-in cabinets hid books, records and even the television. Military trophies, citations and keepsakes littered the surfaces. He had many; he had been a popular officer. We were used to being treated like the laziest and most careless of his men.

At about eight o'clock, I noticed my grandmother hovering outside the den door. Finally she reached out and slowly turned the doorknob. She cracked the door slightly, then slid through it and closed it gently behind her.

I hurried to the door and pressed my ear to it. My mother noticed me and started to scold me, then reconsidered and joined me.

'Mother! You surprised me!' we heard my father say.

'Ian, my dear,' said Sybil in her distinctive voice, 'do you have a light?' There was a pause.

'That was quite a performance at dinner,' she drawled.

'I don't know what you mean,' snapped my father, although he did. Even he had been flummoxed by the sight of me in a plaid dress, hands and nails clean, hair brushed to a shine and tied back in a ponytail with a ribbon that, amazingly, matched the dress. I had eaten properly, using knife and fork impeccably, and even broached two conversational topics, one about the pony club's new mistress and another about the new grocery store in town.

'Rubbish!' Sybil exploded. 'I think Catherine ought to spend the summer with me in Murray Bay.'

'Out of the question. She is doing fine here. You saw for yourself.'

'That was a performance put on for my benefit, Ian, and you bloody well know it. I hear about Catherine from my friends.

She's becoming a legend, roaring around this village like a little hellion, playing with village trash, ignoring friends of her own type and almost drowning poor decent little Meredith Tucker – a more appropriate friend for her I cannot imagine. Your wife, which is not a surprise to me, cannot handle her children.'

'Mother, this is none of your business. I wish you would stop interfering in our lives. Victoria has been doing splendidly these last few years. She has made many friends, has many interests and the children love her. As do I. And there is an end to it. I appreciate your concern, but I assure you it is misplaced.'

'What about Meredith?'

'Victoria told me last night that Meredith insulted us and Catherine defended us. I don't approve of the fight and it was clearly taken too far, but she has been punished enough. And I admire the child's spirit. Lord knows she'll need it in this world of ours.'

'Well, I don't know.' There was another pause. 'I shall leave tomorrow. I am not wanted here, I can see. The Griffiths will take me to the city. I have any number of rides to Murray Bay and I am late.'

'Whatever you like.'

'You will need me in the future, Ian. Don't be too cocky. I can see there is trouble coming. I'm not as blind as you think.'

'Don't be ridiculous, Mother.'

Behind the door, we all were listening.

'What's happening?' whispered Ross.

'He's running her off. It's a rout, a complete rout. We'd better get out of this hallway,' said Mother.

We ran into the kitchen and leaned against the counter, grinning at each other.

'Good for Daddy. I like him better now,' I said. Relief was lifting off me in waves. I had been having awful nightmares.

'That's right. It's a lot for him to stand up to his mother.'

'Not for me!' I said.

Mother hugged me fiercely. 'So I've noticed.'

But our eyes returned to the study door, still shut. It was too quiet.

TWELVE

Summer wore on.

The days were warm, the air caressing, the lake a shimmering welcome, glinting silver as we drove past it on our way to one party or another.

Ross crewed for my father in the boat-club races. His anxious eyes roved constantly between the wind, father's face, the position of the other boats, ears cocked to measure the force of the wind filling the sails.

Their fourteen-foot sailboat, which Ross had sanded and varnished and polished to within an inch of its life, won from time to time. They would reach the dock, Ross would beam from ear to ear, and Mother was there to take the photographs.

She was on her way to becoming ladies' champion at the golf club again, and I was bent on winning junior jumping at the pony club, taking every chance possible to practise in between the classes in the rings.

There were parties every weekend. People had claimed certain weekend nights years in advance and held their party, theme fixed, every year at the same time. That way, people knew what to expect. Women, shopping for the season, would be able to say oh, this will be right for the so-and-sos' dance when they make us eat Italian food and dance outside all night under red paper Chinese lanterns.

I was more committed than ever to my pursuit of such essential information. I hoarded these nuggets. This knowledge was the currency by which we lived and I knew that someday I would need it, especially if the worst happened and Muffie got us.

There were hangover parties on Sunday at lunchtime and Saturday night dances for us kids at the boat club. Ross and Brian spent most of their time together, roaming the hills with a gang of kids on their bikes. Mother had extracted a promise from me that allowed me one engagement with my village friends for each event, including lessons, that I did with the city people. Friday nights would see me struggling with a chart, sucking on a pen, ink dying my lips blue black. She would laugh and stroke my hair. 'It doesn't have to be exact, honey. Just as long as you're fair to both.'

Unknown to her, the plan had already worked. In the village of the rich, familiarity had made us more acceptable. Besides, to my occasional dismay, I could feel myself changing. I had stopped swearing in French slang and my behaviour grew more reserved. Sometimes my village friends would complain that I was acting strange and I would force myself to spit and swear and chew gum with my mouth open. But I wasn't enjoying it as much.

Mother whirled around at the hub of all our activity, managing weekly food shopping, stacks of laundry, meals, parties, driving us to lessons and play, sailing though her own hectic social schedule. She made it look easy. The phone rang constantly and if the cost of everyone being brown and smiling and shining with health was paid by her vigilance, she didn't mind, she said, every night at dinner, beaming at us. We'd beam back, relieved that she was happy.

One Monday morning, I walked into her bathroom, looking for her, and, naked, she confronted me, her hair matted around her face, eyes shadowed with dark rings. I stepped back and she shouted at me. I couldn't make out what she was saying.

'What, Mummy? What?' I said.

More made-up words.

I turned and ran.

It was just one incident, but I was reminded of before, in the little house on Church Street, when there had been whole stretches of days when she was like that, or worse, silent and immovable, not eating or cooking, just a statue lying on her bed.

But I buried it, and concentrated on Daddy. It was easier, not so directly scary. He was dangerous, not her. She was getting better. I crossed my fingers and stuck close to home. It was going to be all right.

She remarked on his attitude after a golf game that Friday morning. I was caddying. I pretended to be talking to Phyllie's miserable son, who had been dragooned into pulling his mother's cart.

'He's usually grouchy by Thursday afternoons and we all hold our breath till the weekend. I don't know what to do. His mother is always on his back. He thinks I can't handle the children. Sometimes I worry myself sick – '

Phyllie sliced off to the right. 'Fuck.'

'Phyllie!'

'What? I swore. Sorree, babyface. Welcome to the real world.'

'What's wrong with you today? How's Jamie?'

'Oh, the kid's fine. Just as long as his allowance climbs geometrically and I send him to the best schools, we live in harmony.'

'What are they saying?' whispered Jamie.

'Shut up!' I whispered furiously.

'Well, what do you think?' said my mother.

'Don't know. Catherine, go find your mother's ball.' She waited till I was out of earshot.

They walked up the hill together, talking furiously. I scooted ahead, found Mother's ball and darted back, but I'd missed what they were saying.

Phyllie hit her ball into the woods. She disappeared after it. A thunderous crash in the underbrush and the ball flew out and bounced a few metres from Mother's feet. Phyllis emerged, leaves in her hair, looking triumphant. Jamie followed her, sulky.

'I say, that was fun.'

We walked up to Mother's ball and she concentrated for a moment, took out a five iron, swung and watched it land demurely on the green.

'How in hell do you do that anyway? It looks effortless.'

'Hours of practice before you summer people get here. And I mean hours.'

'Work away at everything, don't you?'

My mother's mouth tightened for a moment, then she smiled. 'Something you might try,' she said.

They played the rest of the round uneventfully. At the 9th hole, Phyllie threw her putter on to the green.

'That's it for me, sugar. Time for a shandy.'

'You don't want to play another nine holes?'

'And have you shame me every step of the way? No, I need to cling to whatever confidence I have left.'

We threaded our way through the dining room, which was closed to women and children at lunchtime, and found an outside table near the stone wall that bordered the 9th hole. Jamie had caught sight of some friends and disappeared. The three of us ordered, then Mother left the table. Phyllie's shandy arrived. She drained the glass in three long gulps and signalled for another. I was quietly impressed.

'Y'know, Cathy, when your dad and I were kids, he was the quiet one, the peacemaker. It was hard to make him fight. But once he did, if you pushed and pushed, he would suddenly be wrapping his hands around your neck and squeezing hard. His mother picked him up and put him down like he was a toy, dragged him all over hell and gone. I'll bet that all he wants is a normal family life. And the war made them all into raging maniacs. Jamie's father used to foam at the mouth – I mean it. It's why I left him.'

I was struck silent. I struggled to find something to say.

'I'm sorry I'm not much help to your mother. I know she doesn't understand him. But that's what I remember as a kid, this confused, neglected kid with a scary temper.'

'He can be really nice too,' I managed.

'That's the thing, really, isn't it? Jamie's father was mostly a tyrant. Luckily, I had the money and could leave. Sayonara, sweetheart.' She waved her glass in the air. 'I think he lives on rye and potato chips from his club.

I nodded, trying to look wise. This was truly privileged information.

'Of course, your mother could leave too, you know. She has a first-class degree, and had a brilliant career as a journalist, one of the few women journalists in the country. She has ideas, spark, drive! She didn't grow up like one of these little fascists who have never been beyond their own back yard – and take care, Cathy, my dear, that you don't end up like them.'

'I won't,' I promised. 'I'll get a job like Mummy.'

'That's it.' She toasted me with her glass.

'What's it?' My mother slipped into her chair.

'I was telling Catherine that you had a good degree and a terrific career and that you could do it again, if you had to.'

The telltale red flush on Mother's left cheek appeared almost instantly.

'I did not have a terrific career as a journalist. I was a hack on the women's fiction page for about eight months.'

'Which does not mean that Cathy can't follow in your footsteps. Besides, you had a career as something other than a secretary.'

'Not enough of one to get me anywhere, Phyllis,' her voice warned.

'At least you could fight back a bit. Maybe if you left, it would throw the fear of God into him.'

'Hush,' said Mother. Her cheeks were flaming. 'You know why and don't say you don't.' Her voice was low, she was almost hissing.

Phyllis was instantly contrite. She slammed her glass on the table, waved wildly for the waiter. 'Hell, Catherine, I don't know what I'm talking about. I'm sorry, don't listen to a word I say. You neither, Victoria. It's been a rotten week. I'm bored and I'm taking it out on you two.' She reached her hand across the table and gave Mother's arm a quick squeeze.

'Friends?' asked Phyllie.

'*Naturellement.*'

A shout of laughter. 'First time anyone's said a word of French in this hallowed club in decades!'

It wasn't until we were on the way to buy food that she started trembling.

'Mum?' The car was zigzagging on the road.

Nothing. Her mouth was moving but nothing was coming out.

'Mum? Mum, stop. Mum, look what you're doing.' I was bracing my feet against the dashboard. 'Mum!' I screeched.

She yanked the steering wheel and we skidded over to the side of the road and stopped. It was as if she had a massive crick in her neck. Her head was pulled down to her left shoulder and she slumped, her head dropped on to the steering wheel, arms around the wheel.

I put out a hand. 'Mum, are you OK?'

No reaction. I bent down to look at her face. Her lips were still moving. Sounds were coming out. Her hand reached behind her head, massaged her neck. I tried to help.

'Shit shit shit shit shit,' she said. Those were the first words I could make out. 'I'm trying, keep it up.' I guessed she was talking to me.

We sat in the car by the side of the road, I rubbed her neck, and slowly, she lifted her head and sat back. Her eyes were unfocused, her face yellowish.

She was breathing heavily, as if she had been running. I waited, minutes ticked by. Then, without any warning, she started the car and pulled out into the traffic.

I didn't dare say a word. She drove the twenty miles to Cowansville and mechanically did the shopping. I trailed her through the aisles. It wasn't till we were back in the car, on the way home, that she spoke.

'It's just a reaction, Cathy. Don't worry, it means nothing. Ignore it.'

'What happened?'

'Phyllie started me thinking. I got upset. All this cooking and cleaning and shopping and driving everyone around and smiling constantly, no matter what anyone said, and taking your bad moods and your father's bad moods and smoothing them over and not having anyone ever say, "All right?" And if I'm not all right, I'm a broken-down old nag ready for the glue factory. Or ship me off for reconstruction – never mind what's wrong, just make it better.'

I was still scared, but I ached for reassurance. I snuggled up closer to her, and touched her face. 'Mummy?' I said.

'Oh, Cathy.' Her voice was pure despair. I touched her shoulders. They were tight and hard as a rock. I stroked them.

'May I turn on the radio, Mummy?' I was frightened, I wanted her to stop talking.

Tony Bennett, lost love, flowed through the car.

'*No*!' Her voice was jagged. I turned it off. The monologue started again.

'I'm just a stranger here, Cathy. I'm sorry, honey, I'm not a good guide – don't listen to me. Listen to your father, but not all of it. Take the best of both, the things we say that make sense. And remember to think carefully before you fall in love, all right?'

'Mummy?' I was panicking.

'It's all right, honey. Phyllie upset me, that's all.' And she lit a cigarette, settled into a comfortable speed and fell silent.

That evening he came in carrying an armload of presents. We crowded around him, laughing and tugging at the packages.

'What's this for?'

'Aw hell, why not? Bought a new factory today. Celebration. Went to town, went into a store or two.' He was grinning.

There was a set of horse brushes for me, a compass for Ross and a shiny new air gun for Brian.

'Wow, Dad!' he said, mouth open. 'Thanks.'

'Thought I'd teach you all target shooting in the back pasture. Don't know that maybe you'd want to take up skeet shooting some day.'

'Ian, don't you think that's too dangerous for Brian? He's only six.'

'Nonsense. I'll teach him to use it properly. And, wife of mine,' he said, 'a little something for you.' He took a blue velvet box, unwrapped, out of his pocket and tossed it to her. She caught it, and wiping her hands on her apron, opened it.

'It's a ring!' cried Brian. 'Mum, put it on!'

She did. It was a sapphire eternity ring, called a guard ring, worn during the day in place of an engagement ring, she told me later.

'Oh darling, I love it. Thank you for being so thoughtful,' she said, and gave him a kiss.

We laughed nervously and started to creep away.

'Where do you think you're all going?' he said. 'Let's see these things.' And taking them into the den, he sat on the floor with them and started assembling the gun, showing Ross how to use the compass with a map and told me what the salesman at Horse People had told him about each brush and when it was to be used in the grooming process. Each brush had a scarlet ribbing handle and carved green decoration.

'They're beautiful, Daddy, and I *know* how to use them.' I was thrilled by the rare attention.

Mother watched us for a while and left for the kitchen to finish dinner. The brushes had started up a little song in my heart. Everything's going to be OK, everything's all right, it sang, and I felt happy.

Were we safe? Were they happy? I was obsessed with this. I asked my friends how they could tell whether their parents were happy and they looked at me as if I were nuts. It seemed to me that sometimes they were happy, when she dressed up and looked very pretty and he had two of those clear drinks called martinis. Then they joked and laughed and teased each other.

I could hear her talking to herself in the kitchen. 'Stop it!' I heard.

'What, Mum? Stop what?' said Brian.

'Oh nothing, dear. Dinner's almost ready.'

'Great. Dad said I can have some Hush Puppies, if you agree.'

'Why not?'

'I can! In beige?'

She smiled at him. 'They sound nice.'

'Thanks, Mum! Can we watch *The Untouchables* tonight? You

like Robert Stack. And it's Friday. We don't have anything on early tomorrow.'

'Fine.'

'*Yeaay*!!' And he skidded out of the kitchen to tell the others.

I went in to the kitchen and stood beside her silently. She sighed, smiled slightly and rested her chin on the back of her hands, elbows on the counter. She stared out the window, down into the grey-green bower that she liked so much. I stood on tiptoe to see what she was seeing. Her garden looked beautiful in the yellow-orange light of sunset. I kissed her bare arm and her hand ruffled my hair.

Yes, they were happy, surely. For he brought her presents and they laughed and that was happiness, wasn't it?

THIRTEEN

It was Saturday morning. Grey clouds hung heavy over the field outside my window. I shivered and burrowed deeper into my bed.

The door opened and Ross came into the room. 'Catherine?' His voice was muffled and I shut my eyes tighter, didn't move. He pulled the covers down and I pulled them up again.

'Brian's too lightweight still. No, I'll take Catherine. Is she up, Ross?' His voice floated up the stairs, through the open door, directly into my ear.

Ross grabbed my shoulder, shook gently. 'Catherine, I'm too sick to crew for Dad. You have to do it.'

I gave up, sighed and rolled over on to my back. 'What's wrong with you?'

'I have a really bad cold.' He wasn't lying, his nose was stuffed up, his face was swollen and red and he looked miserable.

'I must have caught it up on the Conference last week. Everyone has it up there.'

'So don't go out. Either of you.'

'We have to. We'll lose our place. We're second in our class.'

'Oh for God's sake.' I sat up, swung my legs over the bed. 'I won't know what to do. He'll yell at me.'

'He probably won't, but even if he does, just ignore him. That's what I do. All you guys have to do is finish.'

I pulled on some shorts and a T-shirt.

'Thanks, Cath.'

'I'll find a way for you to pay me.'

I walked down the stairs slowly. Father was waiting at the bottom.

The day hadn't improved by the time we drove down to the boat club. A few people were on the lawn, moving back and forth, unfolding sails and rigging the boats. I had never been here this early and I stood struck by how different the place was without its usual complement of sassy girls with glossy hair and lounging beefy boys taunting anything with legs. I liked it. It was peaceful. The lake sat there, beyond the lawn, vast, still, brooding.

'All we have to do today is finish.'

I nodded.

'Cat got your tongue?'

I giggled. 'I just hope I don't make a mistake. I don't sail much.'

'All you kids have classes,' he said flatly. 'Just listen to me and do exactly what I say when I say to do it.'

I nodded again and saw no point in telling him that I'd skipped sailing for the past two summers.

'All right, just sit back and I'll rig it.' He pulled two bags out from under the gunwales and methodically strung them on the halyards. 'Here,' he said, holding out a sail. 'Put in the battens.'

I managed this successfully.

'Rig the jib.' He handed me a lapful of white nylon material.

'Ross is sick,' he yelled to a couple of enquirers.

'Great for us!' one called back.

'Ross is thought of as a good crewman,' he said.

'What is that anyway?'

'Fast, good at hiking, follows orders, doesn't anticipate them, doesn't talk too much, though I don't have to worry about that with you, do I? Things like that. It's like being a good wife.'

I bent my head to sorting out the jib sail.

'That was a joke, Catherine.'

'Oh.

'We won't have to use the spinnaker today.' He squinted at the sky. 'The wind is going to come from the north, more or less. Did you bring a jacket?'

'Yes. Ross told me to.'

'It gets damned cold out there.' He was ebullient. He cast off and we joined the other boats milling around the harbour. There was still no sun, in fact the clouds had thickened over the last hour. I crouched up in the front of the boat, trying to stay out of the way.

'There are life jackets in the locker beside you. Put it on for the last part anyway. Your mother nearly dies if she doesn't see one on Ross.'

I laughed then and my spirits picked up as we left the shore and tacked out to the starting buoy. It was cloudy and the only people out were the fanatics, pale with lack of sleep and intensely concentrated. Boat people.

He smiled when he saw my face brighten and began to tell me about sailing on the Pacific when he was a boy, about the ocean swells so high that a boat this size would be lost below the crest and how the harbours were lined with middens, little inverted trenches left by the Indians who buried their refuse on the shore. I listened rapt, then began to ask questions about what we were doing. He answered eagerly and we were into our first real conversation, possibly ever.

I found in myself on that long day a hunger for facts unshaped by emotion or hidden meaning. And he, flattered by a long-time recalcitrant child, was delighted to feed that hunger. I liked statistics – each class had a size and weight of boat, a square-footage of sail – and I absorbed them, and sat staring at each boat. I memorized their names and factored in the relative efficiency of each crew member and asked more questions then. He gave me the answers immediately, adding facts he thought were pertinent, and we sat there, rolling on the viscous water, intent on conversation.

A horn sounded and we brought the boat around and lined it up with the others. He explained the course and that a few of the boats would be ahead of us right from the start and would remain ahead for the entire race, because they were bigger and faster. But the boats to watch were others like ours.

Our boat was painted dark green and its decks were varnished to a beautiful walnut brown, shiny and deep. There were five other Scorpions out that day. The wind was slow and was blowing low, right along the top of the water. We were sunk deep into it, as if we were sailing on oil. I did what he told me to do.

The rain started before we rounded the first buoy. It started in a drizzle, and I shouted to him. 'Where's the bailing cup?'

He pointed at the floor. 'We have an automatic bailer.'

Sure enough, below my feet, beside the centreboard, was a small metal object, making sucking sounds. 'It's new,' he shouted.

We were shouting at each other because the wind had come up and a small gale was blowing into our sails. We jerked and ran in front of the wind.

'Shall I pull up the centreboard?' I yelled. I knew that made the boat plane if it was running in front of the wind.

The Flying Dutchman, which ran out in front of the pack in each race, peeled off and headed for home.

'Chicken!' I shouted at its crew, but they couldn't hear me.

He smiled at me, water dripping from the end of his nose.

'Sure, pull up the centreboard. Only half-way.'

The sail flapped out and caught the wind and the boat pulled herself up and whisked along.

He was shouting something and pointed at the floor. I looked down. The water level was creeping up, spilling into the boat from the sides.

'Yikes!' I said, but he couldn't hear me. I tried using my hat and he waved at me, pointing at the locker. I rooted around inside and grabbed a plastic cup and began bailing fast.

Three more boats broke formation and ran for home.

I didn't yell at them this time. My shoulders were soaking wet and so were my shorts. I had taken my shoes off long ago and my feet were white and puckered like prunes. I didn't dare suggest going back.

Rain pelted down and thunder shook the sky.

'Isn't it dangerous?' I shouted to him.

'Ready to come about,' he shouted back. I loosed the jib and we swung wildly.

A jagged bolt of summer lightning clove the sky and dived for the water.

'Jeeze,' I breathed.

'This is great!' I heard him laugh. 'Catherine, hike out, for God's sake.'

I leaned back holding on to the jib sheet. The water kissed my back, but I was so wet, I hardly cared.

Another boat broke formation.

'Why are they going back?' I shouted to him.

He pointed at the deck and I saw that the water had risen again. We both bent to bailing furiously. 'It's the new bailer that's keeping us afloat,' he said above the shrieking wind.

Another bolt of lightning hit the water and two more boats tacked out for home.

We rounded the second buoy and headed for the finish. There were about a dozen others left in the race, all bigger than us. He laughed into the rain, his face running with a sheet of water.

'Don't you love it, Catherine? Isn't it wonderful?'

It was. It was dangerous and fast and unpredictable. I looked over my shoulder. We were out in front, by a nose.

'Dad! Daddy! Look!' I pointed at the boat behind us. They shouted back at us, jubilant.

'Perseverance, Catherine. We're going to win.'

I was shivering. I pulled on my jacket and it helped a little, but I had never been so cold. Soaking wet, bending into a wind, pelting endless, unstoppable rain, and my father, crouched at the tiller, laughing, refusing to turn back.

His muscles were coiled tight. When we needed the weight, he hiked out with me and the little boat planed above the water with that peculiar singing buzz that only wooden boats and wind and a confident skipper can produce.

'Life jacket!' he shouted, cupping his hand over his eyes.

I pulled one out and, with real difficulty, fastened it over my jacket. We sat, afraid to change position, spoil our luck. Another few hundred yards of straightforward sailing and we were in. A gun went off, a swift crack dulled by the rain, and there was a mournful toot on the club foghorn. The beach wasn't too far away and he jumped out, pulled us into shore.

There were a few people out waiting under enormous golf umbrellas, my mother among them.

'Ian! I can't believe you didn't come in!' She muffled us with thick towels, then threw a blanket around my shoulders. I was shivering so hard, my teeth were chattering.

'At least she had a life jacket on. When that lightning struck I was terrified. Everyone on shore was. The commodore was going to cancel the race but a couple of fanatics persuaded him not to.'

'Damned glad they didn't. We had a whale of a time, didn't we, Catherine?'

I nodded, teeth chattering, a drowned rat of a pre-pubescent girl, head over heels in love with her father.

FOURTEEN

It was almost the end of summer when the local sheriff turned up at the door. It was seven o'clock, the hallowed hour of dinner. The interruption astonished us. We crowded into the doorway to look at him.

He stood in the hallway on the black-and-white-tiled floor, looking at the sixteenth-century grandfather clock, wearing his beige khaki uniform and leather holster with some discomfort, I thought. He was a cartoon sheriff, as exact and correct as his uniform, his manner laconic and deferential. Still, he looked as out of place standing there as an Elizabethan pirate.

He and Father disappeared into his study. We huddled around Mother, who retreated, almost stumbling over us, so close to her were we standing, into the kitchen. She bent over the sink, refusing to talk to us. Then she put the food back into the oven, turned the dial to the 'warm' setting, and sat down at the counter, observing us.

We shuffled. I was innocent of any wrongdoing, and knowing this, escaped on to the back steps and looked in through the screen door. This one action made Mother stare at the boys harder.

We didn't have long to wait. There was an echo of words from the hall, the front door opened and closed and he appeared. He was not happy. He had that look. The look that sent men into battle, that had watched friends die in agony in front of him. The look that scared us all so much that we would do almost anything not to provoke it. Except of course what we had done to provoke it.

The boys had been playing with the air gun. For weeks Ross and Brian had gone out to shoot at the streetlamps in the lower village at night. The past weekend they and their friends had visited a large house on the Conference which had just been built by the owner of a car rental company. It had reputedly cost more money than any new house built in the village for a very long time and it boasted a series of seven giant plate-glass windows. Ross had put a hole neatly in the centre of each one.

They were not allowed explanations. Not that there were any, of course. He just grabbed them by the back of the neck and dragged them into the den. I followed and cringed at the doorway, unable to take my eyes away. They stood cowering against the bookshelves, while he, wordless, and white with fury, threw open a desk drawer and found his strap.

I don't know where that thing came from, but I remember its shape and size. It was leather and it was cracked with age and use. It was dark brown, except in the centre where the colour had worn to a tawny mid brown. It was peeling and it had a leather thong threaded through the triangular top. And it hurt like hell.

He came over to the door where I stood and gently peeled my fingers back from the doorjamb, then closed the door in my face. I stood there, waiting.

Enough has been written about the humiliation and pain of being strapped by your father. Even writing the words makes me wince. Ross was loud in protest, howling his way through the ordeal like a hurt and angry dog, and Brian whimpered every time he was hit. Twenty-five times. At the end they pulled up their pants and went to the room they shared. Eating was out of the question. Besides, they could not sit down.

Dinner was silent. Mother merely served the food and made the odd careless remark about the garden show and some party they'd gone to last week, as if nothing had happened. I escaped upstairs as soon as I was able, but neither Ross nor Brian answered my calls.

Their door remained firmly shut. I went downstairs, but they were talking while she put the dishes in the dishwasher and fell silent when I walked into the room. I left, went upstairs and paced through the hall and my room until, finally, I calmed down.

Afterwards, for I crept to the top of the stairs, they went into the living room and talked for a very long time.

I couldn't hear a word, but my terror that night was absolute, overwhelming beyond what was appropriate, despite the expensive and renegade nature of my brothers' actions.

Such are the small tragedies that make up a larger. Things unravelled fast after that. Ross was sent off to school the moment it was possible. He wrote me a tragic, tearstained letter, in which he described being driven to the school by my grim father. He shook with sobs, then was slapped on the back, a little too hard, he reported, and almost hurled at the housemaster. Written off.

After the horse show, where Cedar, my little brown-and-white circus hack, was trounced by an extravagantly expensive hunter direct from Ireland, owned by Susan Spencer, I was more withdrawn than ever. I increased my surveillance of my mother and I abandoned my pact to halve my time between summer and winter people and started to study.

That fall, my face was always in a book. So was Brian's. We would meet every night under the hall light on the second floor at the doors to our rooms at the opposite end of the hall. We would each hold a flashlight, a book and a pillow and we would lie there until the small hours, reading, augmenting the pale overhead light with our separate flashlights. We would exchange not a word, not even when one of us would finally tire and go off to bed.

Brian and I knew there was something wrong one Sunday morning in early fall. We came downstairs and breakfast wasn't ready. Back upstairs, we found Mother lying across her bed, half dressed still. His closet door was still open and I looked in. It was completely empty, not a single shirt or pair of shoes left.

She spent the rest of the weekend dragging herself around the house. The phone rang. She leapt for it, unable to hide the note of desolation that crept in when it was not him.

'Oh no. Just a wicked hangover. How was Ronnie's?' she said.

'Sorry, we can't. Ian had to leave on a business trip and I feel I should be holding stock in Gordon's. Yes, I have a hangover. What do you think?'

Brian and I were suspicious and accepted her explanation with reservations. We had started trusting him that summer, but his withdrawal had the inexorability of an ice pack, slow, silent, sure.

We didn't know. We knew it was our fault and we crept around the house like whipped dogs.

We were used to his silence by now and we had begun to understand his anger and how to divert it. We missed him. What we didn't know, what we couldn't, was how his restricted view of things, his clean perception of the necessity of form, made her safe and that without him, the world shivered with threat. He was her ballast and, more importantly, he was interpreter, when her own perceptions couldn't be trusted.

Phyllie called Tuesday evening around dinner. I answered the phone.

'Hi, darling, Mummy in? Thought I'd drop by. I'm in the village anyway. Be there in five.'

She hung up.

I went into the kitchen to tell Mother. She went white but nodded as if everything was normal.

She served us dinner at the kitchen counter, and checked the fridge for tonic and soda.

No one knocked in Foster. They just walked in and stood in your hallway or living room and shouted until you showed up to greet them. Sometimes they even walked into the den and switched on the TV or read a magazine, figuring that since you knew they were coming, you'd find them eventually.

'Where do you want me?' Phyllie was here.

'I'm in the kitchen!' Mother called.

Phyllie swung on the swinging doors. 'Hi, honey, I'm home! Hi, kids! Yum, fish sticks!'

'Don't do that. Ross has already brought those doors down twice.'

'I would have thought more, with all that goes on in this house.'

'Now behave yourself, Phyl,' said Mother. 'Kids, you can put your dishes into the dishwasher when you're finished. Then you can watch TV till bedtime.'

I took my plate and disappeared around the corner and up the stairs so I could listen.

They had already poured themselves a drink.

'I got into the School of Music in Montreal,' said Mother.

'You can stay with me. Terrific! You must be so happy. Congratulations.'

I heard the clink of ice cubes.

'I haven't told Ian yet.'

'That would be a bit difficult.'

'What do you mean?'

'Well, he's left, hasn't he?'

'What?'

'It's all around town, Victoria.'

'It is?' She sounded slow and stupid.

'It's your mother-in-law. She was so delighted she lost no time in spreading the news. Everyone knows.'

'I've got to get the kids away from her and from Foster. They'll grow up into these precious spoiled little heathens. It's too unreal here, Phyl.'

'Precisely.'

There was a pause. I started to worry that they'd sensed my presence.

'What are you going to do?' asked Phyllis.

'Don't know. Hold out, I guess. Try to teach the kids about the real world, and hope he can talk when he gets back. I don't really know why he left. I mean, we've been having some problems. The kids; his mother hates me; but what else is new? She's hated me since she first laid eyes on me.'

'Jealousy.'

'Why?'

'Oh it's common knowledge. She had Ian picked out never to marry and to be her support in her old age. You know, four sons, each had a role to play. Then along came sweet innocent beautiful you, and she was left to age alone, just another old bat without enough money.'

'You see, I don't even understand that way of thinking. I don't think he'll ever think I'm good enough. I'm not like these other women here. He'll come back, then he'll leave me again. I just can't measure up. Ever. You know why? I don't believe in it. I just don't care.'

Phyllie laughed. 'I still love your naivety, darling, but it's a bit tiresome when you're fighting for your life. More please.' Ice cubes clinked again.

'So she's been trying to get rid of me ever since,' Mother said slowly.

'The light bulb came on, eh? Yes, and she's nearly succeeded. Next thing is, she'll want your kids. Oh, not to mother, she'll hire a maid, but she wants Ian's money. You can go back to work, see them once a month.'

I felt as if a sheet of ice had slid over me.

'Can't be possible.'

'Oh yes, it is. Think.'

I thought for her. Mother loony. Father at the end of his rope. Children need a stable female influence. Grandmother there and willing. Solid community position. Probably knew all the judges on the bench, had dinner with them once a month. Yes. It was possible.

'Oh God,' she said out loud.

'Precisely,' said Phyllie. 'But.'

'But what? What, Phyllie, is there a way out?'

'Yes there is, Victoria. But you have to be strong and not fall to pieces or I'll hate myself for ever. Promise to be a tough girl like me?'

Mother muttered something. I crept closer to the bottom of the stairs.

'She's started court proceedings to have you declared unfit.'

I crawled up the steps to the top of the stairs. Just in time. Mother scurried into the powder room off the hall. I heard a rush of liquid hit the water in the bottom of the toilet bowl.

'You promised you wouldn't get upset!' Phyllis said, mock reproachful as she settled Mother back on to the sofa.

A mumble from Mother.

'It doesn't have to happen, Victoria. Come in to town, see this man I know. He'll help you. He'll declare you healthy and able. Then file for divorce, on the grounds of alienation of affection. Cite his mother. Fight back. You can keep your kids and get some money. You don't have to put up with this tiptoeing around, pretending to be perfect.'

A gasp.

'Ian can't really stand any strain on him at all. I told you that. His mother just works away on him. Drip. Drip. Drip. What with the kids, travelling constantly to the city and back, he snaps. And your illness – well.'

Mother broke into hysterical sobs. I listened hard and finally caught a few words. 'It's not true.'

I couldn't stand to hear any more. I took my plate into my room, then climbed out the window, slithered down to the ground, around to the back, and signalled Brian.

It was still light out and we went for a long walk to the lake.

A few weeks later he came back, whistling and cheerful, put all his clothes back in the closet. And about a month after his return, after a steady escalation of fighting, there we were, on the Midnight Ride, and Brian and I were walking down the road at three in the morning with our mother, jaunty and hopeful.

We didn't see her for months after our precipitous arrival at the McDougalls'. And when she came home, for the next two years, I bounced between her house and Muffie's city apartment, starting school in the city to brush up my schoolwork in preparation for the rigours of boarding school and only coming home to Foster for big holidays, the major ones. I began to feel as if the guest room was my own room and Muffie filled it with all kinds of proprietary touches. Little bits of her various collections started turning up on my bedside table and photographs of her and me at various events and parties in worked silver frames mysteriously arrived on my desk and bookshelves. I had a whole new separate wardrobe for city life. Muffie didn't like to be alone, so every evening that I didn't have to do schoolwork was busy. We whirled around between school and weekends in the country at various houses, always the invited. I grew used to being the guest, I sang for my supper and made friends easily.

I came to love the smell of the concrete in early summer, the look of people who seemed to know it all and understand, the laughter that seemed to light the city, the slick, shiny, ebony surface of urban life. I adored the echoing grey-and-white marble hallways and ponderous mahogany front doors of the apartments in the Linton. The apartment building on Sherbrooke Street had been built a hundred years before, while the city whirled in a social frenzy. It had two enormous red-and-gold brocaded reception rooms, and a ballroom, with a massive gritty-with-dust chandelier, empty, always empty. My mind peopled those rooms with grand parties, with ladies dressed in costumes the world had never seen. I loved the Ritz, I loved the galleries that were strung along Sherbrooke like shiny black-and-gold beads, I loved Holt Renfrew. I loved all the parties. I began to bob along the surface of life, happy, carefree, oblivious.

Muffie watched this transformation with a sharp eye. On one odd, rare evening that we had alone, she pressed home her point.

'You belong here, Catherine,' she said one evening while we were alone. 'You should see yourself. There is a flush on your cheeks and you look happy.'

I looked up from the dining-room table and glanced at myself in the mirror over the sideboard. My dark hair was pulled back in a ponytail and I wore a string of add-a-peals around my neck. I didn't recognize myself for a moment, I was so glossy and new. My eyes snapped and I felt sad, thinking about her.

'Do you think she needs me?' I asked. 'Perhaps I should go, you know, for Thanksgiving. And I miss Brian. I haven't seen him for months.'

'Nonsense. You need to be away from that house. It is too gloomy. You need fun after all the work at school. Besides, the Morgans have invited us to the Seignury Club again this Thanksgiving. You know how you like the stables there; that forest has dozens of riding trails. Those two girls will be your friends next year at Compton. You should get to know them better. And Brian is an eight-year-old boy, busy with his friends, running around like a wild animal. He'll completely ignore you.'

It was true that last summer Brian had hardly been home. He was popular in the village. Worse, he had started to call me Miss Fussy. My heart hardened. It was also true I loved the Seignury Club. What I didn't admit was that I knew the reason our house was sad was because my mother missed her children. She knocked around, mostly alone, with very little to do. I still spent summers there and she never complained, but I sensed she was bored and unhappy. And I didn't want to think about it.

'Will you tell her?' I said, despising myself.

'Certainly. No trouble at all.' And she picked up the phone.

I sat during the call, feigning boredom, squirming inside. She asked to speak to me and I was reluctant. Muffie held out the phone, eyes stern. She wanted to hear my betrayal.

'Hi, Mum.'

'Hello, honey, how are you?'

'I'm fine. I got an A in geography yesterday.'

'We were so looking forward to seeing you at Thanksgiving.'

'I know, it's just that Elizabeth and Jennifer are going to be at Compton next year like me and Muffie says the more girls I know the better off I'll be.'

There was a pause and her voice was muffled when she finally spoke. 'All right, I'll tell Brian and your father. But come down the following weekend. I miss you.'

'All right.' But that weekend too, I asked Muffie to make my excuses. Every time I called, it grew easier to say no, and her acceptance of my excuses became perfunctory, as if she expected and deserved my rejection of her. My coolness began to echo hers, and over the next five years, we became strangers. I confided in Muffie, always, about my little triumphs and my hopes, and when Muffie died, I sat in the front row with my parents, feeling as if my last connection with my family was going to be buried along with the casket. Muffie left me a little money and I used it to leave home right after boarding school. I insisted on putting myself through university. I didn't need my mother any more. I didn't want to be like her and the more distance I put between us, the better.

PART III

APRIL–JULY 1988

FIFTEEN

Washington, DC

I took a job at the firm. I performed a clutch of odd jobs that none of the associates or clerks had time for. As they moved towards a trial date, they needed more help with press relations. I did that. I acted as liaison with the Canadian Embassy in Washington. I did research. I made enough to cover expenses and I worked fifteen-hour days.

I took the train and bunked with friends, then after a month of three-hour train trips twice a week, I had a long talk with Mark and sublet an apartment near Dupont Circle. It was within walking distance of the office. Not that I saw much of it, at least during daylight.

At first Mark was happy that I could face the sheer awfulness of the case. He was fascinated by the shadow play of CIA counsel. Our bunch were throwing punches at ghosts. After eight years of research and discovery, there was so much evidence they hit the mark more often than not.

After the first month, the novelty wore off and he started to complain about weekends broken by a late-night phone call from the office that sent me off with a brief apology and a kiss. His visits grew less frequent, and to me, the thought of going to New York was tantamount to climbing a mountain. He was distant on the phone, noncommittal. I couldn't blame him. One day, he had a normal girlfriend, or half-way normal. We were even talking about marriage. The next day, he had a girlfriend who was one of the walking wounded and permanently out of state.

It wasn't that I didn't care about him or about us. It was just that I, as I had conceived myself, didn't really exist any more. I had finally accepted that all this did not happen just to my mother, but that this story, this nightmare, had formed the climate of my childhood and that it could be fought.

My version of reality had been worn down by the sheer weight of evidence. The horror of reading my mother's file shifted into even greater horror, as document upon document upon subpoenaed CIA file proved that what had been done to her had been done to hundreds of patients of Dr Ewen Cameron. It had been done without their informed consent. It had been done cruelly, without controls, without any thought to their well-being or their future or their families. It had been done, wittingly, by a so-called friendly foreign government, with the tacit, if not full complicity of the Canadian government. It was a lot to get around.

Like my mother, all these people had been educated, productive, caring members of their community who for a brief time had ceased to function efficiently. They had gone to the top man in their country to help them out of depression or chronic anxiety or a drinking problem. Not one of our plaintiffs was truly psychotic or schizophrenic; none had irreversible mental problems. But after a spell with Dr Cameron, their sanity was permanently weakened, if not destroyed. Horror was at the door. Wolves howled. No one was safe.

While my rational mind accepted this, was forced to accept it, given the reading and interviewing and flat-out selling I did all day, my emotions shied away and hid.

To Mark, I lied. I told him that if I could just keep my head down and get this over with, behind us, life could go on as it was before. I made him promises, time-based promises.

Then I broke them.

Maybe I should have shouted and screamed more. But I'd been trained, by school and by my military father. Emotion was an embarrassing luxury, a fur coat worn on a sightseeing trip to the slums. Cold dull reality was far preferable.

On the upside, my health had improved. The concentration on something larger than my little bundle of neuroses had shoved illness on to the back burner. I did the work. Clinical detachment, that faint buzz you get from late-night library work – that's the state I went for.

There was a lot of catching up to do, tens of thousands of pages of reading, all dry and dull with the occasional throwaway admission that was sheer gold.

One morning we were sitting around the oval conference table, drinking bad coffee, coloured caramel with Coffee Mate and sweetened with white sugar. It didn't do anything for the excess acid in my stomach.

The team had given me a difficult reception. They had seen me as an interloper, and someone without much to offer. Every one of them hated the press for its power or its stupidity. I got saddled with all the prejudice they carried.

For the first three weeks, I had been ignored, unless I asked a direct question. After three weeks, little digs started to greet me at the copying or coffee machines. Now, there was an undercurrent. I imagined that Tom Wheeler's attention to me gave the impression that I was a favourite. I felt angry and isolated.

Tom had called us together. He and his assistants had been flailing for weeks, trying to find psychiatrists who were contemporaries of Cameron's, able to speak to the man's methodology. It was critical to prove that his so-called treatments were, in a clinical situation, cruel and unusual, way outside generally accepted practice for the time, and far beyond what was needed for treatment of the illnesses of our plaintiffs.

Wheeler bustled into the room, followed closely by two tall pale young men, who blinked at us behind thick glasses. They placed a pile of documents on the table.

'Pass these around,' Wheeler said, beaming with satisfaction, shoving a stack to the left.

A technician entered the room, pulled down the screen and started to set up an old-fashioned film projector.

The paper pile reached me and I picked off a paper-clipped stack.

'This is good stuff, people. I am very excited by last week's developments. As you all know, Dr Donald O. Hebb was Chairman of the Department of Psychology at McGill University at the same time as Dr Cameron headed up the Department of Psychiatry. He worked extensively with American and Canadian intelligence.' A nod at the projectionist and Wheeler moved to switch off the overhead lights. A flicker, then the countdown in black-and-white came up on the screen. 'This was made just before Hebb's death in 1985.'

The old man was slumped in a yellow armchair that looked suspiciously like naughahyde. He was dressed in the uniform of an off-duty shrink or a professor – tweed jacket, tatty dark shirt, corduroys. His clothes looked too large for him. His white hair was wispy, but his blue eyes were clear and the black irises focused and sharp. His voice was a bit shaky, but you could hear him just fine. He sounded rational. A judge would believe him, I thought.

The questions were practically inaudible. We had a sweep of the campus, a recital of his accomplishments and publications. I doodled on my notepad.

Suddenly, his voice changed, became sharp.

'Well, that was an awful set of ideas that Cameron was working with. It had no intellectual demand; it called for no intellectual respect. If you actually look at what he was doing, and what he wrote, his proposals, it would make you laugh; that is what I meant by awful. If I had a graduate student who talked like that, I'd throw him out.'

My attention was captured. This man was still jealous, thirty years later. Hell hath no fury like an envious academic. The voice sharpened further.

'Arrh!' Hebb was practically spitting. 'He stuck to the conventional experiments and paper writing for most of his life, but then he wanted that breakthrough. That was Cameron's fatal flaw. He wasn't so much driven with wanting to know, he was driven with wanting to be important – to make that breakthrough. It made him a bad scientist. He was criminally stupid. Criminally stupid and irresponsible.'

The interviewer led Hebb back to safer territory and the droning started again. Research procedures, proper controls, drug companies paying for experiments at the Allan – the usual chronicle of humans abusing each other for profit and power.

Was it all a simple case of hubris? Dr Cameron had wanted the Nobel Prize and would do anything to anybody to get it? Could it have been so simple? I had grappled with Cameron's compulsion to cure when I'd researched his early career.

He had written dozens of papers both before, during and since he'd taken up his post at the provincial facility in Brandon, Manitoba. It was the beginning of the Depression, and at first, the choice seemed suicidal to his young colleagues at Johns Hopkins and the Burghoelzli Clinic in Zürich. But Cameron's father had died and his life as a brilliant young psychiatrist in training was over. He had to put his siblings through school.

It was the best thing that ever happened to him. He developed his practical skills and found his strength. Out on the prairie, blasted by successive years of crop failure, he became the born organizer he was, always on hand to put together a conference, to write the paper that broke an idea into the mainstream, to cobble together a bunch of iconoclastic, arrogant *über*-professionals into a foundation or an association to campaign for some change or other. Faced with the human devastation brought on by economic depression, he was first overwhelmed, then invigorated. He experimented, he published widely. He became even more of a workaholic, with one overriding principle. He wanted to help, to heal. Which seemed admirable. But why and when did his passion to help turn him into a torturer?

Hebb's voice was climbing the register again.

'Cameron's experiments were done without the patients' consent. Cameron was irresponsible – *criminally* stupid, in that there was no reason to expect that he would get any results from the experiments.

Anyone with any appreciation of the complexity of the human mind would not expect that you could erase an adult mind and then add things back with this stupid psychic driving. He wanted to make a name for himself – so he threw his cap over the windmill . . .'

A quaint, old-fashioned expression. I started drawing windmills on my yellow pad in the light cast by the screen. The projector wound down. The room became dark, then light flickered and grew strong. My eyes were watering.

'In your folders,' Wheeler said, 'you'll find corroborating statements from two men who worked closely with the CIA in the brainwashing field in the fifties and sixties. Yet they merely studied the Chinese form. They were never asked for their opinion about Cameron's work, nor was Hebb. Hebb was in an excellent position to check on Cameron. He was almost literally across the hall and he too had a long-time history with the Agency, even had a special security CIA clearance issued to him in the early sixties.'

I was barely listening. I was too busy with this new idea. My mother had been sacrificed, her mind tortured and life dismantled for vanity. My family's life destroyed at the whim of some over-endowed asshole with a lust for power. Was that all it was?

'If you'll all turn to page 1132, you'll see the statement made by Dr Osmond Solandt of the Canadian Defence Research Board. As chairman, Solandt had regular contact with the CIA and British intelligence. He knew of Cameron's work and let him know that any application Cameron made to the Defence Research Board would not be looked upon favourably. I quote: "It was my view at the time and continues to be that Cameron was not possessed of the necessary sense of humanity to be regarded as a good doctor."'

'Great stuff,' said Thea, one of the associates on the case.

'Catherine, are you all right?' Tom looked at me.

'Of course. One illumination after another, huh?'

'We need a lot more doctors like this. A half-dozen would do. We need them to evaluate Cameron's methodology and go on the record saying that what he was doing was outside the accepted practices of the time,' said Tom.

'Won't they all be dead? Cameron died in '67.'

'Look for his residents, his interns. Lord, he trained half the current heads of psychiatric departments in the United States. Get on the phones, people.'

There was a general buzz and a line queued up to talk to Tom.

I edged my way out of the room.

I had an interview next week with a senior executive producer at CBS. The story of the experiments and the public action suit had been reported, but no American television show or newspaper had done any in-depth coverage of what actually was done to the plaintiffs, and how it was carried out. Part of the reason was the usual deafening snore that greeted any Canadian problem or issue. But we kept pushing. There was a slight chance we could get the story on one of the news-magazine shows. We needed that more than almost anything else. We needed public outcry. Concerned citizens indignant and calling up their congressman. But for some reason, the networks yawned when I pressed them. The story didn't have the punch it needed, they said.

My presentation was designed to scare them into finding the punch. If I was lucky, I could get them to see the depth of the abuse of public trust. These men, these CIA guys, were so fucking callous. Didn't care then. Didn't care now.

I dived into my work, without making a splash, or even a ripple. I didn't make any phone calls, I didn't speak to anyone on the team and I ordered lunch from the local deli. It was eleven-thirty at night before I even thought of going home.

'Catherine?' Wheeler poked his head around the door.

'Yup? Whatzit?' I was distracted. The screens flickered and I reached for the remotes, put them both on pause.

'What are you doing?'

'Just going over these depositions. We need to get a few new depositions.'

'Good, good. From whom?'

'Oh, what you were talking about today, you know, damaging effects on patients. Tie it in to these guys – counterpoint the horror to their carelessness.'

He pulled up a chair, sat down and looked at my notes.

'Oh, you're running Gittinger and Lashbrook.'

'Just looking for the right clips for the CBS meeting next week. I want good juxtaposition.'

'Only three days away. Great. Let me see what you've come up with.'

'All right.' I picked up the pad that had the tape-counter numbers on it, tinkered with the two remotes for a few seconds, setting the tape. 'We're not going to edit, if we can help it. But it would be real useful if we had another tape deck and monitor.'

'Sorry, Catherine. Can't afford it. Can't afford to pay you much, can't afford to buy new TV equipment.'

I shrugged. 'OK. Gittinger. CIA Project Monitor for Cameron's experiments. We have a choice.' I pushed 'play' on the first remote.

John Gittinger's bony head defuzzed and started to move. The camera was focused in tight. He was wearing a green golf sweater and a polo shirt with Ralph Lauren's polo player glued to the breast plaquet. Retired operatives go to provincial golf courses. That was where we found him and taped him. In a meeting room in his golf clubhouse.

'You didn't have the slightest interest in Cameron?' asked an off-camera voice.

'That is absolutely true,' said Gittinger. His fish eyes rolled back in his head for a minute. I wondered at this peculiar response to stress.

'You didn't feel responsibility to find out what Cameron did to the subjects of the CIA-funded experiments?'

'No, sir,' answered Gittinger. He looked tense, but he didn't crack.

'OK, that's one,' I said. 'Give me a second to find the next.' The green golf sweater blurred by for a few moments. 'Here it is.'

'Did you ever make a check on whether Dr Cameron was doing it unwittingly?'

'I certainly did not, because I had absolutely no interest in that area, as far as he was concerned.'

'You weren't interested – a Canadian citizen might be unwittingly given LSD, with USA money?'

'I was not.'

'And then,' I said over the tape noise, 'we have that famous thing you guys mentioned when we first met – ' I pressed 'fast forward', then stopped as the tape counter indicated the right number.

Gittinger's creaky voice started again. 'Now, that was a foolish mistake. We shouldn't have done it. But there were not the same attitudes about CIA money and government money at that time; that would have caused us to have thought differently. As I said, I'm sorry we did it. Because it turned out to be a terrible mistake. Our motivation in doing it was largely in terms of cover . . .'

A muted question from the interrogator.

'Well, you misunderstand me. The business of going ahead and doing it in Canada was the cover – '

I pushed 'pause'. 'That's it, essentially. We have the Deputy Director for the MKULTRA programme, Lashbrook, saying something interesting here.'

Robert Lashbrook swam up to greet us. Younger than Gittinger, he looked like any retired businessman you'd see tooling around a local shopping mall, aimlessly looking over the hardware section at Zeller's. Harmless, bald, tired.

'Did you ever at any time hear a conversation at the CIA concerning the question of whether the persons who were experimented on must be told that they were being experimented on?'

'Not that I can recall. It wasn't felt necessary really to go into a lot of detail as to exactly how they were handling the subjects – in general patients would be of low interest.'

My hand clenched around the remote. 'That's all we have of him,' I said.

'So not only did they not inform the patients that they were experimental subjects, they didn't supervise the project. They didn't ensure their safety.'

'Yep. And Helms . . . Wait till you see Helms on the subject of LSD.' The whole MKULTRA programme was Richard Helms's idea in 1953, when he was Director of Operations for the CIA. I truly loathed this man. I pressed 'fast forward'.

Richard Helms's saturnine features blurred then focused. 'LSD was regarded at that time as a particularly insidious substance . . . because you couldn't see it in a glass of water. There was concern that the Russians or Chinese might use this on our people . . . Then along came the episode when Ambassador George Kennan came to Berlin from his post in Moscow, and at the airport or someplace on his way through Berlin, he made a most extraordinary series of statements which were regarded by people in the State Department as quite uncharacteristic of Mr Kennan's normal behaviour.'

'There's more,' I said. The image blurred into 'fast forward', then stopped.

'My recollection is that there was a discussion at one time about the need for using unwitting people but there was no way to establish the exact reaction of individuals to certain substances if they were warned beforehand that they were going to be taking the substance. There was going to have to be some experiment sometime with unwitting participants.'

'Don't you just love the syntax? Do these guys ever say I said, I thought, I discussed?'

Tom pressed both hands down on my shoulders and started to massage them. 'Are you going to use the quote from Stansfield Turner's book?'

Admiral Stansfield Turner had been Director of the CIA, under Jimmy Carter. He had written a book called *Secrecy and Democracy: The CIA in Transition*, which detailed his attempt to transform the CIA from an agency that specialized in covert action into an apolitical intelligence-gathering agency.

'I could, but it's not on tape. You know Joe Rauh's secretary took the dictation.'

'So put it in the press kit. It's pretty damning. The CIA insisted that the passage be excised from his book.'

'Here it is: "How could this have happened? The unit conducting the experiments simply had such autonomy that not many outsiders could look in and ask what was going on. In this case the system just could not provide that kind of detached critical review and a few well-intentioned, but terribly misguided, individuals badly abused the CIA's privilege of keeping secret so much of what it does."'

'We hope it's admissible. A former head of the CIA admitting they had no controls over these cowboys is pretty great.' He leaned over me, reading my list of interviews. 'What's on the other tape deck?'

'I told you, stuff on the effects on patients. Expert evaluations.' The screen had long since flickered into darkness. I pressed the 'play' button. 'But we need more.'

'Incontinent of bowel and bladder . . .' said one individual. I pressed 'fast forward.'

'. . . would cause her to suffer significant and continuing psychological impairment as well as likely causing continuing memory deficits and cognitive impairments.'

'. . . incurable organic brain syndrome.'

The phrases flashed by, just as they'd been doing for the last ten hours.

'Think they're strong enough?' I asked.

'They're strong. If we have to go with just them, we can.'

'We need someone whom people can identify with.'

'I may have found someone. His father is one of the plaintiffs. He's a psychiatrist at Stanford, and he's both personable and articulate.'

'That couldn't be better.' I smiled slowly, but the information wasn't sinking in. I was a little dazed.

He sat down in the other chair and leaned forward, a deep crease between his eyes.

'I'm going to see you home,' he said. 'You're exhausted. And if you aren't, you should be. This is taking an emotional toll on you, has to be. You are overdoing it. I know we encourage that, but this performance of yours is ridiculous.'

He held my arm as we made our way down in the elevator and stood me in the lobby until he had hailed a cab.

'You know, I forget you're not trained in the law,' he said, once in the cab. 'We can pull together lots of damning evidence but they can still get us on procedure. Don't forget that.'

'Everyone knows that. Don't baby me.'

'Sorry, I was just wondering if you wouldn't do better to spend your time focusing on your mother.'

'Why? Do you think I'm wasting my time here?'

'No, listen, I put it badly. I mean, have you thought about another way in? Could I come out with you and talk to her? I still think she could really help.'

I sighed. 'I'm still getting furious weekly letters from her: Stop, go back to Mark. Don't drag us through this. For God's sake, quit. Please, darling, don't do this and so on. It's hard enough to stick with it here. Besides, you have nine plaintiffs already.'

'But from what you tell me, she sounds lucid and articulate – '

'Hah.' I laughed.

'Besides, we need someone who can talk about the Grid Room. As we told you on the first day, we think that she was in the Grid Room in 1962–3. We think that the procedures that Cameron developed in the Grid Room are still being used in interrogations in every ghastly hot spot in the world. We want it all out in the open. The writing we have of hers is from her hospital record and they are about her '57 hospitalization. If she could tell us about what happened to her in 1962–3, in the Grid Room, lucidly, clearly, her testimony would be unanswerable. Do you know about Mrs Olson?'

I shook my head, in part to clear it. Mrs Olson. The name was familiar.

'Her husband was a biochemist in the employ of the US Army. In 1953, someone spiked his drink with LSD. Five days later, he threw himself out of a hotel window in New York. That someone was a friend of his, who happened to work for the CIA.'

'Yes, I remember reading about her.'

'Mrs Olson is a compelling witness, and utterly terrifying to the CIA. She is bright, personable and angry. She has three successful grown children. As a witness, your mother has the same power. She has more, if she is as articulate as you seem to indicate.'

'Oh, I see.'

I turned away from him. I hadn't thought about Brian's revelation, that the torment hadn't stopped in the sixties. I had deliberately pushed it into the background and filled up my mind with millions of bites of new information. I was shivering.

'Catherine!' He put his arm around my shoulders and hugged me. 'Please, tell me what's wrong.'

I told him what Brian had told me. Everything, the opened mail, the phone calls, the bumped cars, the suspicious fainting in Safeway, and the flu, even the phone call I had intercepted at home. 'Do you think my brother is paranoid and imagining things?' I finished. It was my secret fear. I was terrorized by the possibility that both my mother and brother were locked in a paranoid psychosis.

He was silent for a long time.

'No, I don't,' he said finally. 'In the fifties and sixties, the agency was a rogue force, answerable to no one. That CIA is on its way back. These people who are harassing your family are probably hold-overs from that time. My guess is that they're semi-retired, working on their own, without any direction from anywhere. They were probably only part-time during the sixties, worried about exposure and clumsily trying to scare you guys off. Cold-war cowboys, unwilling to retire.'

'Which means you can't stop them.'

'No, no, it doesn't. Joe has a million connections in this town and lots of favours owed. We'll check it out.'

SIXTEEN

I got to work late the next morning. Tom had called a conference for ten-thirty. I slipped in and stood against the wall. The whole team were there, researchers, clerks, associates.

'Welcome, Catherine,' said Tom.

I smiled at him. A dozen sharp eyes watched us.

'Welcome, Catherine,' said another voice, dripping irony from the chair in front of me. 'It's eleven o'clock in the morning, by the way.'

'Mary, she was here working till midnight last night,' said Tom.

'Yeah? What do you think the rest of us are doing? Taking a holiday?' It was Thea, Mary's best friend. Her voice was sharp.

Tom shrugged. 'We're all working hard. Come on, let's get on with it. Joe received a call this morning from our opponents. If we don't excise certain passages from Richard Helms's deposition, Joe will be charged under the Espionage Act,' he said.

'What sections of Helms's deposition?' I said.

'The passages you were going over last night.'

'Why were you going over them last night?' said Thea.

'I have a meeting with a top guy at CBS news.'

'Oh right, so we're going to be turned into some fucking circus,' said Mary. A couple of others chuckled and the rest of them stared at me, eyes flat, questioning.

'Stop it,' said Tom. 'Now look, as I just said, Joe is going to handle this latest shot across our bow. What we need now are more psychiatrists. Who has come up with anything?'

'Why not ask Catherine?' said Mary. 'She's around so much, nosing into everything. She probably phoned that stuff into Langley last night.'

There was a silence that no one seemed to want to break.

'Mary, are you hallucinating?' I said finally.

She hunched her shoulders. 'I'm not saying anything that everyone else isn't thinking. You've cut a deal.'

'What deal? What the hell are you talking about?' said Tom sharply.

Mary scrunched down in her chair and scribbled on her pad, mulish, silent.

'Anyone? With whom has Catherine cut a deal? I'm not going any further until we get an answer.'

'Oh, for God's sake, it's just gossip, sheer nonsense, Tom,' said Timothy, one of the clerks. 'Someone started a rumour that Catherine has cut a deal with the Agency for her uncle's money as long as she reports on what we're doing.'

'That's bullshit,' I cried.

'I know, I know,' said Timothy. 'But we're all paranoid as hell. This case does it to you. You guys wanted to know what was being said.'

Tom looked around the room. 'Guys, we have to be careful here. Rumours tear us apart and that just may be the purpose of this one. We have to remember who we're dealing with and the kind of disruption they are capable of. Mary? Aren't you being a little counterproductive?'

'Sorry, Catherine,' said Mary.

I shook my head, too shocked to reply.

A sick sound came from her throat, a croak that was meant to sound like a laugh. 'We know you're not really,' said Mary.

I nodded at her, gave her a weak smile.

Slowly the room returned to normal. People chattered to each other and Tom's attention focused on the people in front of him.

I shook myself. Don't think about this, this is unimportant. Besides, I had an idea and I didn't need to sit around and be treated like pond scum by a bunch of underaged overachievers.

I left the room.

A few nights earlier, I had been combing through ancient Allan Memorial Institute records. One name kept popping up. Peggy Zylin. Peggy had been witness at many meetings with patients and Cameron. She had observed many dangerous procedures. She was young when she worked as Cameron's right-hand nurse, only twenty-four when she started in '56. Which meant she was in her fifties now. Ideal for the press, mature enough for credibility, but young enough for a modern audience to relate to. I couldn't fight on procedure but I could try to fight using public opinion.

According to the records, Peggy Zylin had married a man named Liscomb and had moved. I had called every hospital in Canada and the northern US that claimed a substantial wing for the mentally ill. Nothing turned up.

On the way to work that morning, I'd had a brainwave, so now I dialled a hospital that wasn't in any major city. The Mayo Clinic was close enough to Peggy's home town of Moosamin, Saskatchewan, for comfort, and world class enough for a top-flight psychiatric nurse.

Bingo. A sweet voice came on the phone, with a warmth that sharpened to intelligence when I told her what the call was about.

'I've been reading about it,' she said. 'You can imagine the fire you all have lit in the community. I can't believe what we used to do to patients and how much it has all changed.'

Better and better. Someone who saw what had happened and who could comment on it, seemingly without professional guilt. She had her head screwed on straight. She had been barely out of school; Cameron was the god of his profession.

After some prevarication she said yes, she would come to Washington and talk to me. She wanted to see the Smithsonian.

I promised to take her. We made an appointment four days away.

She was still a blonde and looked young for her age. She was dressed in a boxy tweed suit with a dozen colours in it and was wearing a red hat, which was what she had told me to look out for. She bounced along the platform towards me. Her face was kind, but thin, and her mouth was disciplined – no softness there. She had taken the train from the airport and we had agreed to meet at Union Station. We sat at the Grill and had lunch.

I told her that my mother was one of Dr Cameron's patients. Peggy didn't remember her.

'I know it must sound funny, but we saw so many. And so many cases were tragic that we learned how to forget. The lobotomies, those were difficult to forget, though some people thought of them as the "heroic" contribution of psycho-surgery. We loathed performing them, but sometimes there was no choice, or at least we thought there was no choice. I remember one beautiful girl, about twenty, so sad. I doubt we would have done it now, almost certainly not.'

'What would you have done?'

'Oh there are so many new drugs. Long-term therapy. We were just coming out of the dark ages, remember, out of purging, leg-irons, bleeding, electric eels. Neuroleptics weren't developed till the mid-fifties and they changed everything. They were introduced into North America just down the road from us at Verdun University in 1954, by a man Dr Cameron had turned down for a job. Dr Cameron was furious for months.'

'I'll tell you the problem we're having.' I cut her off. 'No one can believe that someone, anyone, could get away with the procedures Dr Cameron got away with in the fifties and sixties. How did he manage to stop gossip? Lots of people who worked for him said they thought he was wrong at the time. Why didn't anyone stop him? We have all the reasons, but they don't make the reality seem any more real. Can you help us on that?'

'I think so.'

'Can you remember the atmosphere, the way he gave orders, how he kept control, what kind of man he was?'

'Oh dear, yes. He held us all in thrall. I still ask myself what would Dr Cameron say about that. I have to say I almost loved him. I was so sad when he died in '67. He was like my father.' Her mouth twisted in a wry smile. 'The bad father.'

Her honesty surprised me and I began to hope. 'We need colour, detail. What was the Sleep Room like? Did you ever suspect anything about his connection to Washington? Did you even know about it?'

She smiled at me, her thin lips pressed tightly together. 'After the Smithsonian,' she said.

We finished lunch and I took her to the museum for a couple of hours. She was fascinated by the dress collection, particularly the inaugural gowns of the First Ladies. Finally, after tea in the cafeteria, she consented to come back to the office and give her deposition to me, a recorder, and a videotape camera. I called the office and asked the receptionist to have the room set up for us, then I bustled her out of the museum. I was feeling very impatient.

When we arrived at the office, she settled herself and took a sheaf of papers from her handbag. 'You see, I prepared for this interview.' She asked for a few minutes to review, and while she was reading, she began to look distressed.

'I'm ready,' she said finally.

As soon as the room was darkened slightly and the recorder poised his fingers over his keys, she straightened her back, and started to talk. She was a skilled story teller and her memories were acute and detailed. I lost myself in her world. Brian had just been born and my mother was Ewen Cameron's patient once more, just a year after Peggy had begun working at the Allan Memorial.

'You don't know how much your call upset me. I couldn't sleep – I thought of calling you back and declining, but my husband insisted that I come here and talk to you. He says I need to do this; morally, that is. The things I saw, well, they were no more painful or difficult than what any psychiatric nurse sees every day. Except that, you see, we believed. We felt we were making history in that clinic.

Reality was heightened. Even the lights in the corridors he worked in seemed to burn brighter than on any other ward. I remember wondering why it was so bright. No shadows were cast and light bounced off every surface.

'He demanded silence. We stood like posts, staring at our charts, entering, checking, filing, waiting for his approach. He was on a strict schedule, but often he turned up unexpectedly. We were always at attention, backs stiffened, faces rigid with tension, anticipating or dreading his arrival.

'He would arrive already talking to us, mid-sentence as it were, issuing orders in short sharp bursts, a fighter pilot attacking an enemy bomber. We listened, our faces carefully attentive, fingers flying as we took notes. He noticed every deviation from perfection in his nurses.

'Then he'd nod curtly and he'd veer away. Only then, could we relax.

'I always obeyed him unquestioningly. When I was first assigned to him I found it hard to cope with his attitude towards the patients. When they were in the darkest pit of desolation, he would be at his more distant. I found that puzzling, because I had been taught that a psychiatrist should bring understanding and insight to his patients, but also compassion. The thing to do was to make oneself available. Dr Cameron was almost never available. He'd brush off questions from patients. But I began to see why. He saw many patients, hundreds a day, and some twice a day. That's a lot of cases to hold in one mind. He worked late into the night, every night, writing.

'He was like royalty. He strode unsmiling through the corridor, his duty nurse and resident trailing, trying not to get too close, but not too far away either, both continuously negotiating precedence. Silly, but he induced competitive feelings in everyone.

'I'll never forget the first day I was assigned to him as duty nurse. It was around the time you were speaking of. Early 1956. I had arrived a year prior, from a small town west of Winnipeg – nowheresville, in the parlance of the time. I had gone home after finishing my training in Toronto, to see to my dying father.

'At my training hospital, which was a public hospital, the patients were worse than wild beasts. They had become unreachable on any human wavelength, though using all my brand-new knowledge I tried and tried. They foamed at the mouth, attacked me, drooled, pissed against the walls, went around naked, smeared themselves with their own and others' faeces and more often than not had to live in restraints. For me, in that place, getting a patient to brush his teeth would be a victory, and the glow would last for weeks.

'It was a terrifying place and, after a few months, I realized that all I was or ever would be was a glorified prison guard. That was the profession then, everywhere, for the large part. Hopeless, endless misery. Warehousing humans.

'I started writing to research hospitals or institutes connected with universities, where I could learn something, looking for somewhere where something was being done to solve this horrible hidden problem. I wanted to work in a hospital where people were fighting for the mentally ill, really searching for a cure. That was what, in my naivety, I really wanted – a cure. After almost a year, blessedly, a letter came.

'When I received a job offer from Dr Cameron, I couldn't believe my luck. He was famous. He had been trained at the Universities of Glasgow and London. He had been a staff member at Johns Hopkins, the most prestigious and progressive hospital in America. While in Baltimore he had studied under Adolf Meyer, the most eminent psychiatrist in North America. Dr Meyer's theory of psychobiology had burned like grassfire through the profession. While I was taking care of my father, I had stayed up late at night puzzling through Dr Meyer's work. He believed that mental illness didn't knock someone out of the running completely. He thought that successful treatment depended upon rooting out and mobilizing the functional assets the person still had. We optimists were also optimistic about the work of a Viennese psychiatrist, who turned out to be Dr Cameron's hero, Julius Wagner von Jauregg, who was the first (and only) psychiatrist to win the Nobel Prize for Medicine. Wagner von Jauregg had discovered that psychotic patients who suffered a high fever seemed to be better after the fever had run its course. Following on from this theory, it appeared that any shock – and many kinds of shock followed: induced malaria, insulin coma, electric-shock treatment – however administered, seemed to interrupt and even arrest the course of mental illness. We didn't know why that was, but someone was going to find out. The fifties were going to be the breakthrough decade in psychiatry and I wanted to be in on it.

'By the time of his letter to me, Dr Cameron was easily overtaking Meyer's reputation, becoming the foremost psychiatrist in the Western world, the most published, the most sought-after speaker, friend of presidents and politicians. He was President of the American Psychiatric Association and, of course, the Canadian Psychiatric Association, and he was in the process of founding the World Psychiatric Association. He had helped the US government during the war, and had been the psychiatrist chosen by the OSS to evaluate whether Rudolf Hess was fit to stand trial in Nuremberg.

'I was thrilled by the breadth of his thinking. I read all his papers, once I got to Montreal. You see, and I include myself in the profession, we were desperate. The imperative to treat was overwhelming. It was treat or watch the patient devolve. The basic ethical principle of *primus non nocere* – first of all, do no harm – seemed like cowardice in the face of such misery. Dr Cameron had fought the incursion of psychoanalysis into his profession. It took too long, was too expensive for all the really sick people we had. He wrote that he believed that reorganization of the personality could be brought about without the necessity of solving of conflicts or abreaction, which is the reliving of past experiences. He believed that repetition of verbal signals provided a tool where direct, controlled changes in personality could be made. One put the old ones "out of circuit" and allowed for the direct building of new personality traits. There were streams of visitors from all over the world coming to see his work. Are you following me?'

She looked up from her notes, and her eyes gleamed at me. I nodded.

'I'm not going into too much detail, am I?'

'No, please go on. It's fascinating.'

'He called me girlie. He called every other woman lassie – why I do not know. He said, "Girlie, we are going to cure schizophrenia." And I believed him; my heart would sort of leap up, and I couldn't catch my breath. In the hospital, we were all imbued with the spirit. We were not unlike a group of – ' She shook her head and stopped for a moment. 'We had this sense of privilege – that he was on the verge of a discovery and that we were going to be there with him. So when he started the LSD experiments, his psychic driving – we all just accepted it. When one looks back at it now, it's kind of horrifying, but he had us believing that all the people he was treating were people everyone else had given up on.

'We'd think: Isn't that great, here we are – everybody else has given up and we're going to help these people. And in the psychic driving – these people were put to sleep, of course, and they had this combination of chlorpromazine and barbiturates, this cocktail, this whole big cocktail. And with that they were given ECTs and the Page-Russell ECTs, and the button was often pressed several times, and they were given Page-Russells at least a couple times a day, until the point that they were confused in all three spheres which were time, place, and self. Which is totally horrifying to look back on.'

'What are Page-Russells?' I interrupted.

'A form of shock treatment named after its English inventors. Instead of a single shock, a single press of the button, a doctor hit the button six times, one after the other, causing a multi-peaked convulsion.'

'I remember reading about them now.'

'Sometimes we would administer a hundred at a time to recalcitrant patients. In retrospect, that fact alone is disgusting.'

We were both silent for a moment. She gave herself a little shake and continued.

'I'll never forget that first day I went to the Sleep Room. At our approach, the heavily guarded door was unlocked and opened by a security man. We passed through it, one by one; my eyes adjusted slowly to the gloom. The heavy door clanged shut. I listened to the bolts being shoved roughly into place behind them. My heart was in my throat.

'The Sleep Room was circular, with tiny cubicles around the perimeter dividing it into shoebox-shaped cubicles. In each box, a patient lay silent, immobilized. The windows were shrouded and barred.

'In the centre sat a table and chairs. I was to learn that we would sit the patients who were suitably awake at this table. We would get them up, lift them, sit them down and we would feed them and care for them. A black-and-white television stood on a stand, for the night nurse.

'The room stank of faeces and urine. I learned that the patients, kept in a chemically controlled sleep for weeks, or sometimes more than a month at a time, would defecate in their beds and lie, aware of what they had done, but unable to summon help or even to form the words that would call for help. The smell had permeated everything, had formed part of the atmosphere of the room. The Chief called this the ultra-paradoxical phase of treatment. We were stopping the madness in its tracks during this stage. In the loony bin, things just spun out of control as the patients devolved into wild animals.

'I told myself that the smell was something I would change when and if the Chief allowed me to become a nurse in here. A good daily scrub down was called for and I looked forward to it.

'We started rounds. In the first bed was a young man, thin and tall, his head partly shaved to accommodate the electrodes. His eyes were closed and his mouth worked convulsively, presumably repeating the words he was hearing on the tape recorder inside his helmet.

'"Medication correct," said the Chief. His resident took a note and we moved on.

'In the next bed lay a woman in her early fifties, by my guess. She was not so placid. Her head lashed from side to side, trying to escape the words resounding tinnily from inside the football helmet on her head.

'"Please, please, make it stop . . . can't stand it any more . . ." she whimpered at us, eyes rolling in her head.

'I guessed that the patient was menopausal and the hot flashes often experienced by women going through the change of life had flushed the drugs out of her system. She had been left fully conscious, listening to the messages endlessly repeated through the speakers in the football helmet locked on to her head. I had heard from another nurse that the patients hated their messages and that it was torment to them if they were not properly medicated.

'He was not pleased. I craned my neck and caught the words he was reciting to the resident. I overheard, "Recidivist, regression, punishment, curare." The resident's eyes widened as he took notes.

'I was afraid to object, but I was repulsed. He must know about the flashes, he had to, he was a physician – but still, curare! The drug caused total paralysis. But I didn't dare to say anything. We moved on.

'In the next bed was a beautiful young girl with long blonde hair. She too was whimpering, but not consciously. A long, low keening bubbled through an almost perfect pair of rosebud lips. The two men stood staring down at her.

'"Pity," said the Chief eventually. "Up her Semyl 10 milligrams four times a day. See if we can stabilize her. Otherwise, I don't know. Isolation, leucotomy. Pity." This was said with no expression. A scientist's regret at a failed experiment.

'Leucotomy! My heart clutched for an instant, but I pushed the feeling away firmly. According to the chart, they had been working on the girl's case for nearly a year.

'The team inched around the room, inspecting each of the twenty-four beds in turn. Many of the patients, while unconscious, muttered rabidly or moaned, and some of them, before their medication was correctly adjusted, would plead piteously for me to remove the helmets. Like children asking not have a needle, I thought. I stopped two or three times; I would take their arms and fold them across their chests, patting and smoothing the skin. I remember noting that if I worked in here skin lotion would be one of my contributions. Then I'd run to catch up.

'Some of the patients were semi-conscious and they shuffled around in the dank gloom of the chamber, like ghosts trapped in the nether world. They reached out to me, begging for contact. I brushed their hands aside, patted them on the back and sent them on their confused way. Exercise was good for them, said the Chief.

'As I crossed the room behind the doctors, inspection finished, I heard a long low moan from one of the beds behind me.

'The sound amplified suddenly into a shriek. I felt a rush of wind and someone was on my back, clutching at me. The woman's head (it was a woman, I could feel the long hair drape across my neck and the body was soft, frail) sought shelter in the hollow of my throat. She burrowed into me, like an infant snuffling for her mother's breast.

'I froze. Not panic. Not panicking was everything in these situations. I pulled the woman closer, and half carried her, half dragged her to the table and chairs in the centre of the room. The woman – it was the fifty year old who had just been prescribed curare as punishment – scrabbled at my chest and then buried her head in my bosom. I sat down on the chair, pulled the woman on to my lap and sat there, rocking her back and forth, back and forth, as gently as if she were a newborn baby. The woman whimpered, and slowly her cries began to subside into soft sighs of contentment.

'I felt rather than saw the Chief's eyes on me. I looked up. He was watching me, his blue eyes icy. My heart sank. Then he nodded and smiled at me and said something to the resident who furiously started scribbling down notes. "Re-mothering" was a word I heard.

'An intern approached carefully from behind, needle at the ready. He plunged it into the woman's bare arm. She shrieked and slumped, defeated more by the end of comfort than by the barbiturate which was already taking effect.

'My eyes stung. I surrendered her to the nurses who pulled and carried the woman back into her bed. I rejoined the Chief's train.

'"Good work, girlie," I heard softly above her head. I bobbed my head at him, unable to meet his eyes.

'Outside in the corridor we stopped.

'"Again, I say, well done, girlie." He fixed me with his cool eyes. "That is precisely the kind of initiative we need from our staff. Kindness, sympathy, quick rational action. You were truly inspired." He turned smartly on his heels and strode on.

'I was thrilled. You see, he did care. He used to say that you have to risk if you want to get anywhere – you've got to risk. And he was willing to risk in order to cure schizophrenia. He was convinced and he convinced us that he was going to find the cure. After that day, I never for a moment doubted his motives. I think he was good. I do not think he was a malevolent man, in any way. Maybe misguided. And if he was misguided, we all were misguided.'

I cleared my throat. 'Was this a typical day in the Sleep Room?'

'Oh yes. But let me tell you what happened next. I've never quite got over it.

'As we walked down the hall, the Chief turned to look back. "I want you both in on this next event. Come on. What are you waiting for?" And he strode off down the corridor towards the senior staff room. The resident looked at me, shrugged and took off after him.

'We followed the doctor into a small lecture room in the hospital. The others, senior medical staff only, were already seated. I crept into a place at the rear of the hall. From the moment of my appearance on the Chief's heels, I had received a few dark looks. I stiffened my back. If Dr Cameron wanted me here, I belonged here.

'The room crackled with hostility. The Chief was not known for running a happy operation. He didn't believe in it. Nor did he seek popularity from the medical community in the city or from his staff. He encouraged infighting and divisions between the juniors. "Makes for increased creative activity," he would chuckle.

'He took his seat at the front of the room. I noticed for the first time how carefully dressed he was. Usually he looked rumpled, as if he had worked all night. You know his wife lived in Lake Placid, and he had a bachelor flat in Montreal. He wanted to keep his US citizenship. People hated that. Anyway, this day, he was perfection: arms folded, shirt-cuffs visible in all their starched whiteness, one ankle crossed over the other, socks held in place by suspenders, each shoelace identically tied with a reefer knot. His face was white and still; his blue eyes fixed on some point over our heads made him look a little like one of El Greco's saints – all cheekbones and sublimity. He was forbidding, intimidating and something else too. I searched my mind for a word. Menace. He radiated menace. I wondered what had happened that had made him so angry.

'I studied the doctors carefully. I knew some of them did not believe in Dr Cameron's work as fervently as I did. There was so much gossip. I'd heard that the golden rule among his medical staff was "Put up or shut up". Dr Cameron was known for turning on less than enthusiastic acolytes.

'According to my roommate and only nurse friend on the floor, Cameron had refused to support research grants for physicians who had offended him, had moved a senior scientist to smaller quarters for the same thing and had banished a doctor to one of the workhouse asylums in the city for failing to carry out a treatment exactly as directed. At the time, I dismissed the rumours. I thought that gossip attached itself to great men like lint to sweaters and that, if the doctor had done such things, he would have had very good reasons.

'He nodded sharply at the technician, who stood beside him, waiting. The man started the tape recorder on the table beside him.

'A tinny voice explained that not only was what we were about to hear top secret but that any violation of secrecy would lead to prosecution by the United States government. Dr Cameron lifted his hand. The tape stopped. People looked at each other, mystified. The anxiety level in the room climbed.

'Cameron nodded to the technician. The tape started again: "We, all prisoners, solemnly appeal to you as follows. The armed intervention in Korean internal affairs is a barbaric aggressive action to protect the benefit of the capitalist monopoly of the United States.

Let us fight for right against wrong, bravely opposing those of our leaders who would lead us into a war against Russia."

'The voice made me shiver. It sounded like a young man, a college football player, young but no longer innocent. And American: "Dachau, Auschwitz, Hiroshima, Nagasaki. What extreme ferocity capitalist regimes can unleash! The Second World War made that so clear. Anguished humanity cried out in unison. Never should such cries be allowed to happen again. But they have. The highest technological achievements of the United States and all the resources of its capitalist industry have been used to bring new horror. We, all prisoners, appeal to an international body to impose the respect for law on the capitalist and reactionary forces. Let moral condemnation of such actions be clearly expressed . . ."

'It was spooky. The young man sounded no older than my young brother, who had just graduated from high school. Timmy's only thoughts were of girls and the new Pontiac he was buying on time by working at the gas station nights and weekends.

'". . . re-education and not punishment – that is the fundamental difference between our system and that of other countries. Thanks to the system of re-education, it has been possible for me to be integrated into a new world. Please be aware that this re-education has not meant preventive detention as happened to the Japanese in the United States – during the Second World War . . ."

'I listened, bolt upright, transfixed by the voice on the tape.

'". . . we ran our own lives. We held weekly meetings to discuss how we were all doing and every month we would hold a more formal meeting at which it was decided who would get commendations, rewards and then release. We all worked very hard to develop a new consciousness . . ."

'I knew that every so often Dr Cameron would abruptly depart for Washington, and just as suddenly reappear on the floor. I wondered whether this tape had anything to do with his visits south.

'The tape stopped again. Cameron sat, glowering at us. Finally he began to speak, his voice low, the Scots burr more pronounced than usual, a sign that I knew indicated his anger.

'"The important thing to remember here," he said, "is that the

American laddie on this tape has been brainwashed. The Chinese succeeded in creating in the poor lad's mind 'a sense of participation', convincing him they were deeply in earnest about their thought reform."

'He nodded to the technician again. The tape was rewound and started. Dr Cameron went through the tape, pointing out just how effectively the prisoner's mind had been re-motivated. "Yet you all know from our work here that the man's new attitudes are not completely divorced from his former self. What happened was that he had himself refilled the Inner Void his captors had carefully carved out of his mind."

'Dr Cameron stood up. His voice became loud, strident, the burr even more pronounced. He sounded like a chieftain psyching himself up to go to war: 'Does not our success depend upon unravelling the unconscious so that the hidden traumas of our patients become known to them and they can then be liberated for more productive living?"

'There was murmured agreement from the gathered senior staff. Yes, yes, I thought, but what has that to do with the tape?

'"I am primarily interested in mental motivation, and discovering the laws that govern it. But so are the Chinese. They are also studying suppression and repression, projection and displacement, to achieve conversion. There has been some questioning about what I am trying to achieve here. Some doubt, but none have asked for an explanation. Criticism without knowledge. It disgusts me in the extreme. That you dare to call yourself scientists!" The scorn in his voice was withering. "What I am attempting to achieve in the laboratories in the stables is essentially no different from what the Chinese have done to the prisoner on the tape – with *one significant difference*. Their techniques are meant to harm. Mine are meant only to be beneficial. Do you understand? *Beneficial*. I want an end, here and now, to the rumours. What is happening in the stables and the basement is positive treatment." His voice resounded around the room like a whiplash. "Positive treatment. And you'd all better understand that. Now. Here and now." His eyes were hooded, unblinking, filled with threat. He held us for one long moment.

"Now, here and now," he repeated quietly. And rising to his feet, he stalked out of the silent room.

'I waited a few moments. No one spoke or moved. They had been stunned by the ferocity of the Chief's attack.

'I remember smiling, pleased by the effect he had on his detractors. Then quietly, I slipped out the door and followed him.'

SEVENTEEN

I felt triumphant after the day with Peggy. The next day, Wheeler came into my office.

'I read your report on Peggy Liscomb. The part with the Korean War Vet places him firmly in the loop. I don't know how we can use it, but it will sure trigger interest from the press. Great stuff. Congratulations.'

'Thanks.'

'We need something like this to cheer us up. Everyone feels as though we're getting nowhere. We've been waiting for months for a decision on further discovery.'

'The waiting is getting to all of us,' I said.

'Did you hear that one of our plaintiffs, Flo Langleben, died?'

'Delay and attrition,' I said, trying for lightness in my tone. 'It's plainly the strategy, has been since the beginning.'

'Right. Rauh wants to see you.'

My heart did a little flip-flop. 'Why?'

He shrugged. 'Don't know. C'mon, I'll be your witness.' He led the way to the great man's office.

The rumour was that the legend was dying by inches. His heart was bad. That summer he had had a double hip replacement and was still in a wheelchair. None of the clerks on the case had seen him for months and there was a lot of gossip. The firm worried about the future without him.

Even knowing about his disability did not prepare me for the shock of seeing him. He wheeled the chair from behind his desk briskly and was shaking my hand before I knew it. The handshake was the usual rocklike experience, but he was different. His face was a whitish grey and he'd lost a lot of weight. He was sitting uncomfortably in the chair, a bit like a sack of old, ill-fitting clothes. The face still shone. Words that Lillian Hellman had used about him sprang to mind: 'Shrewdness seldom goes with an open nature, but in his case it does and the nice, unbeautiful, rugged, crinkly face gives me confidence about the mind above it.'

He motioned us to chairs and rang for coffee without bothering to ask us if we wanted any.

'I'm getting better now.' He wheeled himself back around his desk.

'You look terrific.' My lie lacked conviction.

'I look like hell and you know it. That's exactly the sort of wishy-washy response I would expect from a Canadian.' He lowered his eyebrows and glowered at me.

'I'm sorry.'

'I still need your mother, young woman.'

I shook my head. 'I understand, sir, but she won't even speak to me these days. Just "Happy birthday" and "The weather is glorious out here" – stuff like that if I call, then impassioned furious letters that order me to go home to New York and let sleeping dogs lie and that I'll kill my father if he finds out.'

'Proves my point about your nationality.' He sputtered and shuffled around with the papers on his desk. 'I just want somebody to explain all this to me.' His voice was plaintive, a frustrated child's.

I looked at Tom. He rolled his eyes.

'Explain all what, sir?'

'You'd think, wouldn't you, that the Canadian government would be our ally?'

I nodded. I knew what was coming now. The Canadians had been dragging their heels since the beginning of the case. There had been the usual exchange of diplomatic notes between the Americans and the Canadians. Then Rauh had requested that the matter be raised during a formal session between George Shultz, the then Secretary of State, and Joe Clark, Minister of External Affairs. It was right after that meeting that the Canadian Ambassador became outright hostile, ignoring us, delaying depositions from Canadian officials.

'Well, they're not,' he said. 'They're a bunch of lily-livered assholes who bend over whenever they see a member of the US government on the horizon.'

I stifled a giggle.

He looked at me. 'No protest there, I see.'

'Sir, I left Canada as soon as I graduated from the University of Toronto.'

'Gee, I wonder why.' He practically snarled his sarcasm.

'What's happened, Joe?' Tom's light tenor was a relief.

He threw a piece of paper at us across the desk. 'I've been waiting for this decision from that asshole Judge Penn for eleven months and I find this, this! in the internal office mail. It's been sitting there for two days.'

Tom and I huddled over the document.

In 1977, the Church Senate Committee had ordered Stansfield Turner, then Director of the CIA, to find all the victims of the MKULTRA experiment in Canada, notify them and apologize. The Senate also ordered the Agency to apologize to the Canadian government.

The apology to the government had taken the form of a letter. And, shortly after the news broke in 1977, Stacey Hulse, then CIA station chief in Ottawa, visited John Hadwen, Security and Intelligence Liaison director for the Canadian government, and apologized. Both forms of apology were critical and could break the case open. It meant that the CIA had admitted liability. I had sat in on the motion that would allow us access to the apologies and make them admissible the first day I'd met Rauh and Wheeler. We had been waiting for this decision for more than three months. It could make all the difference.

Now, the Judge had disallowed Stacey Hulse's testimony on the grounds of national security.

I sneaked a look at Rauh over the paper. He looked caved in, collapsed.

'I'm sorry,' I said.

'It's a real blow,' he said. 'A real blow.'

We sat in silence for a moment. Rauh shook his head.

'But I don't see what that has to do with Canada,' I ventured finally.

He exploded. 'We've been dicking around with the goddamned Canadians for two years now. They say they never got a letter. They back down every time the CIA bares its teeth at them.'

'Your Minister of External Affairs, Joe Clark, has denied us access to the letter of apology and to John Hadwen's testimony,' interjected Wheeler.

Rauh shook his head. 'Jesus, I could carve a better man than Joe Clark out of a banana. Everyone *knows* the CIA apologized. Everyone!'

Tom and I looked at him. He knew better than anyone and certainly better than I, that 'everyone knowing' didn't mean a thing if that fact couldn't be admitted as evidence.

'We invade their territory, forget to inform them, perform uncontrolled, unthinkable experiments on innocent, unsuspecting citizens that they have sworn to protect and all they do is write pleading letters to the State Department. It's disgusting and I can't stand it.' Rauh wheeled his chair around to face the window, staring down at the anthill in Farragut Square.

I shook my head and looked at the floor. Tom patted my arm and got up, pulled a chair close to Rauh and began to talk to him.

My mind veered away from these unsolvable problems and I stood up and took a tour of Rauh's mementoes. I had seen them all a half-dozen times by now, but they still held my attention. I examined the photograph of Rauh with the Mississippi Freedom Democratic Party. Rauh had represented them in 1964 and won the promise of desegregated delegations to future conventions. The inscription read that the delegates were grateful that they had 'met a man like you who like us burns with the desire that all mankind be free . . . a white man who was also concerned with freedom for all.'

But this case was defeating even this man.

He wheeled himself back to his desk and Wheeler came and sat down. Joe pushed two letters at me across the desk. I picked them up.

I started to read. They were both to the Canadian Prime Minister, Brian Mulroney:

> Dear Mr Prime Minister,
>
> Although I am seventy-five years old and have been a lawyer for almost fifty years, I have never before considered writing to a head of state in connection with a law suit in which I was engaged . . . In all honesty, I was reluctant to undertake so massive a struggle against so powerful an opponent as the CIA in the twilight of life and career . . . In deciding to take the case, I assumed, of course, that I would have the full support of the Canadian government on behalf of its citizens and have been thunderstruck watching the opposite happen . . .

The letter went on to detail every instance of Canadian behaviour that Rauh viewed as detrimental to his case.

The next letter was even angrier. It was dated the previous day:

> I write this letter on an aeroplane from Los Angeles to Washington. Yesterday in Ventura, California, I took the testimony of a former CIA official who participated in delivering CIA support to Dr Cameron's brutal experiments upon unwitting Canadian citizens. Anger wells up inside as I ask myself why I go on overtaxing my strength with cross-country trips and seven-day work weeks, and I risk bankrupting my small law firm to help Canadian citizens whose own government works against them . . .
>
> For your government has now, even after my personal appeal

> to you, inflicted the worst blow of all in the form of the so-called Cooper Report which will take its place among the shabbiest, most mean-spirited and error-ridden official documents ever produced by a government following Anglo-Saxon legal principles of fairness and due process of law . . .
>
> The whole purpose of the Cooper exercise was to prepare a press release for the CIA.

I finished reading and placed the letters back on his desk.

'What about that goddamned Cooper Report, young woman? What's your explanation?'

'Well, from my reading of the summary, sir, the Canadian Justice Department commissioned an independent study. The committee members interviewed psychiatrists about Cameron's procedures and they concluded, to a man, that, while extreme, they weren't outside the generally accepted procedures of the time.'

Rauh exploded. 'It's a damned whitewash. Independent, my ass. I tried to go down to the embassy yesterday when I got back and throw it in their faces, but Tom wouldn't let me. Jesus, the shrinks they hired didn't even see any of Cameron's patients, just used Cameron's records. They said, "We must not condemn as negligence that which is only misadventure."'

Tom and I were silent.

'Well?' he said. 'Can you explain it? You're a Canadian. Your family was damaged by this. Why aren't you mad? I've watched you. You're competent. You're committed. You work hard, stay late. But you aren't angry. Why the hell not?'

I cleared my throat. 'I think,' I started tentatively, 'that the anger would make me useless to you and to my family.'

'Well, Miss Ramsey, let me assure you that it won't. But it may help spur you to action. God knows, we need it.'

He wheeled back to his window. 'Get out of here, both of you. I have some thinking to do.'

'What happened?' I leaned against the wall outside his office. 'I feel like I've been mauled by a lion.'

'We've all gone through it. A rite of passage for you. He'll forget about it by tomorrow and remember only that, somehow, he feels closer to you.'

'Lucky you're here to interpret that,' I said drily. 'The question is, will I forget it?'

He grinned at me ruefully.

'You know I can't get her to help, Tom. You understand, don't you?'

'You are pretty clear about what happened, Catherine. I believe you. She has to be protecting someone. Your father, no doubt.'

I nodded, wondering at that new interpretation, and we walked down the hall towards the bull pen. 'Something else is eating at him too, isn't it?'

'Yeah. We don't have any money.'

'But that's always been the case.'

'It's worse than ever. The firm is thousands out on expenses alone, let alone thousands of hours of billing time. We signed on as a hundred per cent contingency and can't expect any payment until there is a settlement. None of the ex-patients can afford the expenses.'

'But what about the Orlikows? He's an MP and she's pretty feisty. Weren't they raising money?'

'It's what we were counting on. David hired a professional fund-raiser after *The Fifth Estate* programme was broadcast in Canada. They sent requests to thousands of likely supporters. Hardly anyone sent money. Orlikow was so depressed he couldn't do anything for five months. Rauh is furious that they can write letters but can't send money. It bewilders him.'

'There's something else too, though, isn't there?'

His face looked tired suddenly. 'We need a breakthrough. We're dying on our feet here. The worst of it is that this is exactly what the Agency wants. They want us to give up, fold our tents, steal away.'

The receptionist was waving at us from down the hall.

'Catherine, your brother's on line three. Take it in Harry's office,' she called.

'OK. Thanks.'

Tom patted my shoulder. 'See ya, kid.'

I nodded.

Ten minutes later I stumbled out into the hallway. No one. I called down to the receptionist. 'Where is everyone? Where's Tom?'

'He's in with Joe. All hell's broken loose.'

'What's happened?'

She shrugged. 'They don't tell me, honey.'

Somehow I got back to my desk and started making calls.

Tom hurried into the room. 'Meeting in five minutes, Catherine, in the conference room.' He came over to me. 'That judgment has really got the old boy rocking. We'll see some action now. What's wrong?'

The airline had me on hold. 'I have to go home.' I looked at him, lost my focus and went back to the pad.

'What? Why?'

'My father's been in an accident.'

'How bad?' When I didn't answer, he crouched down and squeezed my hand. 'Catherine, how bad?'

I shook my head. 'Brian called. He says Dad's going to be all right. But I didn't believe him. I don't know. I bet he's lying. He said to come.'

He sat by me, while I completed the booking. People walked by us on the way to the conference room, looking at us curiously. He was holding my hand. 'I'll take you to the airport. How much time do we have?'

'Less than three hours.'

'Why don't you sit in on the meeting? It might take your mind off it for a little while. Time enough to worry.'

I nodded, got up and followed him blindly out into the corridor. Inside, I found a seat near the back.

Rauh wheeled himself into the room looking as if he were in training for the Special Olympics. Whatever inertia he had suffered a few minutes ago was gone.

He positioned himself at the front, fixed us with his eyes. Immediately the room lapsed into silence.

'We're going to have a motion to dismiss in front of us in a few days. I've just had a phone call from the happy people at opposing counsel's office. I hope you have all read the Cooper Report. The CIA are retaining all the psychiatrists who supported Cameron in the Cooper Report. The damned Canadian government has done the CIA's work for them. There is rejoicing in the halls of Langley today.'

His secretary walked into the room. 'Ah, Glenda, pass them around. Glenda is passing out copies of the most damaging assertions.'

His secretary slowly and methodically distributed papers around the table. Each associate grabbed the document and started to skim it. Explosions of frustration and anger and even a few laughs sounded as they read.

Everyone was there. They perched on the edge of chairs, those who could find a place to sit down. My neighbour had smoked his cigarette down to the filter and someone in front of me had half chewed his Styrofoam coffee cup to little white pebbles. Rauh never called full meetings, even before a trial.

His voice was the only thing we heard. We were mesmerized by the growl of it. All except me. I was thinking of the tone in Brian's voice.

'People, you've heard of Iran Contra?'

A few nods.

'This is where the years we've put in on this come to fruition. We must demonstrate that the law has to serve as a check on a secret agency. The CIA and the National Security Council have been caught playing games that only excessive secrecy and power allow. These psychiatrists did not interview any of Cameron's patients, much less our plaintiffs. They used Cameron's files only, the hospital and medical records he invented for each of his patients.' His contempt was infinite. 'In all my years I've never seen such a blatant government whitewash.'

There was silence in the room.

'All right.' He spun his way over to the front of the table.

'As I said, I've had word that the CIA lost no time in retaining all these shrinks as witnesses for the defence. When you read the stuff, you'll see what they say. They all conclude that Cameron's practices were not outside the acceptable practices of the time, that informed consent was not in operation till later, that what these poor sick people signed was a blanket release – you can do what the hell you want to do to me – that Cameron acted incautiously but not irresponsibly, that it was a *misadventure*, for God's sake.'

I stood up and started for the door.

'What have we got to refute?' he barked. 'I want everyone on this issue alone for the foreseeable future.'

I opened the door and stepped into the hallway. I leaned against the wall.

Tom poked his head out. 'Catherine, why don't you go home and pack. I'll take you to the airport. I'll be at your place in an hour. I'll fill you in then.'

I nodded, grateful. I was feeling like a dumb animal.

He waved at me. 'Get going now. It is Dulles, not Baltimore?'

I nodded again. 'I'm sorry, I just can't listen.'

'I understand. Now, go, for God's sake.'

I stumbled down the hall to my cubicle, shoved some papers into my briefcase and was downstairs, out on Connecticut, hailing a cab, before I could stop my teeth from chattering.

I was glad to see him when he showed up forty-five minutes later. His eyes held a glitter, and he gave me a huge hug. 'Do you want me to do anything? Call anybody?'

'No. What happened?'

'Hang on.' He put my luggage in the boot.

'Well?' I said as we pulled into traffic.

'This should take less than an hour. Traffic's not bad today.'

'Thank you for doing this.'

'No problem. All right. We reviewed our case, starting with Olson's – you remember, the government scientist who was given LSD without his knowledge, and then threw himself out the window?'

'Yes.'

'That introduces the idea that the Agency knew how dangerous the drug could be – negligent failure to supervise. Second, negligent funding of extra-hazardous experimentation, or brainwashing, and third, the consent charge, that Cameron's patients had not volunteered to be experimental subjects.

'Thank God for the Nuremberg Code. It will save us. It is a crystal-clear set of boundaries for research and experimentation on human subjects, including clinical and field-drug trials. First adopted in '49, after the Allies saw the death camps. Then refined in '54, and again in '66. We have Robert Jay Lifton, who is *the* expert on Chinese brainwashing, reviewing the Cameron funding application to the CIA front.'

'What does Lifton say?'

'I'm paraphrasing here, but he says the grant application closely paralleled the techniques of thought reform, or brainwashing, used in Chinese prisons and elsewhere. His colleague, Leon Saltzman, said the application proposed a mind-control project with no safeguards, no discussion of risks, dangers and potential destructiveness.

'There's the Termansen Report, out of the Allan, which studied Cameron's patients, seven years later. He said memory loss was higher than for standard ECT, and that psychic driving resulted in memory loss, and damaging effects on cognitive functioning. Half of Cameron's patients relapsed in a year.'

I was silent, watching the cars jockeying for position on the freeway.

'Catherine?'

'I'm sorry. It does sound very convincing. Will we get the case to court?'

'Probably. Eventually. Then the Agency will appeal, take it all the way to the Supreme Court, which has been tipped all the way to the right by Reagan's crowd. We're looking at another five years, minimum.'

Five years. Five more years. We wouldn't last that long, me and my family.

'Tom, I can't stop thinking. What if my father's accident was intentional? What if someone was trying to kill him?'

EIGHTEEN

Brian was waiting at the exit gate, car keys jingling in his hand. When he saw me, he started to move towards the door.

'Tell me what happened,' I said as I raced to catch up with him. He grabbed my bag and threw it in the back of his car.

'It's worse than I said on the phone.'

'I knew it. He's dying.' My world cracked.

Brian shook his head, and instantly I felt a wave of relief. 'First of all, he has a chance. At the Vancouver General, they're calling him a medical miracle. It's been twenty hours and he's not dead yet. He's on full life support, in an iron lung. Brain stem severed. All the bones in his face broken. "Does he have a living will?" some bitch asks.'

'What did Mum say?'

'She just shook her head. "He's going to pull through," she says. She hasn't been home since it happened. She met the damned helicopter when it landed on the roof of the Vancouver General.'

'All right.' I paused and digested this information. 'What happened?'

'I was up north with him, at Pender Harbour where he keeps the boat. He had discovered some dry rot in the hull a couple of weeks ago and he put it into dry dock. It was coming out and we were going to check it out, pay the bill and so on. So, we took the ferry up there, walked to the marina and hung out for a while. There was nothing to do, which suited me fine.'

'But he doesn't like to sit around.'

'Exactly. So he goes over to a government dock to help some fishermen bring in their catch. You know, one of those huge netting operations with winches and pulleys. They swing the fish, a quarter ton of it, out of the hold into the factory tanks.'

I nodded. I'd seen it once or twice.

'The winch slipped. A huge lump of iron smacked him in the back of his head. He went down like a felled tree.'

I shuddered.

'I'm watching from the sidelines, when all of a sudden, I hear a big shout. Two or three men yelling, then a surge of them, five maybe, push out of the way. And there's a guy on the ground. I'm standing now, trying to see. A couple of guys break ranks and run down the dock, then disappear up the road into the village. I'm surprised, 'cause there's a clinic on the harbour. Another guy runs to the clinic and the doctor comes. We think Dad's dead, but he's not. Then we call the helicopter and I fly down with him.'

'Do you think it was an accident?'

'The fishermen said it was very strange. Or at least, they said that they had just checked all the equipment, that nothing was old or functioning badly. One old guy thought he saw one of the two men I saw run away, fiddle with the safety catch. OK, maybe I'm wrong, call me paranoid – but I'm not.'

'And if you're right, why?'

'Do you really think that these secret agencies we're dealing with have changed since the sixties? They want to stop you. They know Dad could kick up something of a stink. War hero, industrialist. Not a kook. He'd be listened to.'

'He doesn't even know what's going on. Mother insisted on that.'

'Do they know that? No.'

I sat, looking out the window. When Tom had asked the date of my return, I shook my head. I didn't know if I was coming back, I said; I probably wasn't. I hadn't even called Mark to tell him what had happened. This atrocity had tipped me over the edge. I fought myself every inch of the way down Granville Street, and it might as well have been a free fall down Everest. I was sick with nerves and Brian was no help. He looked as if he had lost ten pounds since I'd last seen him. He was busy, just concentrating on navigating his taxi through the traffic.

It was the same hospital where I had visited Brian. It was near enough to his apartment, Brian said, so he could just camp out for the next few months. If Dad lived, it would take that long to reconstruct his face.

Brian had spent last night there. Waiting, listening to him trying to breathe, listening to him crying from the pain. Crying without tears because there were no tear ducts left.

He had fallen on his face and smashed his nose, his sinus cavities, his eye sockets, his mouth. Every bone in his face was splintered.

Upstairs in this modern hell, pale-green and pale-yellow stripes on the walls, with ultra-bright, ultra-white counters, nurses, he lay in a glass room, upside down. Upside down, his lungs would work better; his doctors could work on his spinal-cord injuries, the brain stem might heal.

Most of him was covered in a white tent. I couldn't see much. A hand, a bare arm, white hairs on the arm, skin wrinkled and dark from sun exposure.

In the corner sat my mother, watching me look at him.

'Oh Mum,' I said finally, and went to her, kneeling at her feet, holding her around her waist. Her hands came around me, lifted me up.

Brian brought two more chairs into the room, growling at the nurse who tried to stop him.

'Cathy, I am glad that you're here.'

'How could I not come?'

'He's going to be all right, you know.' Her face was serene.

Brian reached for her other hand.

The doctor came in. 'Mrs Ramsey?' he said.

'Dr Hanesh, this is my daughter, Catherine. She's a journalist working in Washington.' Her tones were almost social.

The man looked tense and worried. 'Mrs Ramsey, I'd like you to go home now and sleep for a little while. Come back in four hours. I promise you that nothing, neither good nor bad, will happen while you are gone.'

She nodded at the doctor. 'All right. But will you leave us for a moment now?'

The doctor left.

'Kids.' She took both our hands. 'I'm sure this wasn't an accident.'

I heard the machines around my father gurgle and hum and whine.

'Brian?'

'No argument from me, Mum,' he said.

'Catherine?'

I shook my head.

She put her hand in her jacket pocket and pulled something out, held it out to us. In her palm was a tiny metal key. 'It's for my safety deposit box. The number is five four six six. Both of you are listed.'

Brian's face went white. 'What's in it?'

'I think you'd better go and open it now. Go carefully. Take the documents to your place, Brian. Catherine, take me home, I need to rest. Then meet Brian and we'll speak later. I think you are right. I think it's time I started to fight back.'

It was a mark of just how stunned I was. Her statement didn't surprise me at all. Brian stood staring into space for a few seconds, then shook himself, nodded and took the chairs back out, smiling at the nurse.

'I'll call Mum's neighbours. They'll stay with her while you come to my place,' he said as he waved goodbye.

I drove her car slowly and carefully up the hill. We talked little. She was cheery, putting a good face on it. Exhausted as she was, I began to see her as old, for the first time. She was getting old – sixty-five is old enough compared to thirty-five, but I had refused to see it. She was stuck in her role as mother/tormentor and that person was always in her prime.

I took the car around to the lane behind the house and locked, under her instructions, the garage door. Then, to further instructions, I made her a fat-free, salt-free, taste-free lunch and carried it upstairs. I sat on the end of her bed as she picked at it. She asked about Mark and she told me a bit about the phone call from Pender Harbour that had changed her life.

'It was the harbour master, not even Brian who called,' she said, shaking her head. 'They brought in a helicopter immediately. It was very efficient.'

'Did the doctor give you anything to take?'

'You know I won't take anything, Catherine.' She picked up a bit of salad. 'Then Brian got on the phone. He was trying not to cry, but I could tell he thought Ian was dead. I knew he wasn't.'

'How?'

'When you're married forty years, you know these things.'

I smoothed the hair back from her brow and kissed her.

'You're treating me like the daughter now,' she said.

I smiled and tucked her under a mohair blanket, patted her cheek and drew the curtains.

'They want to destroy us, you know,' she said, her tone almost conversational. 'I have to fight back. This accident that isn't an accident . . . and when you said that Brian tried to kill himself because he thinks his birth caused my illness, and you won't have children because my madness might be genetic, I can't forgive myself – ' Her eyes filled with tears.

I kissed her cheek. 'Mum, hush now. Try to rest. We're going to fight this together.'

'Like we fought Muffie?' She smiled.

'That was just a skirmish, Mum. This time we're going to win the war.'

I went into my room and unpacked my bag. Then I walked downstairs and did the lunch dishes. I wandered outside. The garden was in its usual pristine state. I wandered back inside, pacing. Where were the neighbours? I thought. They should be here by now.

Around two-thirty the doorbell rang. I ran to answer it, not wanting to wake her.

I skidded down the four steps to the foyer and pulled open the heavy door. I grabbed for the door knocker, which, I remembered, had a tendency to bang whenever the door was opened. I caught it and heard a laugh.

It was a repairman.

He was young. He was dressed in grey workclothes and carried a toolbox. Sun glinted through the monkey-puzzle tree on to the flower bed that circled its trunk.

'Yes, what?' I was irritated.

'I have an order here to check the hydro.' He brandished a piece of paper.

'Oh.' I was distracted. 'Can you come back tomorrow morning? I don't know where the box is.'

'I do. It's in the basement.' He squeezed past me, saying over his shoulder, 'It'll only take five minutes.'

I followed him down the stairs.

'I don't know if you should be here,' I said. Brian had told me not to let anyone into the house unless he was there. 'I should check with my mother.'

'Don't bother your mother.' He winked at me. It was a sly gesture, one that didn't make me feel any better. He mumbled something. 'Brother's not here,' it sounded like.

'What?'

'Nothing. So are you the daughter?'

'Yes.' I was almost glad of someone to talk to who wasn't involved with this unholy mess.

'You from here?' He turned and smiled at me. His grin disarmed me.

'No. New York.'

'Oh gee. I've never been there. Is it as exciting as it looks in the movies?'

I shrugged. 'If you like chaos and people dying on the streets.' I sat myself on the bottom step and prepared to watch him work. The downstairs level was finished and comfortable with polished pine walls and thick carpeted floors.

He laughed, the same appreciative chuckle. 'Not much, I guess.

I like the wide open spaces, myself. How long are you here for?'

'I'm not sure.'

'Aren't you leaving a job or a husband?'

I was watching him work. He was competent and he moved fast. His tools were new and shiny and his box was filled with wires and cables and little boxes that were shiny and black. He opened the fuse box and started fiddling.

'What are you doing? You said hydro. That's hardly the water.'

'Hydro isn't water. It's power.'

'Right, I forgot. Sorry.'

'So are you leaving a husband? I'd be upset if someone as pretty as you left me and I didn't know when she was coming home.'

I smiled. Then I wondered why he was so interested.

'My father has been in an accident.'

'I'm sorry to hear that.'

He fiddled with his ear, and with a shock that felt almost physical, I noticed he was wearing a tiny ear piece. A wire sneaked down behind his ear into his collar.

'Wait a minute. Who are you? I want to see some ID.'

He looked at me and for a second the friendly mask was gone. 'Look, it's fine. What's wrong?'

'I simply want to see some ID.'

'It's in the truck.'

'So go get it.' I was standing up now, holding on to the newel post.

'Fine.' He picked up his toolbox, shut it and pushed past me on the stairs.

'Why don't you leave your toolbox? You're not a repairman, are you? There's nothing broken here, is there?'

He turned to me and smiled. But it looked like a snarl. 'You're nearly as crazy as your poor sick mother.'

I felt as though I'd been hit. I fell back against the stairwell wall. He pushed his face up to mine. 'Go home, Catherine Ramsey, back to your cute little job, and leave us to our work.'

He rushed up the stairs and out the door, shutting it behind him with a bang. I stood there for a moment, winded, not believing what I heard. It was impossible. I felt as if a layer of skin had just been peeled off me.

I made it up the stairs and, leaning against the door, double locked it and put the chain on. Then I sat down on the foyer steps and gasped for breath.

I sat there for minutes, swallowing air like water, arms wrapped around my stomach. Finally, I swallowed and breathed and swallowed and breathed.

I tried to stand up and, leaning against the wall, scrabbled crab-like up the steps on to the green carpet. I was standing then, looking around me blindly: at the inlaid hall table, the books, the porcelain, the china lamp – I had to get out of here now. Keys, car keys. I opened the drawer of the table. Two sets lay there.

The doorbell rang again and I ran to the window in the dining room to look out. Two little old ladies and a man stood there. The neighbours, at last. Thank God. I let them in, mumbled a few words of excuse, then grabbed Mother's keys and headed out the kitchen door to the driveway.

The garage door slid open easily and I backed into the lane. I knew where I was. I had my handbag. I didn't even remember picking it up.

Luckily traffic was minimal. I drove slowly and finally made it to Brian's warehouse building.

I rang his buzzer. He wasn't back yet. I remembered his ritual last time I was here. I looked around for a key, under the mat, under the broken clay pot, and then, methodically, felt along the top ledge of the little window. I found a key. It worked. I let myself in and looked around.

Brian arrived in twenty minutes. I was watching *Phil Donahue*. Television was my favourite anaesthetic. Brian had no alcohol in his cupboards.

I mentioned this to him as he stood in his doorway, looking at me huddled into his quilts and blankets in the centre of his bed.

'There is a bottle of vodka in the freezer, if you remember,' he said. 'Is Mother all right?'

'She's asleep. The neighbours showed up. Three of them, so I thought it was safe. I told them not to answer the doorbell. I'm sorry, something's happened. I needed you,' I said, but my teeth were chattering and I could hear my teeth click together.

'I'll get the vodka,' he said and disappeared. I turned back to the spectacle of fathers confessing lust for their sons' girlfriends. One had divorced his wife and married a seventeen-year-old blonde. She was pregnant.

Brian appeared with two glasses and a bottle encrusted with frost. He set it down on the bureau and handed me a shot glass.

'Skol,' he said.

I drank it and held out my arm. He refilled the glass and I drank another two ounces.

'Medicinal,' I said.

He wasn't smiling. He sat on the chair, looking at me, waiting.

I struggled into a sitting position. 'Did you get them? I want to see them.'

'First, what happened?'

I reported the strange behaviour of the repairman as accurately as I could.

My brother crouched over his shot glass, nodding.

My mind spun around. I pulled my knees closer, leaned my cheek on them.

'OK, it's not like we haven't guessed at that before. But again, why?'

'Say, for instance, that she was interested in challenging it. Then she was awarded a settlement and she used the money to help out the case in Washington. The case is bankrupt, isn't it?'

I nodded. 'It's no secret.'

'Well?' he asked. 'What's the problem? It's not so unlikely, is it?'

I shook my head slowly. 'Except challenging a will takes a lot of time and effort and money. It can take years.'

'Exactly. So all they have to do is make sure she doesn't have the time or the energy.'

I turned my head away from him, looked out the window.

'You're going to have to face it, Catherine.' Voice gentler now. 'I'm sorry. But I've been dealing with this or not dealing with it for years now. They have this thing, you know, at the CIA. It's called stress creation. It was developed by TSS, the Technical Services Staff, during the fifties and used mostly in Europe. They employed it against people they thought were likely to support the communists, against people they needed to destabilize, and against people they wanted to recruit but who wouldn't bite, till a little pressure was applied.'

'I know, you've said that before, but I keep coming back to the same point. Why would they bother? OK, they don't want this to come to court and they are doing everything they can to prevent it. They're trying to scare us away from challenging the will – but that's a lot of manpower lodged against one family. Why?'

'I'll lay odds there's another answer in there.' He pointed to the box at the door.

'What's in there?'

'It's her journal. I just had time to scan it in the car. There are two parts. The most recent is a meticulous record of every odd encounter, every letter or package that has arrived, every phone call, word for word. The second part of it is from the late fifties and the early sixties. It is a day-by-day reconstruction of what was done to her in the hospital, both times – '57 after I was born, and '62–3, the last hospitalization. That fine mind, all of that energy, has been put to use. She has remembered all of it.'

Light finally started to penetrate my thick brain. I nodded slowly. 'That's why they stepped up activity. The repairman.'

'Why?'

'Because of the Grid Room,' I said. 'Wheeler and Rauh think she was part of that series of experiments. That's why they want her. We don't have much hard evidence about what happened in the Grid Room. What do you know about it?'

'Not a lot.'

'The Grid Room was in the basement of the Allan Memorial. The experiments were an attempt to create a killing machine. They wanted to be able to implant suggestions in the brain, which, when triggered, would cause an individual to kill. It was a logical extension of psychic driving. Destroy a personality, reconstruct a new one.'

'They did that to her?'

'It never worked. Not then, and not in later experiments. You remember *The Manchurian Candidate*?'

'Sure, the movie with Frank Sinatra and Angela Lansbury about a soldier brainwashed by the communists. It was banned for years. But that's science fiction. They wanted to do that to her? To the mother of three children, a wife?'

'She would be the perfect subject. Smart, not crazy, lots to lose – '

I slid down and pulled the covers over my head.

'You do realize how much this has influenced us now, don't you?'

I nodded. 'I did before, but there was a large part of me that didn't believe it.'

'We grew up in a constant crisis. A hidden crisis, one not even the grown-ups knew about. And it keeps coming back.'

'How do you stand it?'

'The woman I loved left me because I was intolerable to be around. I have no discernible profession. I've lived for years in confusion, not trusting my own perception. As I recall you wouldn't even speak to me for a year there because, quote, I was such a loser, unquote.'

'I'm sorry.'

He patted me on the top of my head. 'You're making up for it now. Let's have a look at the journal.'

NINETEEN

First there was a bundle of letters, wrapped in ribbon. They were West's letters to Mother and I put them aside. Next was a file folder, inside it, typewritten notes, the first dated the beginning of the first week in 1983. I set the file folder aside too.

That left five notebooks. Elastic bands were wrapped around them and I started to unwind them. The elastic was rotten and snapped, then crumbled to dust in my fingers. I opened one at random and the words jumped out at me:

23 Sept 1950
I am awakened by the dream. In the dream, my son is dead. His father is returning the body to me in pieces, one limb at a time. I thought I screamed – Ian! I sit up in bed, swallowing air in gulps, as if I was suffocating. I get up, throw the covers back and move towards his room. I want to see him again. I open his door, he is gone. The room is empty. The bed is broken down, folded. It leans against the wall. His basin is there too and all his little clothes are in a bag, leaning against the bed frame. I run over to it, crouch down, and I pull the clothes out, bury my face in them and sit, wrapping my arms around the bundle of clothing as if it

were him. The shadows of his mobile move over my face in the moonlight.

This is not happening, I scream. I can't believe this. I think I have died. Night after night, Ian holds me while I shake and my sobs use up all the air in our room. We lie in our bed and try to comfort each other. My mind can't think beyond last week when he left, that tiny white body as cold as the flesh of the chicken I pull out of the refrigerator at night. Wrapped in his tiny blue pyjamas with bunny rabbits sewn carefully on the sleeves and legs, front and back, tiny stitches that my mother laboured over this winter while we waited. She knew he would be a boy, she said. How is it possible to feel such pain and live? Vicky . . . Vicky? Ian says my name – Vicky, I love you. He sings me to sleep.

I page through this. I feel guilty as if I'm doing something forbidden. There are few entries in the diary. 'Tired.' 'Exhausted.' 'Lunch at tennis club.' 'Tired. Doctor's appointment at eleven. Hope he can make me feel better.' Then manic scribbling, as if she had been given speed. I page through more – I am reading the downward spiral to the Allan Memorial and Dr Cameron. Most is written before she meets him, a few entries in the hospital itself. She is tired, overwhelmed by sadness. I skip the next little bit. Then, 1951:

27 Chesterfield Rd, Montreal, 3 June, 1952

She is a beautiful baby. She blows shining bubbles of sound. She loves music and light and colour and voices. She lies on the floor in pink coveralls and pats the floor so hard in ecstasy that her hands blur. She is a miracle to me.

When I have to go out to some thing or other that I can't put off, I leave her with the maid, to whom she is no miracle at all, and as soon as I get off the streetcar on Sherbrooke, I am running, running up Grosvenor, up the steps, fumble with the key, ring the doorbell, and when she sees me she breaks into a clogged weeping that does not stop until I have her in my arms, rocking and singing for fifteen minutes. I cry too.

27 Chesterfield, 26 November 1956

Please, Brian, don't cry any more . . . I can't stand it another night. I have to sleep. This house is dark and empty and your calls echo off the walls and through my eardrums. Don't cry. Don't cry any more. I'll start to scream and drown you out if you keep on crying. Please go to sleep, don't cry . . . I stumble towards your room. The others will wake, are waking, and I will have three of you to work with and Ian is away again. I switch on the table lamp and put it on the floor so the light will not startle you. You toss your body back and forth, arch your back and wail. I walk to your bed and check your diaper – I try to speak, to soothe, but I start muttering and then I'm yelling and I pick you up and shake you and you yell back scared to death, and I drop you in your tangled blankets. My God, what am I doing?

I drop to my hands and knees and crawl down the hallway. I am an animal. I am so very tired. Ian is never here. The maid is always sick and at her sister's house. Ian's mother torments me and I have no friends left. I hate this city, its cold and its snobbery and its stupidity and distaste for anything it hasn't seen for a hundred years. Oh Brian, I love you, please stop crying. Please let me breathe. I am so afraid of what is going to happen and I can't see any way of stopping it.

I crawl back into your room, where you are trapped in your sheets, and lift you up. You are afraid of me and your baby hands cover your face. I change your diapers and smooth out your bedding. I sit with you in the old rocker and I nurse you until your head nods and your eyes close and you are asleep, when I carefully lay you in your bed, on your back, just like the nurse taught me.

So when I leave the room, switching off the light, closing the door quietly behind me, I clutch at my stomach and drop to my knees again. I make it to the bathroom, and vomit into the bowl. I am afraid. I could have killed you, I was so angry. I could have killed you. And I wonder, in my shame, had I killed the first one? He says I did sometimes when he is angry with me. Could he know something I don't?

The next few months are blank.

27 Chesterfield, 18 October 1957
I am free.

But I am different. I am changed. There is much I have forgotten. I try not to be frightened about this. I try just to be a good mother and a good wife. I work at smiling. I rest at night.

I had to write so much in the hospital I began to hate the feel of my hand holding a pen. I didn't want to use this way of expressing myself. Some days, though, when I am in full possession of myself, I am sad because I've lost that ability. Ewen stole that from me. Writing is imprisonment for me now.

But I have to say, I am not insane. It is taking me so long to recover from what he does to me in there. And I am so lonely. I have no friends. Everyone shies away from me; I have to find new friends all the time. Then my story catches up with me and people are afraid of me and start to make excuses. Then I don't want to force myself on them, so I bow out. It is terrible and I will have this the rest of my life. It is a curse to be crazy. *No*! I am not! It is a curse; better to have a real illness, to have cancer, multiple sclerosis, something so that people don't fear you. What will become of my children in this narrow little city? They are marked like Cain and still not into double digits in age.

27 Chesterfield, 1 November 1957
It was Hallowe'en last night and all the children went out into the street. I couldn't remember last year's costumes so when I suggested that Ross and Catherine be ghosts there was a wail that they had been ghosts already, *Mother*! There is so much I've forgotten that I have to tread very carefully with them. They hate it when I stay in bed all day, have Frances cook dinner and can't remember Cathy's teacher's name. I see her off to school and go to

bed until noon. I can't remember anything of what happened last year. Is this normal? Nothing comes up. I must find a way.

27 Chesterfield, 16 November 1957
I have started to wake up at dawn. My body aches and my eyes don't see very well then. I dress in ski clothes and I leave the house with just a glass of juice and a piece of bread in my stomach. Then I walk. I walk for two hours, up the street, past the boulevards and the crescent, into the little streets behind, and then I am on the mountain and the city is spread beneath me, glass and stone office buildings and church towers. And then I walk all the way to St Joseph's Oratory, where the Catholics walk up 282 stairs on their knees. I try to run up before anyone is making a pilgrimage. I run up and down, up and down.

There was a first snow last week and I walked in it until it was time for breakfast and I was late and everyone was worried. I must get better. I must remember.

27 Chesterfield, 26 November 1957
I telephoned Mother for some of her recipes. My God, they taste foul. Will I still be able to walk when the snow comes? It is late this year.

27 Chesterfield, 28 November 1957
I have started to do callisthenics in my room after my nap.

27 Chesterfield, 4 December 1957
I am getting better. Ian is so patient with me. He is like an angel. Do I need? What do I want? Is there anything, anything at all he can do? I wonder if he feels guilty. It wasn't his fault. I was exhausted and lonely and I lost my grip. That's all. I'm all right. I'll be all right. I'm not sick any more.

27 Chesterfield, 6 December 1957
It occurred to me this morning that if I wanted to reclaim my lost memory, I should try to remember everything. What happened in the hospital, what happened . . . Ian suggested today that we all move to the country. I agreed. A new place, for a new start.

27 Chesterfield, 13 December 1957
Christmas is upon us. I am trying to remember what happened, but I can't. There is a great wash of blankness there. It must be shock treatments. I went to the library and looked them up in the medical dictionary. They erase memory. And what about all those drugs? Memory is like glints of starlight in a pitch-black sky for me. I must make those stars expand.

27 Chesterfield, 17 December 1957
My God, I remembered something from the hospital on my walk this morning. All morning I added detail to the memory.

I remember walking out into traffic in my coat one afternoon. I had escaped and I stood, swaying on the sidewalk, trying to make myself plunge into the path of an oncoming truck. It was raining and the streets were filled with slush and I had on wet bedroom slippers. Did this happen? Did this really happen?

Why didn't I do it? The children, of course. But Ian. I wanted to stay for Ian. There is something between us that is so very strong, even after all this pain.

I must find something, anything, to do with my mind. It must be trained to something. What shall I do? What shall I teach myself? I must try to find something. Something that will stretch me.

On another note, I went to a party at the regiment last night – my first.

27 Chesterfield, 20 January 1958
It is not as if I have forgotten this private project. Christmas eats time. I have been very busy packing the house for the move to Foster. I have been exercising, mostly just walking, every morning, including Christmas, and there are people now who I see and we smile, and sometimes even wave at each other.

But it is more. I remember something. A huge chunk of memory, so bizarre that I can hardly believe that it happened to me. Yet it is so real. I remember three days, four days in the hospital. I have been digging away at it like a pig at a truffle or whatever is their most delicious food. I dig and dig and dig and finally, the jewel, the truffle of memory, is exposed to me. Can willpower alone restore my memory to me? If it can, I will have it all back, even the bad parts.

It is summer, 1957. I think it is July. The air is very warm. I am waiting in my room in the new wing and this young man comes for me and I sit down in a wheelchair. I have still not seen Ewen. He is busy, they say, as if I am asking for more than is due me. What is wrong with me? No one asks this. Yesterday an orderly came for me and took me to a small room, a converted butler's pantry, and a dark thin man, whose name still escapes me, welcomed me and strapped things on to me and asked me questions all afternoon. Three hours of silly questions. Then someone took me to a laboratory and they strapped lots more electrodes on to me and they asked me more questions and a needle-like pencil described a pattern on a piece of paper. Then, still without explanation, or how are you feeling, I was deposited back in my room. None of my questions were answered.

So the next day, I am wheeled silently back to the butler's pantry where the dark man waits with a needle and he plunges it into my arm. What is it? I say. He smiles patronizingly. 'It's your treatment,' he says, and he switches on a large tape recorder on his desk. 'But I still haven't seen Ewen,' I say. 'Oh, he read your answers last night and prescribed this.' I say, 'Well, that must be all right then,' but I am worried.

And while I worry, tiny cracks in the ceiling radiate rainbows in colours I have never seen before. Suddenly they become natural stress lines that measure the vibrations of the universe. The tape recorder whirs and the room trembles. The sound is a seashore of intense sensation. I reach my hand out towards it.

My mouth forms in a perfect O. My hand! Why, I have never looked at my hand before! Look at the bones, skin and bones – oh, it was an X-ray! I look down at the table.

Ewen comes in then. The door shuts behind him with a loud creak, and he stands looking down at me. '*Lassie,*' he rumbles. 'I want the truth now.' And I nod and say, '*Yes*, of course.'

And he smiles and I melt in the sweetness of his smile.

Write, they had said, before they – ! The door opening was a fissure in the universe. And sadness follows. I start crying big tears, plopping down on the pages. I miss him before he even goes.

I stare at the mark my tears made on the paper. Their voices rumble down at me.

The sound of thunder. '*Write, Lassie*!' he rumbles. 'Write your life for us.' And the elegant dark man leans over, his entire body a curve, a punctuation of training and discipline, and *crack*! turns on the tape recorder.

Now how could I write with this hand? I giggle. Honestly, they are the silliest people in the world. Write with an X-ray hand? Which part of me would actually do the writing? I move the X-ray hand towards the paper.

Aaah. The texture. Rough, like whorled sandpaper, like unsanded wood. I move my palm back and forth over it. Ouch, it hurts. Write on this? I pick up the pen, my bones and tendons showing clearly through the skin. The sound magnified, a rushing in my ears, a waterfall, a whirlpool, the sound of a million angels breathing. I sit, pen in hand, frozen, mouth open, listening to the sound.

How can I write? What can I write? How ridiculous.

I will write about that. The ridiculousness of writing when so many other things are happening. I touch my sweater. So soft! A pearl pin has been placed in the lapel of my blouse. The tiny hard shiny surfaces are astonishing. I sit feeling the pin for a good long time.

Well. Down to business.

Writing her life. Let's see. What part? What had he said? 'Your children, lassie; you let slip to the puir young doctorr that you hated your children. Tell us about that.'

Did he sound angry? No, I didn't think he sounded angry, right then. Though he was definitely angry I was here again, wasn't he? He was. I thought back on his face, his blue eyes with the tiny black pupils, yes, angry. For he had cured me before. He was busy, he said, too busy to sit talking to me. Write, he said.

All right.

Well, fine. I sit, pen in hand, bent over the paper, and write. The scratching is so loud!

'Sorry, doctors. Today, my brain is on vacation.' And then I lose myself in a gale of giggles.

The next morning, my body feels stiff and old. I dress with difficulty, pulling my clothes on awkwardly. Fastening my pin takes ages.

My eyes in the mirror are dull and my skin whitish grey. They have taken away my compact, so I can't fix my face. I look around. The world is featureless and flat. The glory of yesterday is gone, vanished in a flash. My night dreams were filled with dark leering figures.

There are three of them in the room, watching me closely as I slowly move from the wheelchair to the chair facing them. I lift my head and face them.

'What did you give me yesterday – it was worse than the strongest martini I ever drank!' I say. The effort of making so poor a joke exhausts me. 'What do you want?' I say. They continue to stare. The tray is in front of me.

'Lassie, we'll try again. Give her another thousand micrograms.'

My sleeve is rolled up, and I wince as the needle enters my vein.

'You know, actually, I think this is wrong,' I say. 'I'm too tired, please, not today.'

He stiffens, leans over the table and gazes into my eyes. I am hypnotized, a deer in his sights.

'This is a stronger dose, lassie. We must get to the root of the problem. You must make an effort today. Write about your family, write about your children. How do you feel about them? Tell us, please. We need to make you better, but you must help us.'

They sit and watch me as I sit, my head bowed, exhausted beyond measure.

'I can't answer any more questions, not today, please.'

They are remorseless. I feel guilty. The doctors know about what I feel about Brian and Ross and Cathy. They are avenging angels. What can I do to please these men?

I wait. They wait. I feel my flesh begin to melt. My bones are melting.

'I'm melting,' I say, panicked. 'I'm melting. Don't you see? I'm melting!'

'That's right, lassie. Your inhibitions are melting, melting right in front of us. You are becoming who you really are. Tell us, talk to us, tell us, please.'

I look up at him. He is towering in front of me, a giant of a man, a huge stone statue, like one of the stone giants on Easter Island.

'Everyone hates me, Doctor,' I say. 'You hate me. Why else would you do this to me?'

I clamp my hands over my ears. 'No, stop them, stop them from screaming at me!'

'Who is screaming?' he purrs, a giant male cat.

'They are. My children. They're screaming. My husband, Ian, is screaming at me. My mother-in-law, everyone.' I break down in huge racking sobs and my limbs began to jerk. I am embarrassed by my body, but I can't stop. I can't sit still. I am zigging and zagging around in my chair, like a hamster in a cage. 'You're killing me. Why are you doing this?'

'Write, lassie. Write.' And they leave the room.

'*No*!' I scream at their departing backs. '*No, no, no, no, no*!'

The room is terrifying. The cracks widen and loom down at me. There is no colour, only grey and black and more black. The table jumps at me. Everything is scary. And all around me are faces, many faces, distorted and horrifying. Flesh melts from bones, dripping on to the table. 'Who are you?' I whisper. Teeth chattering, I pick up the pen and begin to write, speaking each word written into the tape recorder, hoping only that the wall of words will protect me from the terror.

The next day when they come for me, I hide in the bathroom. I can hardly stand up. I don't care if I live or die. I just don't want another injection.

I sit, back braced against the bathtub, legs stretched out, feet pressed against the door, forcing it closed.

'Go away,' I shout. 'Leave me alone!' And they leave.

He comes for me. I can hear his voice whispering outside the door. Finally, I release the door, scrambling somehow to my feet. He comes in and sits on the side of the bathtub, smiling at me. 'Yesterday was so much better. So much – we have something to work on. Come out now.'

He walks me up and down the corridor, soft words echoing in my ear. He is trying to persuade me to take another injection.

'I don't want to. It makes me feel like dying. I thought you cared about me.'

'I do, Victoria. We all do. I've spoken to Ian and to your mother-in-law. We all want you to get better. I've said we are making great strides, great, great progress. Just one more.'

So I go once more to the room and hold out my bruised arm. And then I do it the next day too. And again. This continues for fourteen days.

TWENTY

8 Church Street, Foster, PQ, 28 January 1958

I am remembering it all now. I lie in my bedroom in the afternoons, while Brian naps, and I write it down. The memories are full of life, more real than our routine of school, meals, naps, playtimes here, at home. I thank God we are out of the city, in this frozen little village, in this little cottage.

There was the morning that they didn't come for me. I was actually bruised all over, from where I had fallen during the treatments and been unable to get up. My body was aching. All I wanted was silence. A nurse came in and she asked for my arm. I held it to myself for a moment, then let her pry it out from under the covers. She pricked me and then patted my arm, tucked it back under the covers and left. A gorgeous warmth trickled through me and I fell into a dreamless sleep.

When I woke, a huge white breast pillowed my face. A cup of hot sugared tea was being poured down my throat. I felt very small and very young in the nurse's arms. I was crying, caught in the grip of an overwhelming sorrow.

I grabbed the nurse's arm, choking. 'Am I all right? Is it over?' Is what over? I thought.

The nurse nodded. 'You can sleep now. They'll knock those ideas out of your head.'

'What ideas?' I fell back on to the pillows. 'Where am I?'

What terrible thing have I done? I thought. What terrible, terrible thing? My entire body ached, every joint, every tendon, every ligament, every muscle group. Each of them strained and racked with conflicting energy. My body was separate from me, twitching and jerking all of its own volition.

How long had I been here? I turned my head, eyelids twitching, towards the window. The trees were changing from green to orange to red and some of them had lost their leaves. Autumn. How had I got here?

All afternoon I strained to remember things. I did not sleep. When they brought me supper: scrambled eggs, tomatoes, and jello with tiny marshmallows in it, I was sitting up in the dark, my mind actively sifting and ordering information. The orderly switched on the light. I spelled out his name on his nametag.

'It is October now, isn't it, Jean-Luc?' I asked him.

Surprised, he nodded, swung over the tray and laid my food out.

'What is your last name?' I said.

'Beaudreau.'

'Français?'

He nodded.

'Well, *peut-être . . . je peux . . . essayer de parler le français dans les après-midis*?' I said. '*C'est possible*?' God, how I wanted to stay in this normal place in my mind, where I could talk to someone and even speak French to him.

He nodded again.

'It's not . . . much use if you don't talk back, you know.'

He smiled at me. '*J'pense pas, madame. J'aimerais vous aider avec votre français. Comme d'habitude, ça n'intéresse personne.*'

'*Ça m'intéresse* – a deal?'

'*Oui.*' He gave me another tentative smile.

Every morning I waited for breakfast. Those who were scheduled for the machine only got a piece of bread and butter and one cup of tea. Every morning I got one cup of tea and one piece of white bread and salty butter. I could barely choke it down. Then I sat, staring into space, trying to breathe evenly, choking down the sour taste of my fear.

When Jean-Luc arrived, I could hardly wait for the sedating needle. And when Ewen came, I would not meet his eyes or those of anyone else. I kept my eyes on Jean-Luc and watched fixedly as he found a vein and slid the hypodermic into it. Then I would close my eyes and will myself into unconsciousness.

Every time it was the same. I would wake up, head aching to the sight of the same nurse jolting me awake with tea, giving me pills that prevented me from sleeping through the afternoon. Then I would work on remembering. I found a tiny appointment book with a tiny pen attached that they left in my purse. I stuck it between the mattress and the bed frame and I counted days, made notations about treatments. When I could manage it.

One time, the seventh day, I think it might have been, though my notes aren't exact and time was more elastic than ever, the sedation did not take effect the way it had before.

I was awake when they wheeled me into the room. But not awake enough to open my eyes or move my mouth. I could hear their voices over me. Jean-Luc's sullen and full of doubt. Ewen's crisp and commanding. The technician, cynical, full of himself. They didn't even discuss me, just moved me about, attached wires; I felt the cool of the jelly being smeared on my temples. I couldn't move.

Suddenly a flash of light engulfed me and I screamed at the top of my lungs. Then another flash, then another. With each flash of light, a great jolt slammed me until I thought my bones would smash and the marrow leak out of me for the dogs under the table to smack their lips at and suck on till I was gone completely down their throats.

Geometric patterns flashed in front of my eyes – brilliant colours, and streams of ideas, then nothing, blankness. I ceased to breathe. I fell into a deep dark pit. I was gone.

When I woke, it was much later. I was writhing in the bed, moaning and weeping. I knew what it was to be dead now. Terrified that I was dying, I struggled out of bed, took a few steps and collapsed in a flood of tears. I was dead. I couldn't tell the distance between the bed and the floor, between my foot and the floor. I had lifted a leg to take a step and the distance from my foot to the floor looked endless, hundreds of yards away. That proved I was dead.

I paused, flooded with horror. I could not remember my own name.

I stared up at the stranger who gently reached under my arms and picked me up. I opened my mouth to ask him something, but no words came out. I had forgotten how to speak.

I can't help myself. I page through the diaries until I find the one I'm looking for. 1963. Her last visit to the Allan Memorial. The summer of 1962, when I was eleven and remember her best, the summer we had joined forces, become friends. Then, in the winter of that year, I lost her again. Her writing is very difficult to decipher, spindly letters, no punctuation. I pick through it slowly.

Lakeside Road, Foster, PQ, 15 June 1963
All right. This is an enormous effort, but it is worth it. I can do it. It is possible. I can remember.

Ian rescued me. I owe him my life. It is that simple. He risked ridicule and worse to come in and get me. Something was not right. That stern, strict, terrified man broke out of his self-imposed prison and rescued me.

I look like hell. My hair is grey. I have deep dark circles around my eyes. My children are gone. I may get them back if I am good enough. That's what they are telling me. I am thin in some places, fat in others. I must get better.

I will never, *never* go back in there. I would rather die than go back in there.

I can remember all of the first day I woke up in there. I had a fight with Ewen, screaming at him that I wasn't ill, that I wasn't going to have my brain fried with his electrodes, that all I wanted was to go to school, that I was going to have no more drugs.

I was restrained and held down on the bed while he leaned closer to me. My arms were strapped to the bed.

'Don't you want to get better, lassie? Don't you want me to help you?'

I spat in his face, and as he stood there, wiping my spittle off his face, his grey eyes darkened. Then he said, 'You are very naughty, lassie.'

'I'm not an animal, Ewen. Nor am I sick. I refuse treatment.'

'Your husband has given his consent. It's too late.' Angry, he turned on his heel and walked out of the room, the usual entourage following him.

I don't remember what came next, but I remember waking up. I remember it so clearly, I wonder about their drugs and their tests and their treatments, I wonder about memory and its selectivity. I wonder why I can remember waking up and I can't remember someone giving me a shot to knock me out after Ewen left the room.

Here goes. This is very difficult but it is necessary. I find that every time I remember what happened to me, I am strengthened. But the effort is substantial. I am going to have to give myself some huge treat. I am thinking of a new putter.

My eyes were gummed shut. I tried to open them, but somehow I couldn't. My body would not obey my mind. *Open*! I commanded and waited. Nothing. I was there, trapped in immovable flesh, wide awake inside a body that had gone as inert as any man-made material.

They had drugged me again – I could sense it. Or rather, not sense it. I couldn't feel anything at all.

I lay there for a moment, thinking. My mind was dull and slow. Then, praying, with enormous concentration and effort, I brought one arm up to my eyes, scraped thickly, ineptly, paws scrabbling at furry lids. I felt something wet. What could it be? Tears? No, nothing flowed. I just felt damp slimy material. I thought, prodded. And then I realized. I was touching my own eyeball.

I screamed. Something echoed dully. It was a hollow groan,

more of a growl really. I froze, ears alert, waited. Heard nothing; nothing moved, nothing breathed. Seconds ticked by and slowly I realized that the growl was mine.

My mind skittered into hell.

Where was I? What had they done?

I reached out my right hand, the one that had touched my eye. Nothing. I lowered it. I felt a thick slimy surface. It was soft, padded. I felt along the length of my body. The sound of my hand dragging along the floor was loud and it surrounded me. Time widened, then narrowed.

It seemed to take an hour to find my knees, my feet.

This time they had slowed down time.

I was lying on a mat, dressed only in a hospital nightgown, and I couldn't see anything at all. My mouth widened to shape a scream. Then I lost consciousness.

It must have been a few hours later or it could have been minutes. The door creaked open and a wide square of light fell on to my body. I was instantly awake. Two men stood at the entrance and looked. I stared at them greedily, though I could barely make them out against the light. Their appearance meant I was still on this earth and alive.

'What do you think? Is she ready?' came a voice. The sound was dead, no echo.

'Let's see,' said the other.

I felt a foot insinuate itself under my body. I was rolled over on to my back. Something was strapped on to my arm above my elbow and I felt pressure. I turned my eyes to the side.

One man was short, the one squatting over me. The other man was tall, a long thin drink of water, as Ian would say. I had never seen either of them on the upper floors of the hospital. I looked away from them.

The room looked big, big enough to get lost in if there was no light whatsoever. It was black that reflected no light. The walls had been covered with a slick material and the floor had been treated the same way. Something black covered the window frame and I could see that the glass of the casement window had been painted. The ceiling was very low, barely six feet. It too was black. Before the men came in, I thought I was imprisoned in a very small closet.

'Ya, she's all right.' The tall thin man had an English accent. The squat man nodded.

'You want her now?' he asked.

'May as well. Need a baseline sometime.'

'Fully conscious?'

A snort of laughter. 'Now, what do you think?'

'You want her to walk?'

'Not unassisted, obviously.'

'Obviously.'

This rapid exchange had been whispered above my head. The short man turned to me and I saw him draw a flat leather case from his jacket pocket. He flicked it open and lifted out a full hypodermic. Tapped the cylinder a couple of times.

'A few ccs ought to wake her enough to get her up.'

'Get on with it, you pervert.'

The squat man turned back to the body, drew my arm out from under me and tapped a vein.

Time ticked by and I lay there looking at him. He had a big nose. I could the pores on his nose and they were huge. He had funny eyebrows that were spiked upwards and red in colour. He stared down at me, looking into my eyes.

I felt like moving and I stretched my arms and legs. I raised my fists to my eyes and rubbed at the thick sticky mucus that had crusted on my eyelids and my cheeks. He shook my shoulder. I raised my head slightly, then flopped over on to my stomach.

'Come on, lady. Time for your psychological stress evaluation.'

'What?' I said, but it didn't sound like a word, not a real word.

He repeated himself, then leaned down and lifted me in one motion.

I remember my arms flopping limply across his back as he carried me out of the room.

A thin coat of whitewash had been sloppily applied to the old cement corridor. The stink of 200 years of old house met my nostrils.

My head hung over his shoulders, my hair obscured my vision. But not completely. There was a sign: 'The Voice Analysis Room'. We entered. It looked like it had been made out of the old furnace room and had been plastered and painted to look clean. Stacks of equipment I didn't recognize covered one wall and a glassed-in booth stood in front of it.

The stocky man placed me on the wooden chair in the booth, handcuffed my wrists to the arms of the chair and placed a set of earphones over my ears. I tried to take them off, but the effort was too great. I dropped my arms, slumped in my seat.

He hooked me up to the machine that was bolted to the floor under the chair. He brushed off the nightgown, which fell to my waist, and hooked a microphone around my neck. Then he taped the wires to the back of my neck and back.

The two men started out of the room.

'You forgot to pull up her nightdress.'

'She won't notice.'

'I will.' The tall man came back, pulled my nightgown up to my chin, then fastened it.

The man in the booth started to recite questions. They were the usual ones, questions I had answered over and over ever since I had entered Ewen's care.

'What are your parents' first names?'

A mumble. I still couldn't form a real word.

He repeated the question.

Nothing. This time I couldn't even mumble.

Jones turned to Graff. 'How much did you give her?'

'Five ccs.'

'Double it.'

'What?'

'Now!'

I'm sure that the drug is why I remember everything that came next.

He stumbled towards me, another syringe in his hand. My flesh was unresisting. I was two people, the dirty puppet who sat immobile and the person who observed her.

Slowly, my eyes brightened and my back straightened and my mind became razor sharp.

'What do you want?' I made my voice crisp and filled with contempt. Graff winced. He walked over to Jones's desk. Started sifting the files.

Jones repeated the question. 'What were your parents' first names?'

'Janet and Teddy,' I answered. My voice was sharp.

'That's fine. On what street did you grow up?'

'Queen Street.' Another sharp answer. 'What am I doing here?' I asked.

'We're just testing.'

'Testing what?' I picked at the handcuffs. 'Why have you got me hooked up like this? God damn it. I knew this place was bad, but I didn't think it was this bad. I want to leave. I want to go home, *I want to leave*!'

Graff was already half-way into the booth, needle at the ready. He plunged it into the bare arm while I shouted at him. He moved behind me and waited till I ran out of breath and couldn't shout any more. Then I lost consciousness.

'*Mrs Ramsey.*' They was using the microphone that went directly into the booth. I jerked upright.

'We just need to ask you a few questions. Get things straight. Is that right?' He sounded soothing and gentle.

There he taped a gadget on my upper thigh and lower trunk so that the thing rode over the centre of my hip joint. The technician then strapped to my arm a miniature transmitter, antennae like an insect's, smaller than the size of a packet of cigarettes.

The voice was deafening through the speaker.

'*Sit upright in the chair!*' I struggled upright.

There was a short pause while they both scribbled.

'*Stand up!*'

'*Clap hands!*'

'Touch your right toe!'

'Raise your left arm to shoulder level and wiggle your fingers on your left arm!'

The list began again and the questions went on for what seemed like hours. Finally they stopped, turned off all the machines, came over to me, both of them tall and short, stern and grinning.

The questions were over, the measurements calibrated, they told me. They had baseline, they said, and they shook hands. The only thing holding me upright in the chair was the harness of wires and straps.

This procedure went on the next day and the next and the next until I lost track of the days. It couldn't have been more than two weeks. They measured my voice, my movements, at every hour of the day, under every dosage of whatever drugs they gave me. They were looking for my weakest time of the day, they told me, when my resistance was completely collapsed. Then they would fire a whole battery of drugs at me, breaking me completely, they told me, the squat guy grinning widely, hopefully. Only then would the great doctor come to see me, only then would they start to rebuild me. Then, I would be a whole new person, better and happy.

The tall one squeezed my shoulder. 'Fortitude, Mrs Ramsey. It will all be worth it in the end.'

I didn't have the strength to shake his hand off my shoulder.

The next few days disappeared in a fog of drugs and voices chattering at me – my voice, Ewen's voice, Ian's voice. Then, they brought me back to the Grid Room and started measuring me again.

I pushed the diaries away from me and stood up, paced the room. Then, feeling pulled back, I knelt by the bed and paged through the one I had been reading.

Somehow, my mother had kept returning to consciousness and somehow memorized the process. She had dates and times. She had procedures marked out. And over a period of a year, she had recalled much of what had been done to her. I read about her pain and her fear and her nightmares, constant nightmares, her fear of sleep, her fear of medication, her fear of doctors and finally, I understood her.

My father had rescued her. He had broken in one day with his brother and taken her out. The staff had stood in the hallway of the old Allan house and forsworn responsibility, but he, holding his exhausted, skeletal wife in his arms, had shouted back at them and they had let her go.

He had brought her home to Foster and laid her in bed. Our French Canadian maid took care of her, rousing her every morning from her stupor, for my mother was afraid to sleep and refused to take even aspirin, and forcing food down her throat. Then she would put a record on Mother's hi-fi set and play her favourite sonatas for her, little pieces of music. Symphonies were too much for her nervous system.

Then lunch, then a rest, then he would come home early, dismiss the maid and feed Mother. After dinner he talked and read to her until she fell asleep. This went on for months.

I lived with Muffie and hardly saw Mother for the first six months. Ross was at boarding school, and for those first six months, Brian lived in the village with friends.

All this she had written down, along with her first shuddering attempts to play golf, drive a car, manage a stove, make herself some tea, hold a conversation, shop. All of it. She chronicled the things that she had forgotten. She built a scaffold of events that her memory could walk over, until what she had memorized became indistinguishable from what she remembered.

From the point of view of Tom Wheeler and Joe Rauh, these diaries were pure undiluted gold. I wanted to drink myself into a stupor and never come up for air.

PART 4

AUGUST 1988

TWENTY-ONE

The phone rang the next morning at six. I rolled over in Brian's bed and dragged the receiver off the hook. Even in a half-sleep, I was aware of the danger behind the ring. I began to understand the tentative nature of my mother's telephone voice. What used to irritate me now made me ashamed of myself.

Too many emotions before I was even awake.

'Yes,' I snarled. I might as well be impolite while being harassed.

'Catherine! I called your mother's house and Brian answered. He told me where you were.'

'Here I am.' I still had no idea who it was.

'It's Tom!'

I sat up in bed. 'What's happened?'

'It's Joe. He had a bad heart attack yesterday afternoon, about three hours after you left.'

'Oh God. Oh no. Is he going to be all right?'

'Yeah, we think he's going to make it through. But he's been sidelined. And he'll face a long recovery.'

Hospitals, my life was being spent in hospitals.

'What does that mean to the case?'

'Well, we've had an interlocutory appeal from the CIA.'

'What's that?'

'It's a motion to seek a court of appeals review of the decision before the trial.'

'That's strange. What does it mean?'

'It means the trial Judge, Penn in this case, must, in effect, certify in advance that his decision may be wrong, and the court of appeals must agree to hear the case. No interlocutory appeals have been granted in the last two years and there have been thousands of court orders issued over that period, as you can imagine.'

'So it's bogus?'

'Another delaying tactic. Complete trash. But it's meant a one-week continuance to decide if the section in the legal code applies to this case. Worse, it prevents final discovery and a trial date.'

'One week means two or three or four.'

'Precisely.'

'What else has been happening?' For some reason I was reluctant to tell him about Mother's decision.

'Lots. Harvey Weinstein impressed the guys at *60 Minutes* so much that they've scheduled a piece on it. Remember, he's the psychiatrist son of one of our plaintiffs.

'That is so great. How does the team feel about that?'

'Well, secretly pleased. But more pleased that Weinstein found something fairly amazing in Cameron's papers at the American Psychiatric Association.'

'What?' I heard the sound of papers rustling.

'Cameron, in pre-1956 papers, admitted that he conducted experiments with sleeplessness, disinhibiting agents and hypnosis to achieve, and I'm quoting here, "the extraordinary political conversions that we have seen, particularly in the Iron Curtain countries".'

Ice formed around my heart.

'And Mark called.'

'Oh.' I could barely register the information.

'I told him that there had been a family emergency. Has he called?'

'No.'

'Brian told me they think your father may make it. How are you doing?'

A lump rose in my throat.

'All right,' I mumbled.

He waited.

'I may have something, but I don't want to talk about it,' I said.

'Something we need?'

'The phones are bugged, Tom.'

It was his turn to be silent. He was better at it than I was. The distance between us looped and sung.

'Brian doesn't think the accident was an accident. He thinks it was deliberate. He saw it. The guys on the dock were stunned. The equipment is never loose, always locked. They don't want to injure themselves and they all know the power in the winches. I want us to be safe now, Tom. Do something. You can, and Joe certainly can.'

'Catherine.' His voice was soothing.

'Look, you bureaucratic fuck,' I cut in, 'I have something you need and you have something I need. Get busy.' I slammed down the phone.

It rang again immediately. I snatched it up. 'That's all I'm going to say,' I shouted.

There was a pause.

'Catherine?' Mark's voice was enquiring.

'I'm sorry. It's been hell.'

'Why didn't you call?'

'I'm sorry. I was shocked and frightened.'

'That's what I'm for. To hang on to in these circumstances.'

'I'm –' I stopped. I was damned if I was going to apologize again. 'Aren't you sick of being a male nurse?'

'I'm going to ignore that. Is your father all right? Are you all right?'

I sighed.

'Should I come up there?'

'No.' My answer was immediate and unthinking.

'Well, I guess I understand my place in your life now.' His voice was slow and sad. I couldn't stand it.

'Mark, I'm under extraordinary pressure – I can't even begin to bring you up to date.'

'Why not? Why doesn't it feel good for you to bring me up to date, as you call it? I'm not your boss, I'm not someone you're supposed to report to. I'm your best friend. Unless, of course, Tom Wheeler is your new best friend.'

Jealousy on top of everything else was just about the last straw. Without saying anything else, I gently put the phone back on to the receiver, lay back on the bed and stared at the ceiling.

The phone rang again. I let it ring this time. Finally, I got out of bed, took a shower and got dressed.

I called my mother's house, but there was no answer. Brian must have spent last night there. He probably went with her to the hospital this morning. I'd better get over there myself.

What to do with the diaries? Carry them with me? There were so many. I could jam most of them into my briefcase. I hunted through Brian's closets and, at the back of one, found a dusty old knapsack. I transferred everything to the knapsack and ignoring the car, decided to hike to the hospital. I was completely and totally paranoid. Everyone on the street looked suspicious and I took an odd route to make sure no one was following me.

When I got to the intensive care unit at the hospital, Brian and Mother were nowhere to be seen. I found a chair and sat watching my father.

He was still suspended upside down in some sort of steel and truss contraption, and, I was willing to bet, still held in unconscious suspension by a chemical network of painkillers and tranquillizers. A young man sat near him, clipboard in hand, checking the instruments one by one, in a steady stream of eye and head movement. At least Father was being watched.

By one of us. The phrase popped into my head. Paranoia had permeated my mind. I trusted no one. I set myself to watch the watcher.

My poor father. Over the past months in Washington, whenever I had time to reflect on our family, I had wondered how we had survived all this. Every time I thought this thought, he had stepped forward. He had been the rock around which we all flowed, mostly hating him, or deliberately misunderstanding him, seeing him as an impediment, an obstacle, old-fashioned, soon to be obsolete. While all the time, he was standing up against this giant force that inexorably ate at all of us.

He was a fighter and a drinker. He was the centre of any social situation, able to draw a belly laugh out of a recluse, make any woman smile with pleasure. He was also a domestic tyrant, washing children's fingerprints off white walls when he got home from work.

As he aged, the terror he invoked grew to a gentler fear and a growing respect. For often enough his outrageous opinion turned out to be right.

We were amazed by him in retirement. He sat for a year, staring into space, then one day, picked himself up and slowly, methodically, began to reorganize each of the major charitable organizations in Vancouver. We grew used to quavering or stentorian female voices on the phone. Daddy's matrons. His girlfriends were older, stouter and wore moustaches. Instead of cocktail lounges, they patronized the silent offices of the Red Cross, Meals on Wheels, the Western Institute for the Deaf, alternately dying of boredom or scrambling to meet some dire emergency.

As a child, I had seen him stronger, and taller than he, in fact, was. I was terrified by him and hated him for not loving me. I had stumbled, furious and hurt, out of his house as soon as I could, swearing to make him see how tough and independent I was, to show him that I was as strong as he was. No, by God, I was stronger. I would go further, see more things, love more people, and finally make more money than he ever did.

Now I knew his strength had been necessary to haul my mother out of her terrors and her shakes and her induced illnesses. Necessary to keep going, to pretend to us and to the rest of our world that nothing much was happening inside our moat, all the while trying to stave off a complete meltdown of the core, our mother.

I adored him. My defences gave way and I loved him as I had never been able to before. I admired him and wanted to do anything

I could to help him. I could barely see through the tears that obscured my vision, but I vowed to sit here to see that nothing else would ever harm him in his entire life.

'Catherine!'

I turned, brushed my eyes.

'Hi, Brian!'

'We've been talking to the doctors.' Brian put his hand on my shoulder. 'They've scheduled four operations. The first one is in half an hour. They're going to rebuild his face. They think they can save one eye and some hearing.'

I buried my face in his shirt. He patted my head. 'He'll come through, Catherine. He always has.'

I nodded. 'Where is she?'

'Filling in forms. She's in fighting shape. She wants to talk to us.'

'Good.'

'How are you doing?'

'Better. A bit up and down. Not a bit, a lot.'

'Good girl, just ride them. They'll even out as you get used to it. I promise. I had a couple of years to work all this out.'

'Yoo-hoo!' Her voice from down the hall.

We trotted obediently down to her.

'I've borrowed Dr Hanesh's office. We'll be private there.' She winked at us and led us into a glass-enclosed cubicle, filled with framed diplomas. I lay down on the couch. She sat behind the doctor's desk. Brian sprawled in a leather chair.

'What would you like me to do, Catherine?'

I had closed my eyes and they popped open. 'I don't know.'

'What would your lawyer friends like?'

'What do you mean?'

'Don't fence with me.'

'They want you to testify to all the stuff Cameron did to you,' I said.

'How soon?'

'Well, we have to get your deposition and we're waiting for a trial date. Soon,' I said reluctantly.

'I've got to see your father through this.'

'In fact, there is a delay already. The CIA have filed another motion that will delay a trial date and final discovery. Hoist by their own petard, maybe.'

'I think I can be ready to leave in three weeks, if the doctor is right in his prognosis.'

'Are you sure about this, Mum?'

'Brian and I have discussed this. Short of being hit by a car – '

'Don't dismiss that possibility,' said Brian in languid tones.

'I'll make it down there.'

'I'll wait for you.'

'No, I want you to take the diaries down there, to see if they'll help.'

'I know they will.'

'Then I'm hardly going to trust them to the mail.'

I laughed. 'You've been watching a few movies.'

'I don't have to watch television. My life is exciting enough, thank you.'

'I want to stay.'

'Stay until you feel he's in good hands. I understand that. But, believe me, it's because of him I'm doing this. The notion of privacy doesn't mean much when your husband is lying in intensive care and liable to be there for months.' Her mouth tightened. 'Anger helps.'

I sat up then. 'Don't worry, Mum. We'll get the bastards.'

'I know we will, sweetheart.'

'We need to discuss safety now,' said Brian. 'It is a genuine concern. Catherine let one of them into the house yesterday and God knows what they're planning now.'

We sat and talked for another hour. It was the first time we had been honest with one another for more than twenty-five years.

TWENTY-TWO

I arrived back in Washington two weeks later. Tom was at Dulles waiting and we drove straight to Memorial Hospital. It was only a matter of time before I was going to join my friends and family and check in with emotional exhaustion.

Rauh in hospital was worth the trip. I wouldn't have been surprised to see him smoking a big fat stogie. He had two clerks working in the room and the *Post* was strewn all over his bed. Three clipboards lay stacked on top of each other on his lap and he was barking into the phone.

'Hello, young woman!' he shouted at me when I walked into the room with Tom.

'Hi, sir.'

'Her name is Catherine,' said Tom evenly.

'I know that, I know that. Come to see Virtue Rewarded?'

'I think I have something that may help.'

'Whisk yourselves down to the cafeteria, my young knights,' said Rauh and the two clerks melted from the room.

'What is it?'

Tom leaned closer, then pulled back. 'Sit down, Catherine. She's been travelling for the whole day, Joe.'

'So what? I'm recovering from a major heart attack. You never travelled, Tom? What's with the cotton-wool treatment?' He turned to me. 'Look, we've made threatening noises at counsel and they deny harassing your family. Hog's breath, I tell them. I've put in a few calls, and thrown the fear of God into a couple of spooks I know. I'm pretty sure they'll find which screw is loose. So what have you got for me?'

'My mother kept records. Detailed records of everything. Her way of recovery from Cameron's treatments – '

'Experiments, not treatments,' barked Rauh.

'– was to get it all out,' I continued. 'She worked briefly on the *Montreal Star* after the war, so she had a facility that most of the patients didn't have. She reported. We have a pretty good idea from her work what went on in the Grid Room. It should blow the Cooper Report shrinks out of the water.'

'Ah-ha. Where are her journals?'

'In my briefcase.'

'Give them here.'

My hands were sticky on the handle of the briefcase. 'Wait a minute. What about protection for them? I can't just deliver this. You're going to want her to testify – '

'What do you want me to do? Post armed guards at the door? Come on, girl. I'm just glad we made enough this year to pay my health insurance.'

My shoulders slumped. Suddenly, he was all reassurance.

'You're too visible now, Catherine. You've clearly thrown your lot in with us. They'd be insane to try anything now. You're going to have to leave it in my hands.'

I took the notebooks out of the briefcase and put them on his bed. Then I left the room.

I wandered around the corridors for a while. Hospitals seem to me to be comforting places, as long as they're half-way efficient. There is an awful lot of hope in the air. Hope and acceptance. Trust, faith, whatever you want to call it – everyone in a hospital is vulnerable. I had a talk with a very old man who was writing a book about the old factories of DC before the Civil War, and I went through four issues of *People* magazine in the waiting room before Tom came to fetch me.

He grabbed my arm and propelled me back into the room.

'These are fantastic, moving and detailed. Not the work of someone with a weak mind, and that's an understatement. Joe is thrilled. Will she testify?'

I nodded.

'Amazing,' he said. 'How?'

'The accident made her angry. He was – ' I shook my head, tears filled my eyes.

'There are no grey areas in this diary. This is negligence, pure and simple. My God, you don't even have to cite Nuremberg's informed consent as the key legal standard. This was torture, pure and simple. What was the man trying to do? Don't tell me, I know, he wanted to destroy her brain patterns, wipe the slate clean, then implant his stupid suggestions.'

'We have one of his patients, a plaintiff, testifying that she finds herself, to this day, stooping to pick up a pencil that is not there from the floor. That was one of his first suggestions. What did he try to implant in your mother?'

'As far as I can tell, my father broke in and took her home before anything like that happened. The lab was still trying to break her completely, finding the time of day when she was most resistant, then assaulting her brain with drugs during that period. She was still fighting them.'

'That's why she survived. Did you see this part?' He passed me a book.

The entry was dated March 1957. It was written on spongy grey foolscap, scribbled, as if she had written it in the hospital and smuggled it out:

> I stepped out of the door and nearly fell on the ice. But I had rubber boots on and felt confident that I could make it down to the street. I slipped on the steps, though. This house is so high up. The railing was covered in ice. I was very cold. I hadn't been outside for two months.
>
> I got down to Peel Street and walked towards Côte des Neiges. I knew that was the busiest intersection. Then I stopped. There

were enough cars rushing back and forth. It was the mini-rush, lunch hour. There I stood, ankle-deep in slush, spattered by the cars that careened crazily by. Are there any drivers more reckless than Montreal drivers? I clenched, and prayed. I had to. I had to. I had to. I had to throw myself in front of these cars. I had to die. I couldn't live through another day, imprisoned behind those walls, voices speaking to me constantly.

Then Cathy's face, and Brian's and Ross's. How could I do this? I took a step back, a shuddering breath, and found a lamppost, leaned against it. Surely they'd be better off without me? Surely I am a terrible influence, likely only to get worse, a drain on the pocketbook and the psyche. How dreadful to have an insane mother through all those difficult years of growing up. Yes, better to do it now. The short sharp pain, rather than the grinding endless drain. I walked towards the kerb.

But the impulse was gone. I couldn't do it. I stood there for another fifteen minutes, my toes freezing to individual ice cubes, my fingers losing their feeling, my face covered in freezing salty tears. And then I trudged back up the hill and let myself in through the staff entrance, down into the basement, up into the private ward and into my room. No one had missed me.

I thrust it from me. 'Yes, I saw some of it.'

'Pretty powerful argument for sanity, I'd say,' said Tom.

'What do you mean?'

They looked at each other.

'We received a court order compelling our plaintiffs to undergo psychiatric exams,' said Joe.

'By psychiatrists hired by the CIA. They've chosen former associates of Dr Cameron's,' said Tom. 'It will be hostile, Catherine.'

I was numb; nothing else could shock me. 'Can I be there?'

'We'll all be there.'

'She'll survive it. She's probably stronger than any of us.'

'That's going to be the big question. What were the measurable effects of these treatments on her? If she survived so well, then why are we saying this is a case of gross negligence? What was her initial diagnosis? Why was she in three times? Was she a chronic psycho-neurotic, a terminal case – ?' Tom held up his hand. 'I know, I know, but we have to ask, because they will.'

There was a long pause. Finally, I said, 'I don't think that anyone who hasn't experienced clinical depression can know what it is like. It affects your speech, your movements, you feel burdened, buried under a mountain, everything is slowed. It keeps you awake at night, disrupts sexuality, menses. You can't even read a newspaper, go for a walk – everything is too much effort. You can't eat – pounds melt away. You jump at, or at least accept anything that will break you out of that. My guess is that initially it was the death of her baby, and then the treatments themselves and the shame and the loneliness that depressed her, and she was back inside.'

They were watching me. 'All right,' I continued. 'I think I know her feelings intimately. I know how she felt. Call it some sort of maternal osmosis. This will only be cleansing, a new start.'

Tom nodded sharply. 'We're trusting you here. Are you sure about this?'

'My mother was and is sane. She had the equivalent of a psychic flu. As did most of the rest of your plaintiffs.'

'Well, good. We have to find out from her how these experiments diminished her life.'

I took a deep breath. 'I'm sure that's possible.'

They waited a few minutes. Then Wheeler picked up the telephone. 'How soon can she get here? I'll schedule her in.'

I shrugged. 'Let us know when you need her and give us twenty-four hours.'

Rauh beckoned to me. I walked over to the bed, sat down on it. He patted my hand. 'The days ahead will be difficult.'

I smiled at him. 'Don't go soft on me, Joe. I can't take it.'

'So get out of here and get to work. Those Canadians at the embassy are so screwed up they need shock treatments.'

I laughed, picked up my bag and headed for the door.

TWENTY-THREE

I picked her up at the train station. She and Mark walked through the gate into the main hall, laughing and chattering to each other like lovers. I stood behind the railing, dumbfounded.

'How – What happened? What are you doing here?' I stared at Mark.

Mark stood, an elegant curve, smiling down at us, enjoying my confusion. I whacked him with my briefcase.

'Why didn't you tell me you were coming?'

'We weren't talking, if you remember.'

'Oh. Yes.' I dismissed him from my mind with an effort. 'How's Daddy?'

Mother was smiling at us. 'Yvette has moved in and is taking care of the house with Brian. We hired a nurse and some of Brian's cabbie friends are living in the basement. They sit there, drinking beer and watching ESPN, endless non-stop sports,' she said.

'Yvette?'

'I called her and we met. I begged.' There was a light in my mother's eye I had never seen.

We walked through Union Station and she marvelled at the ceiling.

'It is beautiful, Mother, but let's hurry.'

'Why? I'm here. Nothing can stop me now. I've never been to this city.'

'Aren't you scared?'

'A little,' she admitted. 'But mostly I feel terrific.'

'Let's get you to the hotel.'

'Couldn't we at least see a bit of the Mall?'

I sighed loudly. Mark jumped in.

'Of course. Don't be such a nuisance, Catherine. Go back to the office if you need to do something. Your mother and I will be all right. We've been having a great time.'

Mother's eyes were filled with laughter. I felt like stamping my foot but instead I trailed behind them, watching them behave like two old college sweethearts.

After an hour of driving around Washington in the rush hour, I put my foot down. 'We have to work on your deposition,' I said. 'Come on. This isn't much fun.'

Mark put his hand on my mother's. 'I'll take you round tomorrow if you feel like it.'

Her eyes were still suspiciously bright. 'That would be lovely.'

We decided to have dinner sent up to her room. She unpacked slowly, methodically, putting things away as if she were staying a month, not two nights.

'How's Dad doing really?'

'He's improving slowly, as I said in the cab. The nurse is excellent and is paid for by health insurance, thank God. He still can't see, but his hearing has come back, if he uses two hearing aids. His sinuses need constant irrigation, as do his eyes. One side of his face is permanently paralysed and he has more operations to go.' During this recital, her shoulders slumped and her face sagged and I was sorry I had insisted.

I walked over to her, took her cosmetics out of her hand and set them on the dresser.

'It's going to be fine, Mum.' And I hugged her.

She shook her head. 'I don't know.' She hugged me back, then went over to the dresser. 'These belong in the bathroom. You're getting in the way, darling. Go and sit in the corner.'

I sat in the chair in the corner and watched her. Her movements were economical. Every bottle and jar had to be set in a marching order. Her underwear and blouses were meticulously folded and her suits and dresses (so many!) hung, colour-co-ordinated by length.

'I can't believe you,' I said.

'What?' She turned, followed my eyes. 'Oh!' She blushed slightly. 'That's part of it. I need everything ordered or I worry about it.'

'That's one of the things we have to review tonight. I hope you're not tired.'

'Not at all. Let's order some tea.'

I picked up the phone.

'Just hot water for me. And you, if you want my kind of tea.' She fished around in her top drawer, frowned a little, then brought out a tin. 'I think I'll have linden.'

I shook my head, ordered Earl Grey and a pot of hot water.

'Now,' she said, settling in the desk chair and composing herself. 'Let's go over what we need to go over. Should I take notes?'

I shrugged. 'Can we free-form it? I can go through the paperwork, but essentially this is what they'll go at you for. First, how nuts were you? What were the treatments, in detail? How did you survive if they were so extreme? What are the effects of the experiments? This last question is the big one, because if you survived so much so well, then what, in fact, was the big problem? Understand?'

She sat, staring for a minute, then nodded and nodded again. 'It's like an oral.'

'What?'

'You know, for your thesis.'

'This is a bit trickier, Mum. They will go for every sore spot you have, and some that they've made up.'

'That was Ewen's core theory, the nut of it. He believed that you must find the sore spot and keep on rubbing at it.'

'It's what they do in prison camps.'

'Well, yes, it is a pervasive theory. Break down the personality, inject training, re-form it.'

A knock. I answered the door. A tea tray was wheeled into the room and I scribbled her signature on the bill. 'The firm is picking up the tab for this.'

She nodded. 'Well, shall I list some answers to your questions?'

I stood at the tea tray, stirring the tea bags in the teapots. We were so formal, I loathed it. But we hadn't been comfortable with each other for twenty-five years, so how to start now? How do you say to someone Mum, I want to be your daughter now. I know I haven't for the last two decades, but now, now I can understand you and respect you and finally love you without grudging the time and energy it takes.

I rubbed my eye. 'Yeah, that's a start, I guess. Here's your tea.' I sniffed at it. 'Smells revolting.'

An ironic smile. 'Why don't you get your notepad and we'll do some work?'

'All right.'

We worked for about an hour, going over the key sticking points. Finally, I threw the writing pad on to the bed.

'Whew, that's enough. Can we order dinner? Wouldn't you like a drink?'

The phone rang. It was Tom.

'Yes, everything's fine. We're going over tomorrow's testimony,' I said.

Tom was hesitant. 'Joe's going to try to make it to the deposition. He's resting up for it – he wanted me to let you know. Do you need any help?'

I was unwilling suddenly to share my mother's time. I wanted to be alone with her tonight. 'No, we're fine.' I smiled at her. 'Aren't we?'

She smiled at me. We were a bevy of sweet smiles.

'They're bringing up some big guns tomorrow, Catherine,' Tom said.

'We're going to be all right.'

'Try to bring your mother up to speed on the case and the manoeuvrings about settlement, delay and so on. She'll be better equipped to deal with them tomorrow.'

'All right, Tom.'

We hung up.

'Mark is jealous of Tom Wheeler, you know,' commented Mother.

'I know.'

'Does he have cause?'

'Of course not,' I said sharply. She sat immobile, staring at me. I shook my head, confused. 'I don't think so, anyway.'

'Let's have that drink. I've been thinking of a gin and tonic for about an hour.'

'Ever since we started going over your responses.'

She laughed. 'Let me make it. You're making me feel like an invalid. What would you like?'

'Same.'

She busied herself at the small refrigerator, then turned to me. Her face twisted. All at once, she looked bruised and wilted.

'Mum, what's wrong?'

'I've made things so hard for you children.' Her voice was strained and she was forcing the words out around tears. 'I remember going home when I was six months pregnant with you. I thought: I should stay here and have the baby and not go back. I would be safe at home – no Muffie to measure up to, no Ewen lurking in the background.'

'Oh Mum.' I didn't know what to say.

'Oh Cathy, I've done terrible things in my life.' She grabbed herself around the waist and rocked forwards, whimpered in pain. I got up, walked towards her and knelt down. Her tears gave me the strength to wrap my arms around her.

'You have never done a bad thing in your entire life and especially not to me.'

'But Brian and you – I've almost ruined your lives. I should have left that night for good. Creetie and Donald talked me into giving it a day or two. I should have taken you with me and disappeared from that place.'

I made soothing noises, sat there, waited.

'I'm sorry, Cathy, but I loved him,' she said. 'I couldn't leave, didn't want to, kept hoping that things would change, that he would and that I would. You know, we're happy now.'

'I know.'

'People were so cruel to me. To all of us.'

I was trying not to cry. 'I know, Mum, I was there. I watched.'

'Your grandmother, my God, her tongue. She never let me rest. I felt as if I was in a foot race and both my legs were in plaster.'

'And she kept trying to get us away from you.'

She couldn't speak then, just wept and I held her.

'Look at all you've given us. Brains, courage, strength,' I said.

She raised her tear-streaked face and looked at me. 'I was so confused. I thought Ewen's treatments were what I needed to do to fit into that world and to be with him. God help me, that's how I reasoned it. I was too frightened to fight back and leave. That meant leaving all of you and I couldn't do that. Ewen was always there, saying, "You can do it, lassie, I will help you get better. Just one more treatment, one more pill, one more injection."'

'He was a sick bastard.'

'You know, I want to meet those other plaintiffs and thank them. They are so brave.'

'So are you.'

'No, I'm not.'

'And so is Dad.'

'Yes, finally and always, Dad.'

'What was your marriage like?' I held my breath. Would she answer? It was not the kind of question I had ever asked.

She shook her head. 'I don't know if I can – '

'Try. It's important to me.'

She smiled. 'All right.' She frowned, tried to concentrate. 'It's no use. What can I tell you?'

'Just tell me why you stayed together. What held you to him? You must have wanted to leave so many times.'

She stood up, walked to the window and stood staring down at the traffic.

'I like all those black faces down there. They soften the city, somehow. It would be as dry as paper if they weren't here.'

'Drier. There's a lot of violence.'

'I'm not surprised. Look, Cathy, it was different then. We had real problems. But there were no other options. Money was a very big thing. And you kids. I didn't see what kind of a life you would have as products of a broken family. Then, finally, in '63, as you know, he stood up for me, brought me out of that dark tunnel Ewen had forced me into. Not only did he physically rescue me, but he nursed me through the bad times, taught me how to do the most simple things, then how to live. He had endless, endless patience. I loved him more after that and it was in part simple gratitude. That love helped me to decide to keep going, to do what I could for you kids and for him. To fill the unforgiving minute, to spread as much beauty and happiness around as I could. That became my only goal. That and stability. It was too bad that you were long gone by then and only remember the bad times.'

'I think of how much potential you had. I can barely deal with the anger I feel about the loss of it.'

She thought for a while, took a sip of her drink. 'Do you know the collection of writing, *This Bridge Called My Back*?'

'No.'

'My book group did it at the University Women's Club last year. It's a collection of radical black women's writings.'

'Good Lord.'

'Yes, there were a few who didn't quite see the point.' She laughed.

There was another long pause.

'I guess that's the real thing, isn't it?' I said. 'But what a bridge.'

'I survived it, Cathy.'

'And with dignity.'

Her face grimaced into a smile. 'Some of the time anyway.'

TWENTY-FOUR

We were all sitting in the conference room at Rauh's office.

'But that's what we want. We *want* settlement,' protested Rauh.

'Why do you want only settlement? Why not take it to trial?' asked my mother.

Rauh was thinner than usual, but filled with his usual intensity.

'There are a lot of practical reasons, the most simple being that we know the Operations people at the Agency are implacable. They don't want settlement for love or money. They fear a rash of litigation. This case is only the tip of the iceberg. We know, from our discovery process, and from the work of John Marks, the man who first wrangled sixteen thousand pages of documents on mind control out of the CIA, that the Agency channelled ten million dollars, in fifties dollars, through one hundred and forty-four universities, fifteen research facilities or private companies, twelve hospitals and three prisons for the purpose of research into mind control. Almost all the experiments were performed on unknowing American citizens. If this were known, it could bring down the government and effectively end the CIA as we know it.'

There was silence.

Rauh cocked his head at her.

'Yes,' said my mother. 'I'm beginning to see.'

Wheeler stood. 'Catherine, will you give us some time alone with your mother?' he said.

'Why can't I stay?'

'We need to speak to your mother alone.'

'Joe, can't I stay?' I asked.

'No, young woman, get the hell out of here. I don't want your mother thinking a second and a third time about her answers just because her daughter's in the room. I want you around for the CIA deposition, though. Meet us back here in, say, two hours.'

I left without another word.

I hung around in the corridor for a while, but it was a Saturday and there was no one around. I took the elevator down and sat in Farragut Square, a little pocket-handkerchief-sized park, in the middle of Connecticut, then I wandered up the street, looking in the shop windows. There were a few tourists around, a few workaholics scurrying to their offices. Nothing looked interesting, besides, I had acid burning in the pit of my stomach. The thought of more coffee made me feel sick and I went back to Joe's offices and sat in the waiting area reading back issues of *Newsweek*, one eye fixed on the conference-room door.

Finally, it opened and the three of them came out together. Tom's face looked taut, and his shirtsleeves were rolled up. Joe was holding my mother's hand while his other hand brandished his cane at the overhead lights.

'I'm going to kill the bastards for you,' he said to my mother. She laughed.

I hurried up to them. 'How did it go?'

Joe looked down at me. 'Let me put it this way, Catherine. There is no way that some bunch of hired shrinks can say that that cursed man's procedures were anything else but torture.'

I followed them down the hallway, listening. Just then, the entrance doors swung back and three men strode through. Dressed in full bureaucratic rig, disciplined and groomed within an inch of their lives. They frightened the life out of me. My mother stepped back involuntarily into me and I grabbed her.

'It's all right.'

'It's them, isn't it?' she said.

'Yeah, sure is. I recognize one of them from another deposition. George Winkler, US Attorney.'

Wheeler and Rauh were already greeting them and guiding them around us into the room. Wheeler jerked his head at us. We followed.

There were few pleasantries. Rauh was in full glower. The recorder settled into her chair and set up her machine. I slipped out to the coffee room and grabbed a bottle of spring water and a few glasses and returned.

I sat slightly behind my mother, so that my presence could comfort her, but not distract her. Tom and Joe faced the CIA counsel.

'Why are we deposing this woman, Joe?' said Winkler.

I stared at him. He was a block of a man, forward tackle on the football team, completely bald, huge compacted muscle, mean and hard and very successful. His associate, Hank Gemlisch, was skinny and dour and hadn't even looked at us yet. Just stared at his notes. A third man, young and fresh, sat in the rear, listening. He was not introduced.

'You know the damned reason,' Rauh replied. 'You've seen the journals. Where would we find a more competent witness? I do believe that our business here is the truth.' Rauh's voice was as smooth as 50-weight oil.

'Could we get down to it?' A sharp, almost feminine voice sliced into my thoughts. I looked at Gemlisch. He was as thin as a scrub tree and as attractive, all bristle and hair oil and oversized glasses. The academic. I hated him on sight.

They went through the formalities and the recorder painstakingly took down the correct spelling of all our names, and our positions in the proceedings.

'Why do we have this girl here with us? It is out of order. We have allowed no relatives in depositions. We got a ruling on that six months ago, Rauh, remember?' Gemlisch reached into his briefcase.

The recorder's fingers hung motionless over her keys.

'She is a clerk and researcher on the case,' said Wheeler.

'It doesn't matter. She is this woman's daughter and as such is disallowed.'

'Oh, for God's sake!' Rauh exploded. 'You people are disgusting. Mrs Ramsey is not a plaintiff. She is a witness and her daughter is acting as our clerk. That's all it is. You want a ruling on this? We'll get a ruling.'

Winkler held up his hands. 'We'll allow her.'

'Gee, thank you,' said Rauh.

Mr Winkler began. 'Madam, could you state your full name for record, please?'

'Victoria Ramsey.'

'Mrs Ramsey, could you tell us, please, your age and your current address?'

We proceeded slowly and meticulously through my mother's early employment history, education and her early marriage.

'And do you testify, Mrs Ramsey, that these journals in front of me are written entirely by you?'

'Yes.'

'Therefore, no other person had a hand in putting them together?'

'She's just said that,' said Rauh.

'Would you look through them, please, just to make sure they have not been tampered with?'

There was a pause while my mother leafed through the diaries. She shook her head. 'They have not been altered.'

'Fine. Then, ma'am, would you swear that each entry is correct to the date you list? That is, did you write each entry on the date you say, or did you add them in later?'

'For God's sake,' exploded Rauh. 'Winkler, the diaries are hers and were written by her more than twenty years ago, not yesterday.'

'We can have the ink and paper tested, Joe.'

'Call me Mr Rauh.'

'And you can call me Mr Winkler.'

'Yes,' said my mother. 'I wrote each entry on the date I listed. Well, maybe sometimes I got the date wrong. My mind was very foggy in these years and I often did not know the day of the week. But within a day or two, exact as to date, Mr Winkler.'

The room was silent for a moment.

'Very well,' said Winkler. 'Let us talk about your first admission. That was?'

'In 1950. After the death of my first child.'

'And was it a planned pregnancy?'

My mother shifted in her chair. 'Not exactly.'

'Can you clarify, please?'

'I mean it was an accident, but afterwards a very much wanted child.'

'And you began to experience emotional problems after his birth?'

'No,' she said evenly. 'After his death.'

I wanted to hold her hand, but she seemed to have a force field around her. She sat so still she was a statue.

'That was?'

'Ten days after his birth. And they weren't emotional problems then, I was just very very tired.'

'Would you describe, please, the depression or the symptoms of the depression that you experienced at that time?'

'She didn't say it was depression, Mr Winkler. She said it was fatigue. Common, as I recall, after giving birth.'

'Let me give you an example of what we're talking about. Did you become very quiet and withdrawn and stay in your room for several days at a time or did you become angry and hostile?'

'I was *tired*,' she emphasized. 'All right. I felt down. I felt cut away from much of the life I had been part of. I had been very active, I knew everything that was going on around the city. And I felt – I was living under water, unable to get my head above water.'

'What happened then?'

'My obstetrician recommended I see Dr Cameron and he suggested I come into the Allan Memorial for a week or so.'

'What happened there?'

'I remember long talks in his office. He wasn't the centre of an empire then; he was just a psychiatrist and we got along quite well. We had similar interests. We spoke every day. He talked me into a few shock treatments and they helped. Then I went home and I was better, normal.'

'Then it wasn't an unpleasant experience?'

She laughed. 'No episode in the loony bin is pleasant, I imagine. But that time, he was good and kind to me and I trusted him. So when I returned the next time, I felt confident he could help me.'

'Mrs Ramsey, could you read page two of this letter, the last two short paragraphs and then the salutation, and who this is signed by?'

'You mean starting with – '

'"We plan".'

'"We plan to discharge the patient but advise follow-up psychotherapy. Our final diagnosis was that of a severe character neurosis.'

Her voice shook as she read the salutation. 'It is signed by Dr Ewen Cameron, MD, Psychiatrist-in-Chief.'

'Did Dr Cameron inform you that you had a mental problem or impairment at the time of your discharge?'

'No.'

'Did you believe that you had a mental problem at that time?'

'No. I didn't.'

'Yet you returned seven years later.'

'Yes.'

'Are you aware that the CIA funding of Dr Cameron at the Allan Memorial Institute did not commence until 1957?'

Rauh cut in. 'Don't answer the question. There is no basis for that assumption. The CIA was in touch with Mr Cameron before that time, asked him to file an application – he had every reason to believe that he was going to get the money. Mr Gittinger's testimony in this case demonstrates that the CIA went to Mr – '

'Excuse me, Mr Rauh, you are not the witness in this!'

'I didn't know,' my mother cut in. She had recovered from the shock of Cameron's early diagnosis.

'Fine,' said Mr Winkler. 'Please tell us, Mrs Ramsey, what led up to your second admission.'

'I had just given birth to my fourth child and I was depressed again. I was having trouble coping with the older two and the new baby. There were problems in the marriage and I was unhappy just taking care of children all day.'

'So you checked yourself into a psychiatric hospital? Because you were tired?'

'Well, he had helped me so much the last time, you see. I now understand that I merely had postnatal depression, which is treated these days with drugs and sleep. Then – '

'Cameron's standard treatment for postnatal depression was multiple shock treatments and LSD,' cut in Rauh.

'Mr Rauh, you are not the witness here.' Winkler could hardly restrain himself.

'I apologize, sir, but you people disgust me, harassing this woman here and trying to defend the indefensible.'

'Mrs Ramsey, can you answer us?'

'Yes, I trusted him,' she said simply.

'Then what happened?'

'I didn't see him and they gave me drugs, sometimes forty pills a day. Then the injections.'

'And they were?'

'Well, I looked at my chart. At first it was sodium amytal. Then lysergic acid diethylamide. I had it many times.'

'How many?'

'After fourteen times, I lost count.'

'And you never saw Dr Cameron?'

'No, he was there for the injections. He gave them to me and turned on a tape recorder, said, "Write whatever comes into your mind," and left the room.'

'Was the door locked?'

'No.'

'Describe the experience of the drug for us, please.'

'I felt terrifying panic. I had absolutely no control over myself. I felt all of my bones were melting. And it seemed to me that I was moving in a funny kind of way, zigging and zagging around, and I was a squirrel in a cage. I couldn't get out. I tried to climb the walls. And I felt that, if I were to lie down, I'd never get up.'

'And this was the effect of the LSD?'

'I didn't know anything about LSD. I knew only lysergic acid because it was on the charts.'

'I'm sorry. Did you describe for Dr Cameron your experience of bones melting and being a squirrel in a cage?'

'I can't remember. But I can remember telling everyone that the drug was terrible and made me feel much, much worse.'

'I take it then that he overcame your protestations? Did he persuade you to accept it or did he just hold you down and shoot it in your arm?'

'Dr Cameron would say, "Come on, lassie. We'll walk down the hall." He would put his arm around my shoulders and say, "Now, you want to get better. Come on, lassie, you're going to take this injection for me. You know you are."'

'And I would say, "OK, I'll do it. But I don't want to do it. It's killing me. It's killing me."'

'Christ!' said Rauh.

Winkler shot him a furious look.

'What happened the last time he tried to give it to you that made it different? What made your resolve stronger or what was different? Because you did stop taking it at some point, didn't you?'

'Well, I had two injections, one one day and one the next day, and I could hardly stand up. And I didn't care whether I lived or died. And I figured I was dying anyhow, so if they'd kill me if I didn't take it, they might as well do that. So I just said, "I don't care what you do, I'm not going to take it."'

'And how did Dr Cameron respond to that?'

'He became very cold and stern and walked out.'

'Then what?'

'The shock shop.'

'Pardon me?'

'That's what we called it on South Two.'

'What?'

'The private ward. Sounds like a mountain, doesn't it?' My mother smiled as if she were at a dinner party.

She had been able to keep track of how many shock treatments she had received on her second admission by scratching a mark with her wedding ring on the underside of the bed each time. She'd had 200 in one month.

'What did you remember after you were released?'

'I couldn't recognize the neighbourhood where we lived. I couldn't recognize my house or even – ' She stopped, drew a shuddering breath. 'I couldn't recognize my children. They were strangers.'

'For how long did that last?'

'For about two years, on and off.'

'You couldn't recognize your own children for two years?' Winkler's voice held the tone of disbelief.

'On and off. Yes, that's right. I knew they were my children, but I didn't know anything about them. I used to repeat things over and over to my kids. They had to suffer each episode, because I had what are now called flashbacks when I would hallucinate.'

'What else?' Winkler's voice was becoming gentler, less hostile. He shifted in his chair, which creaked under his enormous weight.

'I couldn't attend to any duties properly and that depressed me, but I couldn't concentrate. I had been so independent and now I had to have help all the time because in the middle of cooking dinner, the food would turn into insects and worms or raw bloody flesh and I'd have to stop and lie down until it passed. I lay in a half-sleep for many months.'

'What symptoms persist?' asked Wheeler gently.

'I still have very bad times, although I can manage them now. I lie on a sofa and stare into space for hours. I follow a series of rituals that control my life. I need order and routine to an extreme. Sometimes I suffer from what are called neurologic side-effects. I am restless, I cannot sit still, my legs shake and I have muscular twitches. The cramps left years ago, thank God. It's all in the diaries.'

'Mrs Ramsey suffers from a low plateau of functioning,' said

Rauh. 'If you study her achievements in her early years and match them with what she could have accomplished, given normal energy, the loss is indescribable and immeasurable. To her, to her family and to society.'

Winkler made a dismissive motion. 'Impossible to measure that, Mr Rauh. How can we know what a person could accomplish, given this and that? There are too many unknowns. Mrs Ramsey, let us follow on to your third admission.'

My mother straightened her back. 'Yes, that was in 1962.'

'And how did that come about?'

'I want a recess,' Rauh jumped in.

'Fine,' said Winkler. I thought they were all looking tense, but I could have been imagining things. My mother was trembling slightly.

'Tom, take Mrs Ramsey out of here for a while. Get her some lunch.'

I stood up.

'Catherine, stay here.'

I sat down again and watched as Tom tenderly helped my mother out of the room. She was a bit unsteady on her legs. They disappeared down the hall.

Rauh waited for a moment. 'Catherine, will you shut the door, please?' I walked over, stuck my head out. Tom had my mother's arm in one hand and was gesturing with the other. I smiled and shut the conference-room door quietly and returned to my seat.

The three opposing counsel were sitting quietly, making no attempt to leave. Gemlisch was doodling on his pad, Winkler was staring into space.

'Let's discuss it, gentlemen,' said Rauh.

'Discuss what?' said Gemlisch, but he was looking at his doodle, adding flourishes. This was a ritual.

'Mrs Ramsey is articulate, she is educated, she is clear. Her testimony, in court, will decimate your case and you know it.'

They were silent and did not even look at each other.

'We need Mrs Ramsey to undergo psychiatric examination,' said Winkler.

'You people disgust me. This woman was persecuted by one of your agents for twenty years and now you want her to undergo a harassing psychiatric exam. I want to lodge a formal protest.'

'So lodged.' Winkler shrugged.

'Permission to dismiss the recorder,' said Gemlisch.

Winkler nodded.

The woman packed up her gear and left.

'Wait in the hall, please,' said Rauh.

'We offer $25,000 per plaintif,' said Gemlisch.

'That is insulting,' said Rauh. 'I won't even tolerate it. Catherine, let us go.'

'All right, all right,' said Winkler. 'What will you accept?'

'One million each,' said Rauh.

'Crap,' said Gemlisch.

'She is a formidable opponent for you, gentlemen. She has an impeccable background. She is sympathetic, sharp. Her husband does charitable work that puts us all to shame. She is another Mrs Olson. Do you want another mess like that on your hands?'

Winkler flinched. Rauh saw it and smiled slowly.

'We won't allow her as a witness.'

'There are a thousand precedents that allow her. Don't play the fool with me. You're stalling. And by the way, call off your hounds.'

Winkler lifted one eyebrow.

'You know what I'm talking about, or Gemlisch does. He looks like the type you'd find under a rock. Those idiots out there in the field bothering this poor woman, that rogue elephant you call your Agency – call them off.'

Winkler rose. 'You're losing your mind, Mr Rauh.' He slammed out of the room.

'See you in court, asshole,' called Rauh.

Gemlisch stayed. 'I don't see the point of all this combative behaviour, Mr Rauh.'

'Listen, you cheap bastard, haven't you had enough? This woman is worth twenty of you and can give you chapter and verse on Ewen Cameron's sins thirty years ago as if they happened yesterday. And it's all in the diaries. It's there, clear, in black-and-white, and when we go to trial, any judge is going to blow your defence into hyperspace.'

'We'll need more from her.'

'Well, not today. Take what you've got back to the pit you and all the other snakes dwell in and come back Monday. She needs a break.'

Gemlisch pushed his pad into his briefcase and stood up. The silent one walked over to me, stuck out his hand.

'I'm sorry,' he said.

Gemlisch's jaw dropped.

I stood up slowly.

'Why are you apologizing to her?' Rauh said.

'I feel like apologizing to someone.'

'A civilized reaction from a rodent. Wonders never cease. Your career is over, boy.'

The man looked shamefaced, beaten.

I took his hand, shook it. 'OK. Thanks.'

He looked grateful. 'Is Mrs Ramsey planning to join the prosecution?' he asked.

'No,' said Rauh, 'and you'd better thank your stars she isn't. But she's a material witness, and if you've done your homework, she's formidable.'

They left then and I sat, feeling drained of every emotion.

'Huh,' said Rauh. '*Very* interesting.'

'Sorry?'

'The little guy. I think he's a plant from William Webster.'

'Who?'

'The new head of the Agency, who is replacing Bill Casey. Not confirmed yet. More humane than old Bill.'

'Oh.'

'Very interesting. We'll just see what happens next.'

I was fretting. I wanted to get to my mother.

'All right, Catherine. Go.' I jumped to my feet, paused at the door. 'Tell her good work today. And to you too.'

I made a mock salute then ran down the hall.

TWENTY-FIVE

Joe and Tom arrived at the hotel that night around nine. Mark, Mother and I joined them and sat in the hotel dining room late while they told us stories about the case, horrible and funny both. The countless tricks of the Agency lawyers, their attempts to delay, waiting for death and chronic illness to fell the plaintiffs, trying to disable Joe, to bankrupt the firm. Mother volunteered a few stories of her own, tentatively at first, then with surer confidence – the bumps in traffic, Brian reading the Book of Revelations to a speechless telephoner.

'We want you both to leave,' said Joe finally, around midnight, when the hotel staff were conspicuously emptying ashtrays and clearing tables.

'Why?' I said.

'Joe received a few calls at home this afternoon. We believe that William Webster will be able to deal with this better than Casey,' said Tom.

'Both the US Attorney's office and the General Counsel at the Agency want settlement,' said Joe. 'In fact they have for a long time, but this afternoon's deposition was the last straw. Mrs Ramsey's diaries are frightening and persuasive both. And the case is just too heavily weighted against them. On their advice, I drafted a letter to Webster, sent it over by courier.'

'One of your famous letters,' I laughed.

'Perhaps not quite as impassioned as the ones I sent Mulroney.'

'I have a copy. Here, I'll read the last paragraph,' said Tom.

Joe shouted and waved his cane over the table in a futile effort to stop him.

Tom cleared his throat, drama in every gesture. 'No, this is serious – listen to the masterful prose of the legal maestro: "Wouldn't the Agency be a stronger organization by some recognition of error and some recompense, therefore? Is it in our nation's interest or tradition to compound the old wrong by continuing the struggle endlessly until many or most of the plaintiffs leave this earth with broken lives and without recognition or recompense? A compassionate people can give one answer."'

I had a lump in my throat and I clapped my hands. Mother effused and Joe frowned at us all.

'Will you proceed with a trial in the meantime?' asked Mark, ever practical.

'Yes, until the deadlock is broken. We have to. But we think Mrs Ramsey's testimony and her diaries have tipped the balance,' said Tom.

'You can call me Victoria, Tom. You certainly know me well enough.'

He reached a hand across the table. 'And I've wanted to meet you for a long time.'

'But now, go home,' said Rauh. 'We'll call you if we need you. But your husband needs you more.'

And so we went.

She took Mark and me home with her the next morning. I was exhausted and frightened and she, by contrast, had never seemed stronger. I stumbled along in her wake, at Dulles and at Vancouver Airport. Mark carried the bags, fetched tea and newspapers and *Vogue*.

For weeks, like my mother home from the Allan Memorial, I lay on my bed in Vancouver in a half-sleep. I ate children's meals, mashed potatoes, green beans, apple sauce. I watched afternoon television and grew familiar with the plots of a half-dozen soap operas, learned the names of the actors and traced their careers, standing on line at the supermarket, reading *Soap Opera Digest*. I listened to the complainants on the afternoon television shows, but too often their lives paralleled my own, and I switched to game shows and from time to time, the *International Hour* on CNN. Mark and I went for walks in Stanley Park and talked.

Mark had taken a month off work. He spent time with Brian, while I retreated, and I grew used to him, Yvette and Brian returning to the house, flushed from some adventure, hiking up Blackcomb or sailing on English Bay. It was late summer and the city was at its most glorious. Yvette and Brian seemed to be inching towards a new understanding. The colour was returning to his face and I could tell his inner demons had been silenced, though when I tried to bring up his fears, he hugged me, and put a finger to my lips. We had retreated to our comfortable distances, but now, in the spaces between us, instead of delusion and rancour, there was love.

I sat in the sun room and watched the needle-fine mist dust itself over the leaves and vines and outdoor furniture. I liked how the edges softened and blurred and I felt myself blur too, and the brutal tension that pulled all the muscles and ligaments in my body into a rictus smile of perennial readiness gave millimetre by millimetre.

Brian came around a few times a week for tea time with Mother and me and we talked. I surrendered and began to drink linden and fennel tea, and eat sugarless muffins, sweetened by dried fruit. Mark drove me to the tennis club and we swam in the pool, negotiating between splashing children and flirting teens. As it did my mother before me, the exercise began to revive me and I could answer some of Mark's mostly silent questions. I praised him for his forbearance and let him complain about how much I had hurt him and I didn't become furious. And then, we were able to talk about what had happened to us and how I was changing. For the better, I promised him, and we were able to talk one night, all night until we were hoarse, in my tiny single bed, down the hallway from my parents' room. After that night, we were familiars again, and were able to understand each other without constant explanation and apology. We began to talk about the future with hope, even anticipation.

I helped with the meals and washing and the relentless detail of care of an invalid. My father was more than half-dead. His face was a ruined mask, the face of a Greek tragedian. He suffered through a dozen operations to reconstruct his face, each one muffling him in bandages. The doctors rebuilt his nose, his aural canals, restored his sight, his hearing. One eye was permanently damaged, left to stare half open, inwards, blindly, for ever. He wore a patch, rakishly, some days, one darkened lens on eyeglasses. Because one side of his face was permanently paralysed, eating was a humiliating, messy experience for him.

One afternoon, he stumbled down from his bedroom and sat on the steps from the sun room, head in hands, helplessly weeping. This was too much for me and I fetched my mother, who sat with him, and said exactly the right things until his head rose and he was helped on to the *chaise* in front of him. She bore all his tantrums and despairs with resolution and grace and I hid in her substantial shadow for the first time since I was eleven, and I learned from her.

I inched back into life. One day, one sunny fall morning, was particularly beautiful, the kind of day that sprinkles fairy dust on the street, the sun and air crystal clean, purified by the Arctic, air never breathed before, giving life and hope.

She walked into the room where I had made my camp, noticed that all the windows were open and the sound turned down on the television. She was holding something in her hand.

'Darling, I want you to have this. It is part of your great-grandmother's watch chain.' And she dropped it into my lap.

It was red gold, and the chain links were squared off and thickly woven. I looked up at her.

'There was a time when I was afraid not to wear it. I believed if I didn't wear it, something terrible would happen to me. But that's gone and it is a pretty thing. You should have it.'

'Thanks, Mum.' And I threaded it around my neck and looped it over twice.

That afternoon I listened as she read a story on Japan's trade balance to my father and the words did more than dance meaninglessly around my ears. I felt curiosity for the first time in months.

Then after he was in bed for his nap, that afternoon she played the piano for me. I lay on the floor in the living room and remembered those winter months in Foster, when Brian, Ross, the dog and I used to doze on the floor near the fire and listen to her play *Scenes from Childhood*, or Chopin Nocturnes. Eric Satie would thrill us all; she would play it and we felt it was composed just for us. I would dance and the boys would laugh, but sometimes join in, all male awkwardness and teasing.

She played one of Schubert's *humoresques* that afternoon, and before I could stop them, tears were flooding my eyes. The notes were colours, and they cascaded around and over me in a riotous paintbox of joy. I heard the fantastic imaginings of a child, the wonder of the all and ever new, then sadness, terrible sadness and loss. The melancholy in the second movement tugged at me, and I wept for all we had lost together and separately. The times we hadn't had and couldn't reach. Simple times, a wedding, a childbirth, a family picnic, shopping for grandchildren, the ceaseless ordinary details of a normal life that everyone around us took for granted and that we could never ever seem to find.

I wept for her loss of an active life, a normal life. Who would she have been? Instead she had lived camouflaged, like a hunted animal, watching every word she uttered, afraid that any honest expression would leave her hooked up to machines, and tortured again. I wept for my father's broken body. And hatred sprang up in me like a bitter herb, sour and nasty and ugly as Satan. I hated. I hated the men who had done this to us, with no more thought for us than they'd have for lab mice. Less thought even, for lab mice they had to dispose of. We were left with the wreck of our lives, not even aware of what had been done to us.

I hated the people who had taken advantage of our weakness, the predators and the neurotics who had drained us, and I hated our culture which had taught us never to question authority, and had let this happen to its own in its own backyard.

As my mother played, the music rewove the strands of my childhood into a message of hope and courage. My tears dried and I remembered good things, eclipsed by fear.

Before, I had been strong, brittle, almost inhuman. And I had broken. Somehow, sometime in the last year, I had reclaimed an entire part of my emotional range, and for that I was grateful. I felt, for the first time, as if I were human, part of that whole ugly, messy, half-divine race that raged around us, outside this wall of music.

POSTSCRIPT

On 2 October 1988 the US Attorney's Office, representing the CIA, agreed to the payment of three-quarters of a million dollars to the nine plaintiffs of Civil Action Suit 806012.

The process was one of negotiations. On the day the trial was set to begin, there were six rounds of offers and counter-offers. By Justice Department regulation, there was a $750,000 ceiling on any settlement the suit could achieve without the personal involvement of the Attorney General. The lawyers involved estimated that given the difficulties, uncertainties, and delays of securing the approval of the Attorney General, as a practical matter, that amount was the best they could do, short of trial.

In the words of Joseph Rauh, 'To our knowledge this represents the largest payment made by the CIA in litigation arising out of the MKULTRA programme. In dollar terms the amount was not huge, but it was a significant lump-sum payment that would make an important difference to the quality of life enjoyed by those of our clients who were impoverished or living on pensions. Equally important to us and to the victims as well, the dollar amount was enough to convey the symbolic message of US government contrition. Regardless of boilerplate denials, everyone knows that the CIA acknowledged its past wrongdoing – no one pays three-quarters of a million dollars unless they did something wrong.'

With an *ex gratia* payment of $250,000 by the Canadian government, as recommended in the Cooper Report, the amount recovered for the victims of the MKULTRA programme was more than a million dollars. In 1991, the Canadian government offered a payment of $100,000 to each of Dr Cameron's patients who were victims of the MKULTRA, subproject 68 series of experiments

At a chance meeting with CIA Director William Webster at a Justice Department reception, Joseph Rauh thanked him for breaking the deadlock. The Director expressed his gratitude for having learned of the case and stated, 'Sometimes you see the right thing to do, and you do it.'

ACKNOWLEDGMENTS

The most important resource for me, as it must be for any researcher into CIA mind-control experiments, was the documentation collected by the attorneys Joseph Rauh and James Turner, for the nine patients of Dr Ewen Cameron who brought the CIA to court in Washington during the years that stretched from 1979 to 1990. The records of Civil Action No. 80–3163 sit in five large cardboard cartons in the National Archives Center in Maryland and make for fascinating reading. I used the depositions of the nine plaintiffs in the case: Val Orlikow, Mary Matilda Morrow, MD, Jean Charles Page, Moe Langleben, Rita Zimmerman, Jeanine Huard, Louis Weinstein, Richard McGarrah Helms and the affidavits of: Mrs Alice W. Olson, Robert Jay Lifton, MD, Harvey M. Weinstein, MD, Leon Saltzman, MD, Omond M. Solandt, Ph.D., Jay Peterzell, Paul E. Termansen, MD, Lloyd Hisey, MD, David J. Rothman, Ph.D., David I. Joseph, MD, Brian B. Doyle, MD, Senator Allan J. MacEachen, Wayne Langleben, Miss Eva H. Bothwell, the Cooper Report, as well as hospital records of various plaintiffs, the transcript of the 18 September 1978 Judgment in Appeal of Mary Morrow, MD, one of Dr Ewen Cameron's patients, and many transcripts of courtroom appearances made by lawyers for the plaintiffs and the defence. Documentation of the MKULTRA mind-control programmes, as well as other mind-control projects, including correspondence, inter-office memoranda and status reports, were received by the plaintiffs during documentary discovery. Stamped 'Secret' and much blacked-out, they make for particularly interesting reading, especially for what they blatantly do not reveal. The depositions of John Gittinger, CIA Project Monitor for MKULTRA, subproject 68, as well as Dr Sydney Gottlieb, the CIA chemist and scientist who directed MKULTRA, and his assistant, Robert Lashbrook, are chilling in their seeming disregard for the well-being of the patients.

The Plaintiffs' Statement of Genuine Issues meticulously documents the plaintiffs' allegations in their litigation against the CIA. Briefly, the statement alleges that the CIA established a programme to explore covert brainwashing, used dangerous drugs on unwitting civilians, failed to control their operatives, who recruited Ewen Cameron, who used injurious experimental procedures similar to communist brainwashing methods. The CIA operatives who provided money to Ewen Cameron failed to take any steps to ensure that only volunteers were being used and failed to supervise Ewen Cameron's work in any way. The plaintiffs never volunteered to participate in experiments. The CIA concealed the project and failed to notify the plaintiffs, after being ordered to by a Senate Committee. The CIA admitted negligence in MKULTRA's brainwashing experiments. The brainwashing experiments financed by MKULTRA were unethical and irresponsible violations of recognized standards governing research with human subjects. The CIA violated accepted standards governing research involving human subjects by financing brainwashing experiments upon non-volunteers.

One masterful piece of non-fiction has been written about the Montreal experiments and the work of Dr D. Ewen Cameron, and that is Anne Collins's *In The Sleep Room*, published in 1988 by Lester & Orpen Dennys. I relied upon Anne Collins's work extensively during the writing of the *Monkey-Puzzle Tree*, though I admit that the book sat unopened for two years in my house while I plucked up nerve enough to read it. It is a harrowing and detailed account of the full extent, the reach and implications of Ewen Cameron's work.

Journey Into Madness, by Gordon Thomas, published by Bantam Press, 1988, is another excellent non-fiction account. Thomas's background interviews with Bill Casey, OSS operative and CIA Chief during much of the eighties, and with William Buckley, Beirut Station Chief for the CIA, who was assassinated in 1986, provided vital information on the link between Ewen Cameron and Allen Dulles and Dulles's thinking, and of CIA intent with regard to the mind-control programmes and the Agency's furious efforts to conceal the results of the programmes. *The Hamline Journal of Public Policy and the Law* published an essay in 1990 called 'Anatomy of a Public Interest Case Against the CIA'. The essay is a summary of Joseph L. Rauh, Jr. and James C. Turner's eleven-year fight to bring the CIA to trial in Washington, DC. The essay was written by Joe Rauh and James Turner. *A Father, A Son and the CIA*, published by Lorimer in 1988 and written by Harvey Weinstein, a psychiatrist at Stanford University, and son of Louis Weinstein, one of the plaintiffs in the case, is a description of the case and the experiments from the point of view of a member of one of the families of the plaintiffs.

Most major newspapers and news magazines in the United States and Canada reported on the Montreal experiments and the Washington trial, chief among them, *The New York Times*. John Marks, a reporter for *The Times*, broke the story in 1976 and wrote *The Search for the Manchurian Candidate*, published in 1980 by Times Books. It remains the definitive account of all the CIA mind-control programmes.

My two years writing, rather than researching, *The Monkey-Puzzle Tree*, were spent taking a correspondence course, coached by Roger Longrigg, Patricia Ryan, the Canadian poet Phyllis Webb, Bruce Nickson, and Laurie Devine. Their patience and care were priceless. Jane Banfield Haynes, favourite cousin and law professor, tried to sort out my legal missteps. Xandra Hardie, Toby Eady, Liz Calder, Mary Tomlinson, Louise Dennys and Jennifer Glossop stepped in when I was most despairing and ran swift and invaluable master classes. Xandra, Toby and Liz were midwives. Without them, the book would never have been written.

ACKNOWLEDGMENTS

Anyone with friends like mine has to give daily thanks to the Friendship God. Mary Vango was my muse. She encouraged and pushed me from the very beginning. Marnie Inskip inspired me and Chris Ogden held my hand during each torturous step. Barbara Kurgan kept me brave and Olga Lange, Tony Gross, Anna Stewart, Thom Oatman, Francesca Longrigg, Liz Corcoran, Gabrielle Schneider, Jim Ware, Ingvaar Starrup, Clive Arrowsmith, Bonnie Smith, Gail Ridgwell, Shaun Slovo, Barbara Amiel, John Yates, Elisabeth Mayall, and Teresa Foubert, Dixie Nichols and Mariette Savoie all offered concrete help, encouragement and tribal warmth at various steps on the way. Lisa Skinner and Julian Griffiths at Griffiths & Wanklyn were always kind and supportive, even when I exhausted their printer and burned out the Xerox machine.

Finally, and most importantly, I thank Willie Wanklyn for his endless patience and faith.

A NOTE ON THE AUTHOR

Elizabeth Nickson is a freelance journalist born in Canada who now lives in Bermuda. *The Monkey-Puzzle Tree* is her first book.